**PRAISE FOR THE**

*Dead Floating Lovers*

"If you love mysteries that toss in lots of local flavor, don't miss this book."

—*Traverse City Record-Eagle*

*Dead Dancing Women*

"Every woman who's ever struggled with saying no, fitting in, and balancing independence against loneliness will adore first-timer Emily."

—*Kirkus Reviews*

". . . debut author Buzzelli is notable as one of the growing number of women writers who use female protagonists trying to make a life for themselves, such as Sue Henry."

—*Library Journal*

"The mystery is well-plotted . . . Emily grows more likeable as the mystery progresses and the town and its residents more endearing throughout the investigation."

—TheMysteryReader.com

"Emily and Dolly's developing friendship, the particulars of small-town Michigan life, and the eccentric characters enliven the story."

—*Booklist*

OTHER BOOKS BY ELIZABETH KANE BUZZELLI

*Dead Dancing Women*

FORTHCOMING BY ELIZABETH KANE BUZZELLI

*Dead Sleeping Shaman*
*Dead Dogs and Englishmen*

An Emily Kincaid Mystery

# DEAD FLOATING LOVERS

### Elizabeth Kane Buzzelli

MIDNIGHT INK
WOODBURY, MINNESOTA

FIRST EDITION
First Printing, 2009

Book design by Donna Burch
Cover design by Ellen Dahl
Editing by Rosemary Wallner

Midnight Ink, an imprint of Llewellyn Publications

**Library of Congress Cataloging-in-Publication Data**
Buzzelli, Elizabeth Kane, 1946–
  Dead floating lovers / Elizabeth Kane Buzzelli.—1st ed.
    p. cm.—(An Emily Kincaid mystery ; #2)
  ISBN 978-0-7387-1265-9
  1. Women journalists—Fiction. 2. Women authors—Fiction. 3. Michigan—
Fiction. I. Title.
  PS3602.U985D44 2009
  813'.6—dc22

                                                                    2009005750

Midnight Ink
Llewellyn Publications
2143 Wooddale Drive, Dept. ISBN 978-0-7387-1265-9
Woodbury, MN 55125-2989, U.S.A.
www.midnightinkbooks.com

Printed in the United States of America

For my children: Kathryn Gibbons, Patricia Mullin, Nino Buzzelli, David Buzzelli, and Cindy Anderson—because you keep me on my toes and refuse to listen to defeat.

For my grandchildren: John Mullin, my intrepid webmaster, and Josh Mullin, who keeps me and my computer safe. To Shawne Benson, Claire Gibbons, Kendall Buzzelli, Alex Anderson, Aaron Benson, Matt Benson, Keenan Gibbons, and Antonio Buzzelli—inspirations and my special loves, every one.

And Tony, forever.

# ONE

Eight thirty a.m. on a pretty May Michigan morning that should
have stayed pretty and pristine and quiet. Far too early for a visitor,
especially Deputy Dolly Wakowski, who stood on my small side
porch thumping with both fists at the screen door, bawling my name
like a little kid calling me out to play: "Emily! Emily Kincaid! Damn
you, I know you're in there ..."

What I didn't need at my door that early, or any time for that matter, was my officious, fully uniformed, square-bodied, thirty-three-
year-old almost ex-friend, Deputy Dolly, of the Leetsville Police Department. There was no way I was going to let her in. The last time
she came to see me she'd been furious about a book I'd written, didn't
like the way I portrayed her, and left in a huff, with a big slam of my
screen door.

Let her stand and wait. I pressed harder against the wall, making
myself invisible while rolling my eyes at Sorrow, my big, ugly, unspe-
cific dog, who did a noisy, tongue-lolling dance of joy at the very idea
of having company. It didn't matter if that guest was Dolly, a Jehovah's

Witness, or an ax murderer. Sorrow was a nondiscriminating creature that loved the world at large and didn't give a flying fig if I'd spent all of the last evening drinking myself into a kind of squiggly fog that left me with a pounding wine-headache, a mouth tasting like dandelion fuzz, and a penchant for growling at any overt noise.

Dolly hammered again, setting my house to quivering and leaky-jowled Sorrow to barking and leaping. I could feel the reverberations inside my poor, abraded skull.

Last evening hadn't been the best of my life. I'd gotten another snide rejection on my recent manuscript. Yet another of those "this didn't excite me" letters that I took personally, as all writing teachers admonish writers not to do. But it was my own story, and Deputy Dolly's. The literary agents had it in for me, I had decided. I now was known in all of New York as the "unexciter." I was the joke of every literary cocktail party. The "poor deluded Michigan writer" referred to at writers' conferences; my name followed by an embarrassed laugh.

Maybe I wasn't really that important, but anyway I'd downed a lot of cheap Pinot Grigio after setting fire to the rejection letter. I'm not one to paper walls with rejections nor get them inscribed on toilet paper. Such weak revenge. Instead, I had sat out on my dock watching ducks fight in angry silhouettes against the fading light on Willow Lake, my own little northern Michigan lake surrounded by weeping willows. The lake was also home to a family of loons I'd fallen in love with, and a beaver who, over my three years up here, had become my tree-chewing, tail-smacking nemesis. I had swatted spring mosquitoes the size of chickens and made a game of seeing how far I could flick them off my arm. In between these important businesses, I had plotted large events of splendid vengeance on all of New York, where I swanned prettily into a party given for my new best seller. The agents who'd scorned me were all there, begging me to come to them, tears of remorse filling the room.

By nine p.m., before true northern spring dark, I had depressed myself sufficiently and gone in to bed with the dregs of the Pinot Grigio and a lot of self-pity.

Now Dolly was at my door. The last time I'd seen her she had come to tell me I better not try selling that book about her. Since it wasn't about her—exactly—and I thought I did her justice, and I was certainly damn well going to try to sell it, we had mumbled and strutted at each other and she'd left in a mighty huff.

For a few minutes all was quiet. Maybe she was gone, I hoped. I lifted the corner of my gauzy white curtain and peeked out the door window. Still there, four-square with both hands hooked in her gun belt, shiny gold badge stuck on her powder-pigeon-blue breast. She looked absently off toward my spring garden of bright yellow daffodils and pale blue windflowers. The side of her face I could see had its usual intent and unappreciative stare. "I don't *get* flowers," she'd once said to me as I had proudly showed off my neat bed of pink peonies. "Plastic's better. Don't die."

She knew I was home. My Jeep was parked in the drive. She might figure I went out walking around Willow Lake; or maybe visiting my friend Crazy Harry across Willow Lake Road, getting him to come take out a wasps' nest or cut up a fallen tree. In either case, she'd sit in her car and wait, not just until hell froze over, but until whatever time it took for me to drag my body home.

Or I could be in my writing studio under the tall maples behind the house, but she had probably checked already. No escaping her. I opened the door.

"God, Emily!" she greeted me, small, homely face tied in a knot. "I thought you were dead." Her voice had a hurt, demanding quality to it; a kind of angry mother tone that got me way down inside, maybe because it had been a long time since anyone—younger or older—had said my name like that.

She threw both her hands in the air, reached for the screen door handle, pulled it open, and came on in, half knocking me out of the way and stepping on Sorrow's big, hairy front paw. "I'm not here because I'm mad about the book anymore. You write whatever you want to, you hear? I don't give a rat's behind about any of that stuff. You probably won't sell it anyway. Never have. I'm over that. Something else. I need your help and you're my friend. You've gotta come with me …"

I didn't get a chance to say hello or even sort out her words. This wasn't the usual Dolly voice. She never asked nicely for anything. This was a mix of pleading and demanding. A dubious face. Fast batting eyes. Evidently asking favors didn't come easily to Dolly. I was thrown, and stood looking at her with my mouth half open.

Sorrow recovered from the foot stomp and leaped to hold Dolly in place, big black-and-white paws placed strategically on both of her ample breasts. Dolly nuzzled his long, wet nose then pushed him away. She leaned close to me, taking in the circles under my eyes that probably made my long face look like a mask. She checked out my curly blond hair caught in a messy ponytail, my paint- and soil-marred jeans, and the new University of Michigan tee shirt that was a gift from Jackson Rinaldi, my ex-husband, whose obsessive philandering had ended our marriage, though we had stayed friends. Well, sort of.

"Emily, I swear to God, something awful's happened. I don't know what to do, where to turn. I'm gonna do something illegal. I got to. And I need you as a witness. Just to say why I did it, if it comes to that."

A shudder passed through me. I could smell trouble coming. Dolly attracted it and I would get the fallout again. My day was all planned. Today was for going over my checkbook and figuring out how many months I had left of food money, while still paying my bills. Summer

4

taxes would be coming in August. I had to prepare. Today was for calling editors I knew at northern Michigan magazines and pitching articles. Maybe calling my friend, Bill Corcoran, at the Traverse City *Northern Statesman*, to see if I could get more stringer work. Something had to be done about my pathetic bank account. The money my father left me was going fast. I'd come up here from Ann Arbor, after the divorce, with what I considered a good stake, certain I would soon sell a novel that would bring a million. I figured that at thirty-four all it would take was one best seller to set me up for life. What editor could resist such quality? Such amazing intelligence? Such creative spirit?

Seemed everybody could.

Dolly leaned in close to get a good look at me. She sniffed and shook her head. "Damn, Emily. You're not drinking, are you? Out here all alone? Taking to drink will be the end of you, like old Cornelia Pund, over to Mancelona. Nothing in her garbage can but cheap whiskey bottles. Garth got tired of picking up those whiskey bottles every week and called social services. Told 'em about her. A guy came out and she pulled a gun. Shot him in the arm. Now she's sober as a monk, staying down near Detroit in a women's prison. Habitual offender. So, you see? Drinking's not going to get you anywhere you..."

"Let's stick with what's going on here," I interrupted the diatribe. "I can't imagine you doing anything illegal." I ignored the sermon I'd just gotten. "You go into spasms when you forget to put on your turn signal."

She lifted her chin from the V of her blue uniform shirt to give me a long, hard look. Those faded blue eyes had never registered neediness before. There might even have been a tear there, if stones can be said to cry. "Have to."

"Maybe tomorrow..." I shuffled into the living room and sat heavily on my brown sofa, bare feet up on the oak coffee table with one long crack running across it. My dad made the table in his woodshop behind the Grand Blanc house where I grew up and where my mom died when I was twelve, and where we lived until I went off to college at U of M. Last piece he ever made before dying. I didn't care if it had a crack across it. It was part of me.

"*Now!* You've got to come see. You'll be out there anyway, soon as the state cops get their hands on it. You'll want to write the story. Please. Truly, Emily, I never asked anybody for this kind of help before."

She wasn't kidding. Her right eye drifted off, leaving the left to stare at me with seriousness drained of any anger or quarrel. I'd never noticed before that Dolly had a lazy eye, or maybe it was brought on by stress. The look was odd, unsettling, until her right eye wandered back and I got my mind on what she was saying.

"What's going on?"

She shook her head. "Can't. You gotta come. Means everything to me. My family…"

"Family? You don't have any, Dolly."

"'Course I've got family. I don't tell everybody…"

"Where are we going?"

"Out to Sandy Lake."

"Nobody there but kids having campfires and making out."

"Mushroomers came on it. You'll see. But you gotta hurry." She stopped to cough and twist her neck nervously from one side to the other. "I was supposed to call in the state boys and I didn't call nobody."

I groaned. "You're not here to get me to witness some gigantic mushroom, are you?"

"Don't be dumb. I'm asking you as a friend."

I started to say something about the editors I had to call, about Crazy Harry maybe coming to rototill my new garden, but her face stopped me. I might have been hung over, but I wasn't heartless.

I ran back to my bedroom and found a purple cotton sweater and some passably clean jeans. In the bathroom, I peed, then brushed my hair out to a wild, blond halo. I was going to put on some lipstick but Dolly stood outside the door hollering for me to hurry. I grumbled at her to be quiet while I dug a pair of sandals out of the closet then put Sorrow on the porch. He'd be fine, kept busy chewing the rope I tied him with, or breaking through one of the screens. I slipped on the sandals and let myself be pushed out the door to her black and white, a new one Chief Lucky Barnard, Dolly's boss, bought second-hand after Dolly had totaled the last one down in Arnold's Swamp.

"Terrible thing." She threw an arm over the seat and turned to watch while she backed up my sand drive. We bounced between silver birches and out onto Willow Lake Road with stomach-turning speed. Once on the blacktop I expected the siren but for almost the first time since I'd met her, the siren stayed silent.

"You better not be getting me into trouble," I grumbled.

She craned her neck toward the front window, watching the road for deer and coyote. I didn't get another word out of her until we'd made our way sedately through Leetsville and bounced two miles down a sandy two-track to a cleared place in an open field. Dolly parked against a big rock and got out, slamming her door behind her. I struggled with my door, got out, and took off after her as she ran up over a rise and down a steep hill toward a flat, blue elliptical lake set against a shore of deep, yellow sand. No cottages. No people. This was a wild place with only a gull high above us, a circle of deep woods behind us, and bright spring sunshine.

I ran hard after Dolly, who held her gun against her thigh as she bobbled along. Up and down her booted feet loped, throwing sand back at me. I began to think this was some kind of challenge, a race she was putting me through. I was a year older than Dolly, but a lot

7

thinner. I reached inside—as runners do—and put on a last burst of speed when, at a small, hidden cove more than halfway around the lake, she stopped dead and stood staring at her feet. I pulled up short and bent over, hands on my knees, panting, eyes closed. Out of shape, I told myself, then opened my eyes. To my right, Dolly's booted feet sank slightly into the water. In front of her wet boots, half buried in dark, wet sand, lay a human skull. At first my mind told me it was a white rock, as I grasped for something ordinary. It was a skull, white and picked clean. As if staring out at the lake, it lay turned away from us. The eye sockets were shadowed, the jaw tilted forward, trying to disappear from sight. Near the top, at the back of the head, a neat black hole with tiny radiating cracks marred the bright white of the naked bone.

That small hole turned the skull from a thing of creepy interest into a chilling relic of violence.

# TWO

THIS WAS NO PLACE for something so grim. Not out here at this peaceful lake. We squatted next to each other there in the damp sand, looking with morbid curiosity at the small skull. Light yellow stains colored the base. At the back, like a bull's-eye, was that round hole the size of a nickel. Dolly moved so she could see the front of the skull and pointed to another neat round hole, an almost perfect bull's-eye between the empty sockets. Awful thing. The skull looked pierced, as if for hanging. Somebody's idea of a weird trophy.

I couldn't help thinking that if it hadn't been turned up the way it was, maybe by an animal; if it had been face down in the sand, I wouldn't have given it a second thought: just an unimportant glacial rock uncovered by receding waters. All the Great Lakes suffered from lowering levels. Some said St. Clair River dredging was leaching our water out through the St. Lawrence Seaway to the Atlantic Ocean. Some said it was the water bottlers, stealing our groundwater. Some said relax—it's the big wheel turning. Part of a natural cycle. We'll have our water back one day and complain then of flooding.

Sandy Lake was down from what I remembered. The shore was much wider. Up fifteen feet in back of us, the old shoreline cut a deep ridge into the sand.

Water lapped gently at my feet, turning my sandals from brown to black. I stepped in farther to get a look as Dolly pointed beyond the skull, out to where the water got darker, murkier, deeper, out to where yellow pollens floated gracefully over more bones: humped rib bones, maybe an arm bone, other scattered bones. And nearby, next to the deeper bones, submerged planks—some kid's attempt at a raft a long time ago.

"Poor thing," I said, feeling protective of the bare bones. "Somebody must've drowned when the water was high. You should have called the state police right away." I kept my voice respectfully low despite, or because of, the wind-slurred silence around us.

Dolly shot me a sideways, disgusted look. "You don't see that hole?"

"Hmm," I said and winced.

Dolly's big shoes dug deeper into the sand. She shifted her gun around to her back and put a hand out to steady herself, fingers digging a deep hold beside her. She lowered her head and looked down as if to talk to the skull. She had that kind of face on, mouth a little open, eyes filled with sadness.

"I was supposed to call the state police. I couldn't call anybody." Her voice broke as she stood up. "I think I know who she was."

"Dolly…," I whispered. There was something deep and ominous around us. We had walked a long way to where the bones lay, off where people who knew the lake never came. There were a few rows of fresh footprints. Two of the rows must've been the mushroomers approaching and leaving fast. The others were Dolly's—when she came out to investigate then ran to get me. Then ours. Like footprints over a hill in the middle of the desert, even these prints seemed out of place here, where everything else was undisturbed.

Three huge crows passed overhead. A shudder moved across Dolly's wide back as echoes of their cawing died away. She pulled her hat off and rested it against her leg as her lips moved and her eyes closed. Dolly was praying.

"Dolly," I said after a few uncomfortable minutes.

Another high-flying crow cawed a reverberating caw. A red-winged blackbird flew slowly overhead, watching what we did. Along the shore around us were the toed footprints of many birds. I recognized the signature print of a raccoon. Nothing bigger. No bears here pawing at the bones. No murderer's footsteps loping away. But there wouldn't be. Too many years ... something happened out here I didn't want to think about.

Sandy Lake wasn't a place many people knew about, and I'd been told it was best to stay away. Before I'd gotten strange feelings out here, I came to watch a mother swan and her cygnets. That was my first spring in northern Michigan. I was lonely then, before I learned to live alone. I didn't yet know my neighbors—Crazy Harry Mockerman; Simon, my helpful mailman. I hadn't yet made friends with people in town like Eugenia Fuller of Fuller's EATS, a genealogy-crazed woman with a proud heritage of ancestral outlaws.

I didn't string at the newspaper in Traverse City where I now knew and respected the editor, Bill Corcoran. And, of course, that was before I knew Deputy Dolly Wakowski, who was bent on making a reporter out of me, or at least a writer of something useful, if it killed her. I had thought this place healing—the silence, the deep, unmoving sand. Maybe, I'd thought then, it was my "road less taken." A place where my muse resided, like visiting the Oracle in Greece. I imagined this a healing spot where ideas for new novels would spring directly from the waters into my brain. Still, even back three years ago I'd felt too exposed, too breathless, too afraid of emptiness out here.

I stopped coming.

Now human bones lay at my feet and the small lake was changed again. Fear. Death. A pile of bones. Dolly's painful voice: *I think I know who she was.*

"She?"

Dolly nodded.

"There's no telling from…" I gave a half wave toward the skeleton.

"Mushroom hunters thought it was some kind of Indian burial they'd come on," Dolly said finally, voice low though there was no one but the three of us, or rather the two of us, and whoever the bones had been, to hear. "I think they called the tribe."

"They're probably right," I said. Picked-clean bones like these could have been anyone.

I wrapped my arms around my body, holding myself tight, as much to be reminded I was alive and had nothing to do with a bare skull, as for warmth.

"Nope," she said. "Don't think so. I only saw her the once but … I know what that is."

She pointed one pudgy finger toward the water, beyond where the skull lay.

I hunched forward and followed to where the finger pointed. Something out there. A small mound of corroded metal with a red bit sticking out.

"What is it?" I asked her, still whispering.

Dolly took a long, deep breath, reached into the water, and, with one finger, dug out a chain with metal dangling from it. And something red. She turned to me, eyes lost in the shadow of the brimmed hat she'd settled back on her head. "I think … it might be my wedding present." She looked me straight in the eye. She let the metal chain play between her hands, running it lovingly across her fingers.

That last part didn't sink in at first. I was too upset at what she was doing.

"You know better … No evidence tampering. I'm not going to be a party to …" I thought a minute. "What the heck do you mean, 'my wedding present'?"

She settled the chain with oblong tags gently into her open hand. All I knew about Dolly's husband was that he'd left her a long time ago. *Just gone*, she'd said and shrugged. I never thought any more about it.

"Chet gave me his dog tags when we got married. All he had. See this?" She prodded the rusty chain, exposing a small red charm that looked like a beer stein. "He was in the army. Motor pool in Germany before we met. Got this charm over there and was proud of serving his country. Talked a lot about being in Germany. About the girls. But …" She stopped, reading my eyes. "I'd better get you home. No sense you being in on … well … I just wanted you to see I didn't do anything else. I'm not covering up for anybody. Not Chet. I wouldn't do that."

"You mean, you think the bones belong to your ex … or whatever he still is … husband?"

"No. Not his," she said, vehemently shaking her head. "Last time I saw these dog tags they was on a real young woman. She was with Chet at The Skunk Saloon in town. I went in there one afternoon, just looking around to make sure nothing was going on. Saw her with these. My wedding present, can you imagine? I hardly looked at the woman, just kept staring at the dog tags around her neck. Walked out of there and Chet came running, trying to tell me she was nobody and why didn't I ever believe him. But he didn't follow me home. Next thing he was gone, and so was she—I guess."

"This is the woman?"

Dolly shrugged and threaded the dog tags into her breast pocket. "If it is, Chet could be in big trouble. If the bones turn out to be male then I'll tell what I know. It would have to be him. If they're hers … well … I've gotta find him, talk to him before I say anything to anybody. Not that I'd let 'im get away but … I guess I owe my family that much. Benefit of the doubt."

"What the hell's going on, Dolly? Unless you've gone completely out of your mind, I can't protect you. Not after what you just did. Put those dog tags back. You're interfering with an investigation. My God, Dolly, you're hiding evidence. That's everything you would never do. And you know you don't have any fam—"

She shook her head, stopping me as she stood and brushed sand from her trousers. "I'll take you home, call the Gaylord post on the way. Then you're out of it. The mushroomers are staying at the cabins on US131, too upset, they said, to hang around. Nobody but you knows anything so far." She set off ahead of me up the beach.

I wanted to protest. I didn't know what I had witnessed, and didn't feel right about any of it. Dolly had pulled me into something I didn't want to be a part of. I felt a chill like the chills that come just before the weather turns; the kind of feeling you get when you know you're in for it but there's no place to run.

I followed along with my head down until Dolly stopped dead beside me. She stood still, not even a breath. Her eyes turned up toward the tree line. The expression on her face, as her eyes stayed fixed on a place among the trees, told me something more was going on.

A dark figure stood there, just before the darkness of the woods. A man watched us from up among the quaking aspen, the new spring leaves making shivering shadows over him as they danced on a strange breeze that didn't reach us. The man was tall, with long, straight black hair blowing around his head and face. He was broad shouldered. I couldn't see his face, only the outline of him as he stood motionless, watching.

"One of the Indians," Dolly whispered. "Mushroomers called 'em after all."

"He saw you," I whispered, not taking my eyes off the man. "He must've been watching when you took those dog tags."

"Naw," she said, but shuffled her feet and squinted hard at the ground.

The man didn't move. I wanted to wave or call out. Anything to break the silence. But even as we watched, he disappeared. As if he'd only been a shadow, he was gone.

"See," Dolly said, but with a catch in her voice. "He didn't see a thing."

"Oh, Dolly," I moaned. I wanted to go home. I wanted to stick my head under a pillow and come out when whatever was going to happen was over.

"I wouldn't be so sure," I said.

# THREE

"YOU GOING TO CALL it in to the paper?" Dolly asked as she pulled down my drive with gravel-hurling speed. She skidded to a dusty stop amid a chorus of pinging against the undercarriage of her patrol car.

"Of course." I held on to the door handle for dear life. Dolly's driving could rattle your bones and your brain unless you prepared yourself for mercurial starts and dead-on stops. "That's my job."

"What're you going to tell 'em?" She watched me with a look falling someplace between rapt interest and challenge.

"That a skeleton was found at Sandy Lake. Maybe something about low lake levels revealing old secrets."

"Nothing about me." Those round blue eyes were pale marbles turned on me. That one lazy eye of hers moved slightly to the left.

"I can't believe what I saw you do," I said. "You, of all people, breaking the law."

Dolly opened her mouth, then snapped it shut. "Sometimes you just have to," she muttered. "I love the law. I believe in it." She hesitated, taking a swipe at her nose with her shirt sleeve. She turned her wet eyes on me. "But there's something even greater, you know."

"Like what?" This little woman exasperated me. She made me sad and she made me mad. I was more than a little pissed. I'd been lectured on the sanctity of speed limits more than once as Dolly stood next to my car window, writing me yet another ticket. And this wasn't about speeding. This was all about evidence tampering. But maybe about a broken heart, too.

"Like what you owe a member of your own family."

I gave up. Dolly Flynn Wakowski was one of those maddening, strait-laced people who live unnuanced lives. There were times I even envied her single view of morality. She spouted the code according to law enforcement classes. Rules were rules. Everything was black or white, right or wrong. Kind of an easy way to look at things—not a whole lot of rethinking involved. But now she spouted this family business. She had moved to a book with two commandments and the highest order had to do with a ceremony she and Chet shared so long ago.

"That man saw. Don't kid yourself." I hissed at her and looked around as if the man might step from my woods.

I got out of the car.

"If the bones are Indian ..." I looked back at her.

"They're not. At least not ancient bones."

"You might be in trouble with the state police. And from the looks of it, with the Odawa Tribe, too. I wouldn't want to be in your shoes when that Indian comes after you. You could lose your job, Dolly. If that guy tells Chief Barnard what he saw ..."

She looked out her window toward my garden, not seeing the beds of nodding daffodils, not smelling the deep pink and blue hyacinths I'd planted near the door. Beyond my garden beds, the woods were filled with glowing trilliums and Johnny-jump-ups. Dolly only looked inside herself, not at the soft spring landscape. She sucked at her bottom lip. "So you're not saying anything about my wedding present?"

"Was it really?" I couldn't help making a face. I wanted to laugh and felt crummy about it. "I mean, is that what he really gave you?"

She glanced down at her watch. "Got to get going. Detective Brent will be out there and expect to find me."

"So." I was like Sorrow—couldn't let it go. "This Chet took his dog tags back and gave them to another woman?"

"Looks that way. Got to wait and make sure the bones are female. I don't know what … I don't want to think about …"

"They could be Chet's," I said, not to be mean but only direct.

She shook her head fast. "Said I don't want to think about it."

"Sorry."

"I'll call you later. There's something else …"

"Oh God. No."

"I don't know how to find him. I need help."

"Check the DMV. Check if he's got a record."

"Yeah, well, we'll see." She nodded, sniffed, and then took another swipe at her nose. "How about dinner later? OK? We gotta talk."

"EATS? The whole town'll be in on it."

"Nah." She shook her head. "Nobody knows yet."

"You think so?" From experience I knew Leetsvillians had an uncanny sense of occasion. Like giant insects, their feelers spread out. Be it danger, somebody needing help, or bad weather coming, Leetsvillians knew long before things happened and brought the news to Eugenia Fuller's restaurant on 131 to chew over with other town citizens. They would have answers before the storm hit, before a person's burned-out house stopped smoldering, before a woman's dead husband turned cold, or before Dolly could tuck her patrol car between buildings and hope to trap somebody speeding along at 40 in a 35.

Dolly said they all had police scanners and that accounted for their rapid knowledge. I wasn't too sure it was that easy.

"Make it seven," she said, and was gone in a choking cloud of dust.

———

Sorrow had pushed the porch door open and had been having his way with my house. One pile of poop under a captain's chair—still steaming. A lake of pee in front of the sink. And Sorrow leaping to be loved. After that morning's events, a little poop and pee meant nothing to me. Mere messy gnats to strain at. I scooped and sopped and patted my loving dog's head. I knew, as Portia knew, that mercy was not strained ... or was that something else? I didn't care right then. I knew what I was getting at. I needed love, and Sorrow gave it with unfettered abandon.

Bill Corcoran was in his office at the *Northern Statesman* when I called, as he was most days—all seven of them—writing, editing, assigning. I could picture him among the usual mess of newspapers, copy to be edited, notes for an upcoming editorial. Nothing neat in his office, but nothing where he couldn't find it. A bear of a man, gruff but caring, Bill was everything a medium town newspaper editor should be: intelligent, aware of his readership, but true to his calling. And always with that odd middle finger he used to push his heavy-rimmed glasses back up his nose. I still didn't know for certain if he meant it as a comment, a suggestion, a criticism, or if it was merely a bad, handy habit.

"OK," he greeted me with his usual bruskness. "So, Emily. What's happening out there at the edge of the world?"

"Bones," I said, meaning to be titillating.

"Human? Animal? Ancient? New?"

"Kind of old. I mean, it takes awhile for bones to become bare bones. Definitely human."

"You mean Indian old?"

"I don't think so."

"So? What's the story?"

"They surfaced out at Sandy Lake, with the receding water. Skull. Other bones. There's a bullet hole straight through the skull."

"Hmm. You calling Gaylord? They'll handle it. Brent won't want your buddy, Deputy Dolly, anywhere near it. Or the Tribe. Wouldn't fool with them. Got a thing about their ancestors. They'll be called in case they're old bones."

"Police are ... eh ... still out there, I think. The Odawa might know already."

"Got a photo?"

Sticky subject. Maybe I'd go back. But the investigators would chase me away.

"No."

"You see 'em yourself or just hear?"

"Saw 'em."

"But no photo, eh?"

"Un-uh."

"OK. Get me the story. Could be front page. Oh, and by the way, your ex called. Dinner at his house soon. Suggested I bring a date."

"He would."

"Might take him up on it."

"Your life." I was immediately sorry I'd introduced Bill Corcoran to Jackson in a weak moment. Something about Jackson that he zeroed in on anybody I might be remotely interested in. Not that I was—interested. It was just that there weren't many available males up here in the woods, which made Bill a possibility.

"So, e-mail the story."

Yeah sure... depression crawled into my head. I hung up. Not smart enough to take my camera. No instincts for journalism. Books didn't sell. Jackson moving in on one of my few friends. Money low. No prospects. What else did I have going for me? Hmm... no use selling my body. Wouldn't bring a dollar and a half.

I let Sorrow out while I grabbed a tuna sandwich then went out to stand in the middle of one of my garden paths, needing to get my head out of Dolly's world and back into my own. I stuck a Detroit Tigers cap over my thick hair and looked around at what I'd created from a patch of pure glacial sand. Neat beds of flowers. Stone paths with creeping thyme planted between them. Spring flowers—no tulips since the deer saw them as cause for celebration and brought their buddies to the banquet. But a wave of daffodils in varying shades. Hyacinths: blue and pink. It was perfect. Spring was always perfect, no slugs, no moles, no leaf rot.

Sorrow snuffled at the base of a birch tree, then hurried to the other side, then back. Doggie business required deep concentration.

I got the pointed hoe from the garden shed and dug around the flowers. At this time of year the cultivating had to be done carefully. In my second spring up here I'd been overzealous, digging and coming up with lily bulbs with tiny sprouts, and damaging late-emerging peonies. I dug carefully then got on my hands and knees and poked around with my fingers, pulling the earth away from rose bush roots and checking around the iris to see if they'd survived the voles. After a while I sat back on my heels and let a few of the thoughts I'd been avoiding come into my head.

How did I begin to process "wedding present" and a set of blank dog tags with a little red beer stein attached? How did I put together a philandering husband who'd fled the marriage thirteen years ago, with Dolly's tearful "he's my only family"? Geez! What she believed came from a place above, below, aside from everything my middle-class upbringing prepared me for. I wanted to laugh at her "wedding present" and her "family," but there was something so painful trapped in those words. Dolly asked for so little. Who was I to judge her need? Me? Family-less Emily with only my own philandering ex to claim.

I yanked hard at last year's Japanese iris foliage, then got the pruning shears and cut it back.

I wanted to call Jackson Rinaldi and tell him what had happened. He would laugh with me. I'd get my head back on straight, and feel better. He would find it ridiculous, as he'd found Dolly earlier. "The simple, you know," he said once about Dolly, "they will inherit the earth and welcome to it."

"It's the meek, Jackson."

"Whatever," he had shrugged, but the idea got across to me. This was not my place. This was not my circle of Ann Arbor friends. This was not a dinner out with professors, a hot discussion of the latest book, the current political fandango; not even a snide assessment of a new reporter come to the *Ann Arbor Times*. This was the empty woods and lakes I'd chosen. Dolly and Crazy Harry and Eugenia. This was Native Americans and their counterculture. This was bones and history.

I whistled to Sorrow who was reluctant to leave the hole he was digging. I put away my tools, wiped my hands along the sides of my jeans, and went out to my small writing studio under tall maples with newly unfurling leaves. Sun shone on my little peaked roof through a mass of knobby, fuzzy spring shadows. It was so unlike winter, when the shadow lines were straight pencil strokes of spare shapes and the only sound the thump of bare tree trunk against bare tree trunk.

The size of a small garage, my writing studio was plain and undecorated, a single open room with windows looking out on a small meadow where I watched deer chase each other, and once I saw a coyote passing through, and once a mother fox with her kits. It was a good place to work and a good place to do nothing but stand at the window and look out—a thing I did a lot of, calling it "mental writing."

Elbows on the window sill was a terrific position, I'd found, for musing. My best stuff came from watching the meadow, and sometimes observing a spider weave a laddered web in a corner of a pane of glass, and sometimes lying on my back on my tattered futon, watching the ceiling, hoping inspiration would droppeth like "the gentle rain from heaven."

I pushed the door open and Sorrow clambered in with a scramble of toenails on the wood floor. He sank down to the rug with a thud and a deep sigh. He was in for a long session of tedium, ending only when the computer said "Good-bye." Then he would leap and pant and be absurdly happy that I'd finished my boring sitting job for the day.

I put an ani difranco CD on the stereo, bowed slightly to my painting of Flannery O'Connor, nodded to the Georgia O'Keeffe photo with Stieglitz, and snapped my fingers at the drawing of Emily Dickinson's Amherst home. Mothers all to me. Women, like my favorite poet, Erica Weick, who held on despite what the world threw at them, their confined lives, their subversive art.

I needed my mind focused on things other than Dolly Wakowski and old bones. I thought about the novel I wanted to write. I pictured it in my head: the scenes, the characters, the setting. My main character would be a man. Contrary to what some misguided writing books preached, I was drawn to see the world through the eyes of men. This man would be an attorney. Elderly. Just out of the hospital after his first heart attack. I could see his grimaces of pain. I could feel his chest grumbling. I could smell his cigar smoke, a brandy stink, and the mothball aroma of his worn wool jacket. I could hear the soft sigh his leather office chair made under the weight of him.

I turned on the computer, lived through the pop-up reminders of downloads waiting, of virus scans expiring, and files I had yet to process. Irritating, especially in my current mood. I wanted immediate access. I wanted a fresh page. I wanted the ceremony of putting truly new words to paper…

*Randall Jarvis pushed his private nurse's hand away from his wrist and fixed her with a look that could make guilty defendants squirm and intractable juries melt…*

In the middle of this—my creative throes—the phone I should have taken off the hook buzzed at me. I felt the usual tug of war between curiosity and blatant indignation. *How dare anyone interrupt what is certainly the next great American novel? How insensitive. How crass. How…*

Jackson. My day was complete. He had followed me to northern Michigan, on sabbatical, writing his important tome on Chaucer's pilgrims. Or maybe he'd come just to drive me crazy. I wasn't sure. He was in a cottage—bigger than mine—over near Spider Lake, outside Traverse City. The sad thing was he couldn't find anyone to transcribe his work for him. Since he took great pride in writing in long hand, as the greatest writers wrote, he saw no reason to change his winning ways now. I was the secretarial service, as I had been when we were married. Some old habits just don't go away. I would type his work into the computer, copy the files on disk, and deliver hard copy for his astute editorial eye. For all of this I'd been presented with a tee shirt.

A U of M tee shirt. A shirt high above others. With all the work I'd done for Jackson, even at ten dollars an hour, I figured it had to be worth about a thousand dollars.

"I must see you, Emily." It was the usual demanding, deep voice not meaning to be demanding. In fact, he would be hurt to think I ever thought such a thing of him ... ever.

"Busy working right now, Jackson. What's it about?"

"I need a sounding board. Some of this chapter doesn't ring true to the ear. You know I'm trying to capture Chaucer's insouciance."

"You mean over the phone? You want to read to me now?"

"No, no. I thought I'd bring dinner in an hour or so. I've got more work for you to put into the computer. Maybe you could run off a copy or two. You do such beautiful work ..."

"Can't tonight. I've got plans."

"Plans?" Snide laughter that could make my skin ripple up into crocodile hide lay just beneath the word.

"Dinner plans. Sorry."

He huffed a moment. I said nothing more. "Then tomorrow. I'll bring what I have and read you this bit ..."

"Tomorrow," I agreed.

"Lunch?"

"Great."

"Do you have things in the house? I could pick up a loaf of bread ..."

A sigh and lunch was settled. I put down the phone and pictured poisoned mushrooms. An omelet. A soup ... ah yes ... who would suspect an ex-wife trapped into endlessly typing her prior husband's manuscript, a Sisyphean task never to be completed? Who would even imagine she might hold a grudge ... ?

I liked the idea of mushroom soup but decided I'd go with morels I'd buy from Crazy Harry. He was an expert in the woods. So maybe one or two weren't quite right...false morels weren't easy to spot. Who could blame me? A form of Russian roulette.

I couldn't get back to my gentleman of the bar. He retreated behind a woodpile in my brain while I stewed over being cornered, yet again, by Jackson, the man I'd sworn to love forever and ever and ever. That love lasted less than five years, unless you counted the motherly fondness I still felt for him from time to time. Who knew why? Old habits, I guessed.

I turned off the computer and endured Sorrow's joy. Dolly was what I planned to think about for the next few hours, until I met her at EATS. Dolly was less complicated. Dolly and her wedding present and her "family" were easier to deal with than Jackson and everything I'd left behind in Ann Arbor. Right then, if it had come to a struggle between my graduate degree, my knowledge of cheap wines, my drunken discussions of the meaning of "circumference" in Emily Dickinson, why, I'd pick Dolly and simplicity every time and feel good about myself in the process.

# FOUR

THE USUAL RUSTY PICKUPS stood at individual angles in Eugenia's
rutted dirt parking lot. I recognized a few, knew the people they belonged to, and could walk in to meet Dolly without feeling like the
stranger I used to be here, in the town of Leetsville, Michigan.

There was Anna Scovil's red truck. Anna was the town librarian
and forever sidled up to me, the local "writer," to whisper the name of
a new book in my ear, savoring the words and keeping them from the
uneducated, the rest of the Leetsvillians. Recently she'd been mouth-
ing the words *A Thousand Splendid Suns* at me from across the room,
glancing quickly around to make sure nobody saw. We were in the
know, the two of us. Anna did a good job of protecting her books.
Even all checked out and ready to go, Anna could give you a powerful
tug of war if she felt you unworthy. Fortunately, because I was one of
those who came from far away, and was blessed with what she called
"a gift," I could get a novel of somewhat recent vintage, or something
for my research, with only a worried frown on Anna's long face, with

only one irritated punch to her upswept hair that didn't move when poked.

In the musty vestibule of EATS hung a new genealogical chart; another of Eugenia's mythical family. I'd found her out last fall, after researching a few of her so-called relatives. I still didn't understand why Eugenia claimed hung or shot outlaws as next of kin. Maybe for the notoriety. Maybe for the sympathy kind-hearted Leetsvillians gave her. Who knew? There they all still hung. Some, possibly the worst among them, with big gold, stick-on stars attached. I told Eugenia I knew what she was doing but she went on hugging the fearsome mystique of the killers and rustlers and train robbers around her like a big hairy rug.

This one looked … hmm … I stood on tiptoes to make out the wide sheet of paper, actually two sheets taped together. A photo of a tough-looking lady hung on one side with text on the other. No gold star. Maybe somebody Eugenia didn't hold in high regard. Maybe she was running out of dead outlaws. The woman looked ordinary enough in the old, grainy photo—dark hair up, unsmiling face staring at the camera as if it were the worst of her enemies. The paper beside the photo read: Ellen Liddy Watson. Not a name I knew. I'd look her up later, when I got back home.

I went in the restaurant and cut my way through Eugenia's non-smoking section. There was no use hoping to breathe clear air in EATS. Eugenia didn't like the state dictating what people could and couldn't do in her place. She put up a dozen "Nonsmoking" signs and ashtrays on every table.

Eugenia stood behind her glass counter filled with cigars, candy bars, and beef jerky. She nodded, gave me a nervous smile, and shrugged her wide shoulders a couple of times. Eugenia was a pillow of a woman. Soft breasts stretched out way beyond her chin and shoulders, and around to her sides. A pouf of bright yellow, curly hair sat piled loosely on top of her head, then left to cascade down her back. There was something motherly about her, but even larger than that. If there was a person in Leetsville who needed to eat, couldn't afford a meal, required help by spreading the word for canned goods or clothes—after a fire or job loss or that time a tornado came through town—that person was big-hearted Eugenia. Maybe she had an opinion on everything and everyone in Leetsville, but when it came to helping or listening there was no one kinder.

Eugenia stood with her arms crossed, waiting for my snide comment on her new relative. "Don't know her," I called over. "But I will."

She threw her head back and laughed hard. I think I'd become her main target, fooling me. I was just as determined to figure out who this new one was. Not just a game between us, but a real tussle for who was smartest in all of Leetsville.

I spotted Dolly in a corner booth, hat on the red Formica tabletop, brown hair bearing the indentation of her hat, a kind of ring-around-the-head which did nothing for Dolly's worn-out look. I cut through the tables, all with mismatched wooden chairs. I said hello to pixyish Gloria, my favorite waitress. Anna Scovil clutched at my denim jacket, as I tried to get past her, pulling me down close so she could whisper in my ear.

"I've got a simply wonderful idea. We've got to talk," Anna said in her librarian's hushed voice. She moved her eyes right, then left, taking note of anyone watching. "Come into the library this week. It is *very* important."

I smiled, nodded, promised I'd do my best, and had to look purposefully at the hand holding me in place before she said "Oh, sorry" and let me go.

I slid into the booth across from Dolly and picked up the thick, sticky menu laying on the table. Though I knew it by heart, it didn't hurt to hope that one day Eugenia would replace her tough sirloin with a piece of fish. Or maybe there would be a fresh bread pudding with a dash of cinnamon rather than glutinous cherry pie in a cardboard crust.

"Detective Brent wanted to know where I got to. Why I wasn't waiting out there for them," Dolly whispered across the table at me, barely moving her lips. "I told him I had to go back to the office, get ahold of Lucky. I said I wanted him out there with me but I couldn't find 'im. Hope Brent doesn't start asking any more questions." She frowned hard at the menu laid flat in front of her.

I studied my salad choices: Salad Bar with cheese ball; Quarter Head of Lettuce with Thousand Island dressing; Tossed Side Salad with those hard little balls of cherry tomato you couldn't get your teeth into. When Gloria came tripping up to take our order, her blond head waggling, her tennis shoes sticking to the tile floor, I ordered the meatloaf special with mashed potatoes and canned gravy and canned corn on the side. Dolly ordered the same thing. It was easier to order the special. I think Eugenia dished it up ahead of time and popped each plate into the microwave to be served in breath-holding minutes, sometimes little more than five minutes from order to customer. You just couldn't complain about the service in EATS.

"Anybody ask about the bones?" I murmured at Dolly, keeping my head down and mouth covered. No matter what she said, EATS wasn't the best place for secret meetings, nor sharing private information. It wasn't just that the townspeople knew everything that was going on; I'd begun to think they all read lips.

She shook her head. "Stop worrying."

I looked at the people seated around the smoky room; at Gloria, standing off to one side gossiping with a couple of old farmers; at Eugenia, whose big eyes traveled back and forth, watching everything and everyone. Usually they were ahead of the news. Not today. I supposed Dolly had stayed off the radio and maybe Detective Brent hadn't appeared at the station yet to talk to Lucky Barnard.

"Got some information though," Dolly spoke through clenched teeth. "Doc Stevenson, the coroner, said he thought the skull belonged to a woman. Something about the way a woman's skull is formed. Wouldn't say anything else except it was murder. Gun shot. Small caliber."

I nodded. I'd seen it.

"Bones went to Gaylord, or on down to Lansing by now. They need to find out what they can about her, and when she died. Bones should say something, but maybe not a whole lot."

I nodded. "Certainly when she died. If she's recent or pretty old. With a gun, can't be ancient. I'll call in the morning, get it all from Brent."

Gloria brought out steaming plates and dropped them in front of us. Six minutes. Not a record, but still very good. I ordered hot tea. Dolly stuck with a glass of water.

"You've got to help me some more," she said, though her head was bent over her plate. I couldn't see her face.

I wasn't sure I'd heard right. Help her? Hadn't I already implicated myself in some pretty serious evidence tampering?

"I gotta find Chet." She glanced up over her meatloaf, eyes red-rimmed and blurry. "This is going to get bad. The tags were his. He was out there. I don't know what happened. He was never the killer type, but I'm gonna have to bring him in."

"You wouldn't protect him, would you?"

She made a face, shook her head, and lost a few kernels of corn from her fork. "Still, I'd like to be the one to do it. He's my husband,

31

Emily. That means something to me. Blood's thicker than water, you know."

"He left you thirteen years ago. And he's not blood. If he were ... well ... that would be a whole other story."

She shrugged and cut her meatloaf into tiny bits. I stabbed mine and marveled at the way it fell apart, just like the stuff I spooned out of a can for Sorrow.

"You don't look at things like I do."

I nodded. True enough.

"Anyway, he's got people down in Detroit. Went to high school at Pershing High. Friends, too. If those bones belong to the woman he ran off with, then where'd he go? I need to find out what happened."

"So, you going down to Detroit?"

She shrugged. "That's where you come in."

I waited, almost scared. Something about a serious and fixated Dolly left me with a chill running up and down my back.

"Department of Motor Vehicles don't have anything on him. Never renewed his license. At least not in Michigan. Found nothing else. Like he just disappeared."

I scowled at her. Where would a guy go without his license? Maybe he changed his name and was living in Montana.

"You're good with the computer. You can look him up. Check phone books. I'll get the names I can remember. I've got an old Christmas card list. But if it comes to finding nothing, we'll just go."

"Can't you do this alone?" My whine wasn't gracious but it came right out. A trip to Detroit, listening to four hours of Dolly worry—it seemed like a kind of penance I didn't owe anybody.

Dolly looked around to see who was watching. They all were, but she ignored them and put a hand over her mouth. "Haven't been much of anywhere, my whole life," she whispered. "Think I'd get lost down there in the big city. I mean, I lived down there when I was small. Got moved from foster home to foster home. But I was still little when one of them moved me all the way up here before dumping me back on the state. All my life, it was foster homes or institutions, then meeting Chet and getting married. You know, you're what you might call 'sophisticated.' People will tell you things. You'll get us around. Save a lot of time. And I think time's what we're not going to have a lot of."

She slid a paper across the table at me. I picked it up. A list of people:

*Chester Allen Wakowski*
*Mother: Mildred Wakowski*
*Lived on Filer Street in Detroit*
*Brother, Tony Wakowski*
*Sister, Elaine*

"You want me to see what I can find?"

She nodded.

I nodded back. Simple enough. With my journalism background, I'd done a lot of research, looked for a lot of people. I had found some. This could come down to a few phone calls. How hard could it be?

"And I brought this." Dolly slipped something from the breast pocket of her uniform shirt. She palmed whatever she had for me in her right hand and pushed it slowly across the table. Her face was blank, but her eyes almost sparkled. "Him," she leaned toward me and whispered.

The photo was wrinkled, as if it had been through a fit of screaming, shouting, and gnashing of teeth. There were creases across the face of the guy standing there, leaning back on a picket fence. Not much to see—he wore sunglasses and a baseball cap. He was tall. Skinny. Held a can of Budweiser out toward the camera. Maybe a cigarette hung from one corner of his mouth. Like a million pictures of guys relaxing, there Chet stood laughing with his friends.

"Want me to keep it?" I asked after looking him over and finding nothing unique there.

Dolly frowned and reached over to slap her hand on top of the photo. She dragged it back to her. "Just wanted you to see. Quite a man, Chet. I've missed him. But what can you do?" She shrugged, slipped the picture into her pocket, gave it a couple of pats, then buttoned the pocket down for safe keeping.

I wiped my mouth, picked up my bill, and slid out of the booth. "Hope I can help," I told her.

"Right away," she hissed. "I'm taking a couple of vacation days. Not telling Lucky anything yet. In the morning I'm going to go talk to those mushroomers. Call me with whatever you find. If we have to go, let's plan on tomorrow afternoon."

I shook my head. "I've got a date tomorrow."

She grinned. "Yeah sure."

"Lunch. Jackson's coming over."

She made a face, then nodded. "Whatever. Make it the day after, then."

"Who's gonna pay for gas?" I stopped, thinking of my sorry bank account.

"Don't worry. I'll take care of everything."

Good deal. The only thing I'd be missing out on was a few days of typing Jackson's Chaucer into the computer. Anyway, with my skill on the Internet, we'd never have to take the trip. How many Chet Wakowskis could there be?

I waited at the counter and thought about the jobs I had to do at home—find Chet Wakowski and plan my luncheon date with Jackson. I figured I'd make mushroom soup after all—but no self-picked morels involved. I thought of Chaucer's Wife of Bath: a funny, bawdy woman now in Jackson's clumsy hands. It was partly for her sake I kept helping him. I loved seeing her take Jackson's self-serving words about her and twist them on their head. One of Chaucer's greatest characters. A "gat-toothed" woman after my own heart.

Eugenia took the twenty I held out and slapped change into my hand.

"Think 'pickle.'" She leaned across the broken and taped counter glass, whispering the two words at me.

"Huh?"

She jerked her head toward the vestibule. "I said, 'think pickle.' It's a hint."

I made a face. As if I needed a hint. "I'll find her as soon as I get home."

Eugenia shrugged and took aim at an early fly with her ever-present flyswatter.

I went out to my Jeep with nothing but mushrooms, pickles, and a bright future in computer research dancing in my head.

# FIVE

THE NEXT MORNING I had a lunch to plan; mushroom soup to make. Part of me looked forward to Jackson's visits—they reminded me why I divorced him. Part of me dreaded them—he made me remember that steady stream of coeds calling, showing up at the front door of our Ann Arbor home, and leaving little things like panties in our car. When you have a history with someone, no matter how checkered, it makes a mark. There was odd comfort in feeding Jackson again, in sitting afterward, having a glass of wine, laughing about people we knew. I wouldn't mention my looming financial crisis to him. Not his problem anymore. We had split everything fifty/fifty in the divorce. I'd taken the money from the sale of our Ann Arbor home and bought the Willow Lake property. I used my inheritance from my dad to live on. How things went for me from here on in was solely up to me. I had resources. I would figure it out.

It was one of those fortunate May mornings when the earth apologizes for winter. There was a warm, soft breeze. Daffodils and blue windflowers bloomed through last year's rusty leaf bed. The warming wind in the garden smelled of earth moving. It smelled of worms and seeds stretching and carving summer niches. It smelled of water and then of powdered leaves. Some of the daffodils were caught and couldn't open, buds bent at the neck, leaf spikes twisted through a single noose-like hole in an old oak leaf. It was my job to police the bloom, free the bright yellow heads. Jobs like these took precedence over soup. I got on my knees, down where the earth was still cold, and freed the flowers. Beneath the leaves were more pale flower heads just breaking through. Even the reluctant double pink peony had little bent spikes coming in around last year's dead foliage.

Days like this were rare. Pure and clean. Nothing to do with dead bones. Nothing to do with sadness. All new life and possibility. I wanted to crawl through the beds and clear and see which of my plants made it—pure joy. And which were dead. I would do some mourning—for a poppy that was black and rotted, with no sign of life. But for the tree peonies I could only rejoice that they'd made it through another winter: my lovely, frilly showgirls of the garden.

I gave myself an hour then sat back on my knees looking wistfully at my filthy, cracked nails. I sighed. I had that mushroom soup to prepare. Shopping to do. Jackson would be here for lunch and I would have nothing.

As I stood, wiped my hands along my jeans, and kicked dirt from my tennis shoes, Crazy Harry Mockerman, my neighbor, came down the drive in his slapped-together vehicle which was half truck, half car, and parts from other things I couldn't identify. The vehicle choked to a halt and Crazy Harry waved as he turned it off. The motor went on chugging. Harry flipped the key again—back and forth. Nothing. The motor coughed a couple of times and went right on running.

Harry climbed down and stood looking at the front of his contraption. He lifted one side of the hood and stared in. I joined him, looking down, without comprehension, at the crusted motor. Harry turned, gave me a grizzled smile, and scratched the back of his gray head.

"Heard of 'em not starting…," he said.

We watched the motor bounce and cough until it finally stopped and Harry shut the hood.

"Knew it'd get the idea sooner or later." He smiled, his lips not moving enough to show teeth but enough to give the idea of merriment. "Came to rototill that bed."

My house sat in a valley cut by water racing downhill to Willow Lake eons ago. I already cleared and planted most of the level back area. Now it was time to begin moving uphill. I was thinking beds of zucchini and pumpkins; stands of tall, heavy tomatoes. Maybe beans and corn. Things I could can and eat as starvation loomed when my money ran out. Or, more probably, give away all those zucchinis as they piled up on the kitchen counter, filled the refrigerator, and spilled out the door. And pumpkins? How many pies could I eat? But there was pumpkin bread, soup, and muffins. I'd live like a queen, right out of my freezer.

Harry had cleared out the trees from the new bed the year before, but still he complained he would be awhile. "What with all the roots." He unloaded his old rototiller, lugged it up the hill to where the bed was staked out, pulled the cord a couple of times to get his machine roaring, then bent his skinny chest into it, pushing hard as the tines dug and cut into the sandy soil.

I was used to the look of Harry Mockerman, ministerial in his black funeral suit (in case he died and no one could find it to bury him in) and to the wry humor he treated me to as he would smile over my latest diagram for a flower bed—all perfectly detailed— scratch at his rough chin, and shake his head. He wasn't one to put things on paper. Maybe he couldn't write, or read. I didn't know and didn't care. He knew the woods and knew the earth and how to live with little to rely on but his wits. Someone to pay attention to, I'd thought from the first time I met him. A lot to learn from Crazy Harry Mockerman, though I wouldn't be cooking roadkill, the way he did, anytime soon. Dead possum stew and flattened squirrel frittata still weren't part of my favorite cuisine.

"Brought you over those morels you wanted," he yelled above the noise of the machine and gave me another smile, a kind of sinking in of his lips over teeth that had to be there somewhere.

"Thanks," I cupped my hands around my mouth and yelled back.

"Six dollars. Cheap compared with what those city stores charge you." He shut off the rototiller and made his way back down to talk. He'd been working all of five minutes. He charged me by the job, not by the hour, so Harry's frequent conversation breaks cost me nothing.

I nodded. "Very cheap," I agreed.

"Better than buying them, you could come out in the woods with me and find 'em. My eyes ain't what they used to be. Other things I could show you. Milkweed pods. Best thing ever when you know how to cook 'em in three boiling waters and fry 'em up in butter. Puffballs be coming soon. Slice 'em up, cook 'em in butter. Um, um."

Almost every recipe Harry gave me ended with "fry 'em up in butter," but whenever he sent over one of his delicacies I had to agree: Harry Mockerman knew how to cook.

Maybe this was just what I needed to learn. Lots of people back in the woods didn't have jobs. Lots of families at the far end of sandy two-tracks didn't rely on a steady income. Some did logging. Some made crafts all winter and went from fair to fair, selling them all summer. Some lived off welfare. They got along the way families have always gotten along. A secret I hadn't learned yet. If I was going to be able to stay up here I had to find a source of income. It wasn't going to be welfare. Probably not logging. I wasn't very handy with string and ice cream sticks. Had to be something else.

I left Harry at his job and drove all the way into Kalkaska, ten miles beyond Leetsville, and bought my salad vegetables at the Cherry Street Market. I bought a pint of thick cream for the soup, and a loaf of Stone House Bread. Jackson had said he'd bring bread but he rarely remembered details like a loaf of bread, a jug of wine ...

A fine mind such as Jackson's spun incessantly with Middle English conjugations and minutia of fourteenth-century dress. No place in there for bread or—when we were married—a lot of other things.

Back home I let my sliced morels simmer gently in butter, onions, and garlic while I called Detective Brent in Gaylord. Each state police post covered a lot of territory up here. They took over in cases too big for the smaller village police departments—like Leetsville, though Chief Lucky Barnard and Dolly fought hard to keep their hands on what they thought of as their turf. Michigan State Police detectives were constantly over-extended but very professional and hard-working. Still, this particular detective didn't much like the press, especially stringers like me, who came and went like the seasons.

"Yes," Officer Brent, of the unibrow, big chest, stiff back, and zipper-straight mouth, said in response to my inquiry about the bones found out at Sandy Lake. The informative "yes" was in response to a question as to where the bones were now.

"No," I said, and gave my little false laugh. "I'm asking you if they've been taken down to Lansing for further analysis."

"And your answer was 'yes,'" he said, sighing at the other end of the line.

"What are they hoping to find? Age of the bones? Are they Native American? Female? Murder?"

"Female. Looks like murder. Bullet hole straight through. That's it. I've given you all I can. We might not know more for weeks."

"Has anyone from the Odawa been in touch?"

"They called us."

"Are they willing to wait?"

"Have to. This is a criminal investigation. Unless we find this all happened a few hundred years ago, and that was a musket ball went through her, we call it current and ongoing."

"If ongoing, do you have any leads as to who the bones might have been?"

"Too early for that."

"Anyone missing over the last few years?"

"A few. We're looking into it."

"So, no imminent arrests, no suspects, no persons-of-interest."

"Nope."

"Anything found out at the lake?"

"Nope. Divers going in as soon as I can get them out there."

"Any idea what they'll be looking for?"

"Nope."

Since we were down to the "nope" answers, I figured I'd better write up what I had and send it to Bill. Tomorrow would be another day. Maybe I'd call the tribal offices, see what their story was. By then I would have found Chet Wakowski. Dolly would have talked to him. We'd get him back up here and the whole thing would be cleared away. Maybe that wedding present of hers had nothing to do with anything. Maybe it was another set of worn-off dog tags with a red beer stein charm attached ... well ... there was no getting around that one.

I hung up and wrote my new story, padded with facts about the water levels in the Great Lakes. Not a big story, but intriguing. Bill

41

called when he got it and asked me to get back to him daily until it was over. The thought struck me, as I hung up, that there might be a full-time job right there at the newspaper. I'd have to go in and talk to him. At least I could make him aware that I was looking. It wouldn't hurt.

I finished the soup and put the salad together, chilled the bottle of white wine I'd bought, and went back to the computer to search for Chet Wakowski. Probably not a lot to find, but I felt kind of sorry for Dolly and wanted to help. This "family" stuff was important to her, for whatever reason. I still had the vision of those dog tags lifting out of the water, a glint of sun on the red beer stein. Made me an accessory. As long as I kept what happened a secret, I was as culpable as Dolly.

I Googled Chet Wakowski, then Chester Wakowski, first in Detroit, and then in all of Michigan. Nothing. I Googled Mildred Wakowski, his mother. Nothing. I did a reverse phone book search. Again nothing. I could spring for a full search from one of those pop-up companies—supposedly there was information on a Chester Wakowski, but I didn't want to. Dolly would be over later. We would compare notes then.

While I was on the computer I looked for Ellen Liddy Watson, Eugenia's new "relative," and found her easily. An outlaw all right. A woman hung by a lynch mob because she dared settle land and buy cattle. What a story! Could break your heart. Good for Eugenia, to claim Ellen. Maybe I'd write up something on her. Had to be a magazine printing the truth about old lies. Or not. Old lies have a way of digging deep into American psyches. But that "pickle" hint ...?

Eugenia was still ahead of me. Maybe there was more than one Ellen Liddy Watson. Nope, there it was on the screen. Her first husband's name: William A. Pickell.

I felt so smug. Nobody could put anything over on me. I might not be able to find Chet Wakowski, but I could sure find a "Pickle."

With the addition of cream and a lot of chicken stock, the soup was ready. I set a table out on the deck. The sky was dark off to the north, but when I asked Harry what he thought he told me not to worry, "Nothin' comin' our way. Blow right on over."

My faith in Harry's nature knowledge was so deep I spread a white tablecloth, set a bowl of daffodils at the center, and put out bright yellow dishes.

The soup cooled. The salad warmed. The bread hardened. The daffodils bent to drop pollen on the white cloth. I sat at my lovely table and waited, yet one more time, for Jackson, thinking seriously about poisonous mushrooms and how everything had its place in the big scheme of things.

# SIX

Jackson arrived in a shower of pebbles and dust, his white Jaguar screeching to a halt where my drive ended and the tall bracken began.

"I couldn't wait to get here," he enthused after leaping from his car to lean his head back, drink in the wine of my lake-washed air, then throw his arms wide and walk toward me.

With his dark hair, long slim body, that superior air, those warm arms—he had me. He always had me; the reason I moved two hundred and fifty miles away after the divorce. I didn't want to become one of those sad, pathetic cast-off wives who hung around, waiting to pick up the leavings—should he care to drop by from time to time.

I guess I'd always been a sucker for a good-looking man with an affected laugh and an absolute belief in his own transcendence over ordinary mortals. Jackson could make my heart do stupid things and make me smile when I didn't want to smile. He could even make me feel better about myself just by putting a hand on either of my shoulders and kissing me in the middle of my forehead. There is something about warm male lips on dry, longing, female skin.

"You're late," I grumbled because he always made me grumble to protect my self-respect.

"I know, but when you hear why…" He folded his arms slowly around me then smiled down as he hugged me gently to him, pulling me very close so I could feel his legs against mine. He turned me back toward my own house then followed, pushing. I let myself be pushed, though I pushed back a little.

"It was for the cause, Emily. I got so much work done this morning. An amazingly prodigious amount. No sense coming over here and then having to come right back again. So, I've brought you ten chapters. Can you imagine it? Ten chapters. The book is flying."

He stopped at the door, gave me a little shove inside, then ran back to his car to retrieve the manuscript pages, all waiting for me to decipher his handwriting, type them into a file, print out a final edit, and then burn onto a CD for his publisher. He held the stack of white paper high and riffled through them. His worn, if still good-looking, face took on the triumphant look he'd once had after sex. Probably still had. Something to do with getting a woman to satisfy a need. Right now his need was for a typist.

The sun on the deck was warm, the clouds gone—as Harry had predicted. Jackson liked eating this way—*alfresco*. It reminded him of our days in Italy, he said, leaning back in the deck chair, hands behind his head.

"Remember Tuscany, Emily?"

I nodded, remembering Tuscany only too well. The days I'd spent trying to keep him out of the clutches of overheated Italian women who admired the scarf tossed casually around his throat and his pale wool cap, tipped at a jaunty angle. *Professori* they called him and virtually swooned.

He'd forgotten the bread so I produced mine, puffing with pride at my efficiency. As we ate, Jackson stopped from time to time to lift his hand from the manuscript pages on the table beside him, pick them up, and flip them at me. "Won't take too much of your time," he smiled, his dark eyes crinkling. "And think of the contribution to literary studies. I will, of course, acknowledge your help."

"I've started a new novel," I said, trying for a little of this bright glare of spotlight.

He set his pages down slowly and gave me a doubting smile. "Not like the last, I hope? What was that one? A new rendition of *Fatal Attraction*?"

"Mistake," I mumbled, stuffing salad into my mouth.

He leaned back, large hands pushing his soup bowl away, and watched as white puffy clouds sailed over the lake. "I'll be glad to take a look at whatever you have. Just to make certain … well … you don't want to make another mistake."

He yawned and reached for a piece of bread, took a bite, chewed thoughtfully, then added, "What about that mystery, the one about your adventures with Deputy Dolly? Anything back on it yet?"

"Yes. Very favorable," I lied. "An agent asked to see the whole manuscript."

"Ah," was all he said.

"In fact, there was more than one." I hoped my nose wasn't growing. "Three, to be exact. I should be hearing any day now."

He lifted an eyebrow and made a noise. "I'm sure you'll be hearing," was all he said.

The phone rang and Sorrow, who'd been asleep at our feet, leaped up to answer. I followed him back into the house.

It was Dolly, wanting to know if I'd come up with anything on Chet. I had to disappoint her.

"I found his mother's address, on that old Christmas list," she said. "We can start there."

"What's this 'we' stuff?"

She ignored me. "I talked to the mushroomers from Ohio. Nice old couple. Very shaken by all of this. They didn't have anything else to add, just that they found the bones by accident. And they did call the Odawa, who don't look kindly on anyone disturbing an old burial site. Brent said they've been in touch with him so maybe it *was* one of them out there. I still don't think he saw anything, but I'd better get moving on finding Chet. We've got to have information fast. They'll be demanding answers."

I looked out at Jackson and the sheaf of papers settled securely beside him. His eyebrows went up in expectation of me getting off the phone quickly so as not to miss a single bon mot of his. I weighed things in my mind: Chaucer? Dolly? Hmm...

"OK, look, I'll go with you," I said into the phone while smiling and nodding through the open French doors at Jackson.

"Er...thanks, Emily. I really mean it. Tomorrow morning. I'm going to Gertie's salon this afternoon. Wait'll you see my new hair color. If I'm going to see Chet Wakowski, I want him to regret the day he left me. I'll be there about nine. If that's OK. And Emily, get Jackson out of there. I know you, Emily. No character at all. Don't even think about going to bed with him."

"Why...I...you..."

She hung up laughing as I sputtered.

I lied to Jackson—that I had to get into town, that Dolly and I were working on another case. I gathered his papers, went back into the living room, and set them on the big desk in the corner.

"Well, if you have to go … And my work? When do you think … ?"

"Soon. As soon as I can get to it." I hurried him along.

"Oh … then, well, dinner at my place next time. I want to cook for you, the way I used to. Something simple, but wonderful. And Santa Margherita Pinot Grigio."

That alone would have done it.

He came closer. I stood with my arms down. Were we going to shake hands? Perhaps pat each other on the back? Jackson put a hand on each of my shoulders and pulled me toward him. He bent just a little while my breath first held, then shook. It had been a long, long time.

He kissed first my forehead, then kissed me full and hard on the mouth. He was so good at this stuff. Why had I forgotten? I wanted to curse my weak knees when he let go. I'd forgotten the power he had over me. Like turning on a switch somewhere inside, I not only got turned on but lit up and more than a bit needy.

"See you in a few days," he whispered down at me, smiling a too-knowing smile. He stepped away fast, leaving me with a silent, *aw shit* … rolling around in my pathetic brain.

All I could do was nod. Nothing much really changed between us. I was so easy, I told myself, as I watched him back his Jaguar out of my drive. Dolly was right about me. A person of no character at all.

# SEVEN

WE WERE ON OUR way to Detroit, me and Dolly, though our leave
taking wasn't without stress. First, I had to find Harry to come feed
and water Sorrow, and let him out a few times a day. He wasn't home
when I went across Willow Lake Road to his crooked little house,
down an overgrown and picker-treacherous drive. His dogs, back in
their kennel behind a high chainlink fence, barked and snarled and
tried to run me off the property.

It must have been all the noise the dogs made, for Harry soon
ambled into his clearing dragging a long mesh bag of morels behind
him.

"Sure," Harry said. "I'll take care a yer dog. You do the same for
me someday."

I'd eyed his snarling, leaping kennel of animals and hoped it would
never come to that. "What neighbor won't do a favor for t'other, I'd like
to know?" he asked.

So I left it there, deciding I'd worry about feeding Harry's dogs the
day he ever went somewhere. Since, as far as I knew, Harry had not

left his house for more than a few hours in his whole sixty-some years on earth, I figured the odds were on my side.

Second, I had to get over my amazement at the dye job Gertie of Gertie's Shoppe de Beaute had given Dolly. Her hair resembled striped mattress ticking. It was still a dirty brown, but with stripes of some shade of blond she called "Topaz Triumph." She took off her hat and bent her head down to show me. I told her to keep her hat on and then she was mad at me.

Next, we had the "who's going to drive" struggle.

"Not you," I said as I loaded the back of the Jeep with my overnight bag and her backpack. She made a face, crossed her arms over her chest, and tapped one foot against the gravel. Dolly was in jeans and a sweatshirt with LAW ENFORCEMENT—YA GOTTA LOVE US across the back. One of the few times I'd seen her out of uniform.

"My car," I said. "I drive." Memories of wild trips with siren blaring were too seared into my brain. I wasn't going to let her pilot my yellow Jeep. We would travel the speed limit, or maybe a few miles over, but this wasn't going to become one of Dolly's trips from hell.

"I'm the professional." She'd planted her body like a tree stump.

"My car," I repeated, got in on the driver's side, stuck the key in the lock, and started the motor. I buckled the seat belt then leaned down to grin at Dolly.

"You can't drive the whole way. Maybe just the first hour. I'll take over after that," she said.

I shook my head, as stubborn as she could be. "I drive. You're crazy behind the wheel."

She looked off toward the lake, then up at the clear sky, then down again at me. "You'll get tired. You'll be begging."

"Yeah," I said, and revved the motor.

With slow dignity, Dolly got in and settled beside me. She gave me a look that said a lot and pulled the seat belt across her body.

"Hope you're not going to be a big pain in the ass through the *whole* trip," she said, as if we were off on an adventure and I hadn't been coerced into going with her on what was probably going to be a big wild goose chase, producing nothing, and proving unnecessary in the end.

"And my hair does too look good. I don't care what you say. You just got no taste. No taste at all."

"Hmph," I answered, and we were off.

A flock of turkeys greeted us near the end of Willow Lake Road. Mating season got interesting in spring. Robins swooped, orioles dived, hawks sailed, sparrows and chickadees and goldfinches acted silly and coy. The deer got stupid and couldn't tell a Ford van from a doe, becoming sad hood ornaments and costing drivers lots of money. Tom turkeys stood along the side of the road with their tails spread like peacocks, trying to attract females more interested in the new grass beside the road than strutting males. And humans? Well, there wasn't a season on human stupidity.

Along M72 the trees were in the little leaf stage that quickly turns to heavily burdened branches hanging to the ground. Always something special about spring, about the first warm wind, the first warm day when I dared take off my heavy jacket, or strip down to a turtleneck sweater. We had about forty miles to go to get over to I-75, the main artery splitting Michigan's lower peninsula in half—east side from west side. I took the shortcut around by the Grayling National Guard base and we were on our way to Detroit.

It was noon when we got to Saginaw. We stopped for lunch at a McDonald's, then had our second fight over who was going to drive.

My car. I drove.

The plan was to stop somewhere outside Detroit and find a cheap motel. From there we could start making phone calls and looking over city maps. We got down close to Detroit by two o'clock, found an Econo Lodge, and took one room with twin beds.

Dinner later was at a nearby Burger King. We picked up an area map at a Barnes & Noble, and went back to our room. Dolly wanted to show me her old Christmas list and a paper Chet left behind, which turned out to be a couple of addresses on a dirty, lined scrap. No names. Just addresses.

I took a shower and got into my tacky pjs and floppy slippers. Dolly was in the bathroom a long time and came out in a camouflage nightgown with camouflage slippers to match.

"Hope I don't have to find you in the middle of the night," I groused. "I mean, in case there's a fire or anything. Between the camo and that dye job, you fade right into the shadows."

"Hmph," she said right back at me.

"You remember any of those addresses? I mean, who they belonged to?"

She shook her head and spread the map on the floor, then lay down on her stomach, legs bent into the air. She began tracing Detroit streets with her finger. "Never knew any of his people from Detroit. We weren't married that long."

"How long, Dolly?"

"Oh, maybe six months."

"Six months! He left you after six months! And you feel you owe him ... ?"

Her hand was up, stopping me. "Still makes him family."

"Dolly, how many foster homes were you in altogether?"

"Ten."

"Did you ever know your mother or your father? Any family?"

She wrinkled her nose and sniffed. "Nope. That don't mean I don't have one or the other. Just that I don't know where they are."

"You ever look? All these years?"

"Why? Never looked for me." She picked at a red cuticle around her thumb, then bit it and spit out the piece of flesh. "Doesn't it seem it's their job? I mean, to come looking for me?"

She thought awhile. "There is one woman I'd like to see in Detroit. If we have the time. She was the best foster mother I ever had. Phyllis Dually. Maybe I was six. Six and a half. Something like that. Seems I remember..." I looked away from Dolly's sad face. "I send her a Christmas card every year so I've got her address. Lives in Utica. East side. Just outside Detroit. If we have the time, and we're not too far from there..."

"Was she your last foster mother?"

Dolly shook her head. "Somewhere in the middle."

"Why'd they take you away from her?"

"She couldn't handle me. I was a troublemaker. Real pain in the ass. But I didn't want to leave that one. Truly sorry."

"Why go see her?"

"Well, it wasn't really her. It was her husband. Mean son of a bitch, if you will excuse my French. He made her get rid of me 'cause I bit his ear hard."

"Oh come on, 'bit his ear'?"

"He...eh...was...one of those too friendly types. Even then, I knew I had to fight him. She understood, Phyllis did. She knew. But what could she do? No money. No place to go. So it was me. I went."

"And you want to see her?"

She picked at the little speckles in the motel carpeting. "I think she kinda loved me. Be nice to see her. I've got some happy memories..."

Rutting around in Dolly's past was painful. I thought I could see why she considered Chet "family." Why she had fond memories of a woman who didn't protect her. There was a glimpse here into a world I could only imagine. I could go along with her. It cost me nothing.

We spent the next hour finding addresses on our map and marking them with big *X*s.

When we had our plan for the next morning in place, she put on the small TV. I got out a book to read but soon gave up because an old *Matlock* was on, and it was on loud.

# EIGHT

THE WAKOWSKI ADDRESS ON the second block of Filer Street, right off Seven Mile Road, was for a narrow empty lot between two burned-out houses. Grass and broken beer bottles were all that was left of whatever had once stood there, and a faint indentation in the weeds where a foundation might have been.

"Wonder what happened? That's where I sent his mother's Christmas card." Dolly stared out the car window.

It didn't look as if we were going to get any help in this place. The next neighbor was halfway down the block, in a house behind a tall wire fence. We parked in front of the empty lot, got out, and walked down there. A few black kids played on the sagging porch. Their mother came out fast when we opened the gate and started up the steep stairs.

"Can I help you?" the thin woman with blond highlights in her hair demanded, standing at the top of the peeling steps, hands on her angular hips.

Dolly squinted up at her. "My husband, Chet Wakowski, used to live right down there." She turned and pointed toward the empty space between houses. "I was wondering if you'd have any idea where the family went."

"Been like that since we moved in. Couple of years now," the woman said, and relaxed first her wary face, and then her taut arms. One of the children, a little boy in a blue Detroit Tigers tee shirt, ran over and hid behind his mother, peeking out and smiling at us.

"Anybody along the street been here a long time?" Dolly asked.

The woman nodded, then came down the steps and pointed. "See that green house across there? Mrs. Gleason. Old lady. Been here forever. Everybody around here taking care of her now. Can't get out to shop or nothing. Neighbors all do turns carryin' her to the doctor. If anybody knows anything it'll be Mrs. Gleason. Go on down. She loves company. Tell her Vera sent you and tell her I'll be over with soup about five o'clock."

The pretty woman smiled and waved us off.

It took Mrs. Gleason a long, long time to get to her front door. She was a thin, elderly lady with short white hair curling around her soft and welcoming face. Dolly introduced us and delivered Vera's message. Mrs. Gleason smiled and shook her head. "My neighbors," the small woman said, pushing her front door wide for us to come in. "They take such good care of me."

We walked into a living room overfilled with "stuff." There were walls of family pictures and small altars to Mary, the Blessed Mother. A Russian icon hung just inside the door. A small votive candle burned in front of it. Every table had a stiffly starched doily under a Swiss chalet thermometer or a painted Chinese statuette or a frame with another yellowed photograph. A green sofa and chair shone under stiff plastic slipcovers. Mrs. Gleason, walking slow and bent forward, pointed to the sofa. Dolly and I sat with much crinkling and crunching.

"What can I do for you?" The old woman sat across from us, hands precisely folded in the lap of her white-collared, blue-flowered dress.

"Well," Dolly said, moving to get comfortable on the stiff plastic, "my husband's people came from here. House right across the street. Used-to-be-house, I guess you'd have to say. I was wondering if you could tell us anything about the people. The Wakowskis?"

The woman smiled, lifted her hands, then thumped them in her lap. "Yes, of course I knew the Wakowskis. Mildred. I never knew the husband. I think he was gone when Mildred moved here. Oh, that was so long ago. She had two boys. And a girl."

"One of the boys Chester?"

Mrs. Gleason smiled. "Yes. Certainly was. Chet. I remember him. Used to walk around in just a diaper, one hand stuck down in and planted on his back cheek. Nose always running. Not what you'd call a...well...an attractive little boy."

"And he had a brother, Tony, right?"

Mrs. Gleason lifted one hand and waved it hard at Dolly. "That one. Always bad. Used to beat up poor little Chet. Mildred couldn't do a thing about it. I told her to get that boy help. He was going to turn out bad. And he certainly did. He's locked up in Jackson Prison. Murdered someone. Don't remember who, just the shock of hearing...well...that a person I knew could do a thing like that."

"Do you know what happened to Mildred?"

"Mildred went to live with a sister of hers. Indiana. I think it was Bloomington."

"And Chet?" Dolly asked.

Mrs. Gleason took her time. She shook her head. "I thought he was moving to Indiana with Mildred, but I heard he didn't. Elaine said Chet went up north somewhere. Elaine was never too friendly but that doesn't mean I can't send her a Christmas card once a year."

"Are you talking about Chet's sister?" Dolly asked.

"Well, yes. She lives out in Warren. I'll get the address, if you want to go see her. If you're a friend of Mildred's, or of Chet's—not Tony's though, she won't like that."

"I was married to Chet," Dolly said.

Mrs. Gleason's mouth dropped open. "You don't say. Think of that! Well ... but then why are you asking me where he is?"

"Left thirteen years ago and I haven't seen him since."

"I'm so sorry." Mrs. Gleason waved a shaky hand then put it back in the safety of her flowered lap. "And now you are hunting for him?"

Dolly nodded.

"Let me get you Elaine's address. If anybody knows where Chet is, she should. And once she finds out you're his wife, she'll surely tell you where to find him."

The address, written in wobbly handwriting, was one of the addresses Dolly'd found in Chet's papers. We might not have been finding out much about Chet, but at least we were moving in a straight line.

———

The Warren neighborhood was upscale, big brick houses set back in the middle of wide green lawns. A far cry from Filer Street in Detroit. Elaine Wakowski was doing well for herself—or had married well.

I followed Dolly to the door and stood behind her as she rang the bell.

The woman who answered wasn't pretty but she was striking, with medium-length dark hair pulled back behind her ears, bright blue eyes, a tanning salon tan, and long silver and turquoise earrings hanging to her shoulders.

"Yes?" she said, looking from Dolly to me. She looked warily, from behind her screen door, as if we could be Jehovah's Witnesses or somebody there to sell her magazines. We weren't dressed well enough for the former, and the latter were usually kids.

"I was married … well, still am, I guess … to Chet," Dolly said, talking through the screen.

Elaine frowned at her. "Really?"

"He left me and I'm looking for him."

"He left you? You mean recently? I haven't heard from him …" Elaine Wakowski shook her head as if flustered. She pushed the door open. "Come on in. I … I'm sorry. You surprised me …"

We followed her back through a living room of neat modern sofas and thick Berber carpeting. She led us through a dining room done in blond modern, to a kitchen with high, narrow windows, stainless steel appliances, and pots of African violets in lush bloom set on every surface.

Elaine waved us to the oak table and reluctantly offered to make coffee. She got cups and saucers and spoons and set the table, nervously arranging then rearranging everything.

"I'm Dolly." Dolly held her hand out, shook Elaine's hand, and then sat down. I was introduced and we all stared at each other.

"Well," Elaine said as the sunny kitchen filled with the scent of coffee brewing.

"You mean you didn't know about me and Chet? I sent your mom a Christmas card every year … well, for a few years after he took off."

"You're *that* Dolly?" Elaine's blue eyes grew big. "We wondered who the heck...from someplace up north. She got a card for a few years there and then you stopped."

Dolly shrugged. She looked uncomfortable. "I figured, since I didn't know you and I never got a card back..."

Elaine nodded. "If we'd known we would of...well...It wasn't like Chet kept in touch or anything."

She got up and poured the coffee, set cream and sugar on the table, and sat back down.

"I haven't heard from him in...oh my goodness...it must be twelve, thirteen years now. Me and Mom, we just figured he'd wandered off somewhere. Not always reliable, Chet. Last we heard he was going up north. I *thought* maybe he got married up there. Could have had kids by now, for all we knew."

Dolly shook her head. "No kids." She looked unhappy. "So you haven't seen him, nothing, in that long. Was that right after he got out of the army? I mean, that he left for up north?"

Elaine frowned at her. "What army? Chet never was in the army, or any other branch of the service."

Now it was Dolly's turn to frown. "Sure he was. I got his dog tags..."

Elaine made a noise and sat back in her chair. "Good Lord! Him and his dog tags. Sorry to tell you, Dolly, but my brother dropped out of high school in the eleventh grade. He kind of drifted after that. But he was never in the army. Loved those dog tags though."

Dolly's eyes opened wide. Something going on in her head. I could see big red placards floating. It wasn't anger. More confusion, and maybe putting old information together.

"How long ago did Chet leave you?" Elaine went on as if she hadn't dropped a bombshell. "I would have thought he'd come back here.

60

That he'd at least call. If I hear from him I'll certainly tell him you're down here looking…"

Dolly shook her head. "Thirteen years," she mumbled and looked over to me, as if I could save her.

"Goodness! Why are you hunting for him now?"

"I just have to…eh…find him. Something's happened up north and he could be in trouble."

"Oh no, not another one." Elaine sank back in her chair. "I'm so sick of this. Got one in prison, as it is."

I sipped my coffee. I figured we weren't going to be there much longer and I needed a jolt of caffeine. The coffee was like dirty, warm water. Elaine hadn't wasted much on us.

Dolly showed Elaine the other addresses we had but she didn't recognize any of them. Dolly promised to call her if and when she found Chet.

"I'll pass on the word to my mother. But I don't want her upset with any of this. You have anything to say to her, you go through me first." Elaine wrote her phone number on a piece of paper and handed it to Dolly. It was an uneasy, not friendly, parting. Neither woman seemed to know if she should be happy or sad that they'd finally met.

Back in the car all Dolly said was, "There. More family. Now I got a sister-in-law."

I drove off, saying nothing.

"Never in the army. If that isn't something. The whole thing a big lie." She shook her head. "Guess I should've figured. No photos from army days. No army buddies.

"What do you think happened to Chet?" she finally asked, settling herself in her seat. "Where the heck did he go? And never calling his mother or his sister? Seems kind of odd, even for Chet."

"If Chet killed that woman he's long gone, hiding out someplace," I said. "Could be anywhere. If he didn't kill her—and you're right—that is the woman he was with at the bar, well, maybe he knew about the murder and took off anyway."

"Or..." She tucked her chin far down into her neck. "He's dead."

I drove back out to Twelve Mile Road and turned into a Big Boy. With a bowl of hot vegetable soup and a stainless steel pot of tea in front of me, I was better able to cope with a depressed Dolly and a dead-end trip.

"I'll tell you," Dolly mumbled over her order of pancakes, sausage, and eggs. "We gotta check out the last of the addresses I've got."

"His sister didn't recognize them."

"Don't mean anything."

I gave in because we were there and it didn't seem smart to leave dead ends unexplored.

"Then I'd like to go see Phyllis Dually," she said on the way out of the restaurant. "Utica's right on our way home. Won't take any time at all."

I think I made a noise; a kind of scoffing sound. "Haven't you had enough of this family tree stuff for one day?"

I wasn't being mean. I was just tired of seeing her hurt. To the outside world it might not look like hurt, but I knew that a surly Dolly was a Dolly in pain, and as far as I was concerned, she'd had enough pain for one trip.

We were on our way back into Detroit to follow another trail of gobbled-up bread crumbs. And then off to see this Phyllis Dually, one more of Dolly Wakowski's sorry connections.

# NINE

ONE OF THE ADDRESSES turned out to be a topless bar on Eight Mile Road, a wide street of defunct businesses and seedy strip joints. The next was an unemployment office on Woodward Avenue. The last was a house in Hamtramck, a Polish suburb in the middle of the city. The middle-aged man at this thirties-built house with a high covered porch never heard of a Chet Wakowski. The place was a boarding house, he said. "Folks come and go." He leaned back in his porch chair and stretched so we'd notice how bored we made him.

"You cops?" he asked, eyeing us. I shook my head hard. Dolly, in the same tee shirt she'd worn yesterday, said nothing. We left him to his ruminative leaning.

After that we had no place left to go except maybe Chet's Mom's in Bloomington, Indiana. Not much point in that since Elaine said he hadn't been in touch with their mother in years, and she had warned Dolly to keep away from her.

"Can we leave now?" I asked, heading out Conant Street, hoping to hit I-75 and turn toward home.

"Utica," Dolly said. "Last place. I just want to let Phyllis Dually know—if she even still lives there—that I've got no hard feelings against her."

"Oh, Dolly." I let my complaint stop right there.

The tiny blue house in Utica sat on what must have once been a street of nice little suburban houses. But those good days were long gone. This house sat back from a dirt road under overgrown bushes and a stand of dead maples. Any one of the trees could take out the peaked roof at the next storm. I thought the place must be deserted, but when we pulled up the weedy drive, Dolly spotted a woman sitting on the top step of the slanting porch, smoking a cigarette and watching us with a lot of squint-eyed suspicion.

"That's her!" Dolly hopped out of the car.

The woman, in her fifties, watched as we approached, cigarette hanging from a corner of her mouth. She didn't wave, welcome, or say a word. We walked to where she sat, her knees splayed out under a faded house dress. Nothing in her worn face moved, but she wasn't expecting anything good out of us.

"Know who I am?" Dolly asked, from the bottom of the steps, in what for her was a merry voice.

The woman squinted one eye through her own smoke and looked Dolly up and down. She shook her head slowly.

"I'm Dolly. Remember?"

She looked Dolly over again then shook her head.

"Sure you do. Dolly Flynn. I lived here with you when I was about six—I think."

"One of the foster kids." The voice was flat. "Didn't you used to send me Christmas cards?"

Dolly nodded, happier again. "That's right. You had to turn me back to social services because there was trouble. Your husband ... well ... I'll just say there was trouble."

"Must've been Mike." The woman offered nothing more. She let out a long, heavy sigh, accompanied by wisps of smoke.

"No, I think his name was Herbie."

"Yeah. Herbie. He was a son of a bitch, too. He do something to you?"

Dolly shook her head. "Remember, I bit him on the ear, and he made you call the social worker?"

The woman looked Dolly over hard this time. "Don't remember you. Lots of kids had to be taken back. Herbie was big trouble for me. But so was Mike, after him. And then came Daniel—he was a bastard, let me tell you. Lots of kids come through here. The girls went fast. Even some of the boys. With Daniel it was boys as well as girls. I divorced them all."

"You cried when they took me away." Dolly crossed her arms protectively over her chest. She looked like somebody shrinking in place. I could see the little girl being dragged off, crying.

I put a hand on Dolly's tensed arm and for once she didn't shrug me off. "Let's go, Dolly," I said, and pulled just a little.

"You sure you don't remember me, Phyllis?"

Phyllis took a long, slow drag on her cigarette, shifted her legs around under that skirt, and shrugged.

"So many of you. I needed that damned money. Those assholes I married was forever messing it up for me. Glad I ain't got no man in this house anymore. But then I can't get kids either. Too bad. Things would be fine now. Might even meet somebody who was different from those others. I thought each one of them was a good man. I guess some women have trouble their whole life long finding Mr. Right."

"Dolly," I pulled a little harder. She stood frozen, staring up at Phyllis.

Her empty-eyed face turned to me. Her mouth dropped open a little. I felt sorry for her. She'd just had the last member of her imagined little family shot out from under her.

Dolly turned without saying a word and walked back toward the car. I let out a lot of pent-up air, trying to think of something cutting to say to the ignorant woman on the porch. But what was there to say that would hurt her? What was there left to say or do to her that hadn't already been said or done?

We got back in the Jeep and headed north.

# TEN

"I DON'T SEE WHY you don't have a cell phone."

We'd been driving a long time. Through industrial Flint. Through Saginaw. We were just past the turnoff to Midland in Bay City—the point where I'd always thought true up-north Michigan began. From here on we would see farmland, a wavy American flag made of cement blocks, and then the woods. I breathed better when I was back among the trees, heading toward Grayling. Not only breathed better but felt an oppressive load lift from my shoulders. Probably memories of all that old stuff—the escaping when our marriage soured, when there were decisions to be made and I didn't know I had options. All things that oppressed me disappeared when I headed north. After my dad's funeral, I hadn't taken I-75 up from Grand Blanc, but it didn't matter as long as the road went north: Claire, Cadillac, Grayling—they sounded like freedom to me. And smelled like freedom when I opened the window and let in the scents of the pines and the leaf mold and the water.

It seemed there was little left to say between Dolly and me. Nothing had worked out for her—no Chet and not even that one good memory from childhood. After our abortive trip neither of us had much energy, not even for arguing.

"I said I don't see why you don't have a cell phone." Dolly raised her voice, but not with the usual aggression. "You'd think, being a reporter and all, you'd need to be in touch all the time."

"Nope," I said, getting the feeling she had an ulterior motive. "Why don't you have one?"

She made a derisive noise. "What for? I've got the police radio in my car. Got a phone at home. Hardly ever anywhere else but those two places."

"Then that makes two of us," I said, and fiddled with the radio knob, trying for some jazz, maybe NPR. Music or talk might fill the emptiness in the car. We hadn't discussed any of what had happened. Dolly was uncharacteristically silent, and I didn't want to walk where smarter people knew not to go. The radio gave me static and a cooking show.

"I'd like to make a call anyway."

"Oh? To whom?"

"The chief. I'm going to have to tell him about Chet. There's no getting around it—Chet must've been involved. Not to call his own mother in all these years. Not his sister. Nobody heard from him. That's not like Chet at all. To tell you the truth I thought he'd be coming back to me long, long ago. You couldn't exactly say Chet was the kind of man who could stand on his own two feet. You know, kind of a sorry soul, was what he was. But if he did this … to that girl …"

"You going to tell the chief what you stole from Sandy Lake?"

"What do you mean 'stole'? I told you those tags were my wedding present. I was just reclaiming what's …"

"Yeah."

"Well, I was."

"Why didn't you mention making a phone call back around Bay City where there were places to stop?"

"There's gas stations ahead."

"Most don't have phones anymore."

"Phooey! When'd they stop having telephones?"

"When people all got cell phones."

"Except you and me."

"Yeah. Except you and me."

"Won't hurt to try."

The next Shell station and convenience store had a public phone inside. Dolly got more change than she would ever use and made her call. I walked the aisles picking out things I'd buy if I were really truly skinny and could afford the calories—like Three Musketeers and trail mix loaded with M&Ms. Dolly came back from the phone busily shoving change into the pocket of her pants and frowning. She glared at me and barked, "Let's get going."

I let her pay for the gas and went on out to the Jeep. Something new was up. Her face didn't hide anything. She was upset all over again. Lips pursed. Nose wrinkled up into something like a knot. This had been a rotten day for Dolly so far and, therefore, for me. I hoped it hadn't just gotten worse.

We were back on I-75, almost to West Branch, before she finally opened her mouth.

"They found another one," she said, half growling at me as she stared out the window at the woods.

"Another what?"

"Another skeleton. In the lake."

"What!"

"Yup. Brought in divers. Found this one farther out, held down by a cement block with ropes tied around it."

"So…" I needed time to think. A lot happening all at once. I would have to get ahold of Bill, call the state police, maybe get out there and take photos of something or other. But a deeper thing nagged at me. Another skeleton…

"A man," Dolly said, voice low and sulky. "Medical examiner's pretty sure about that. Teeth—first and second molars. And other stuff. The chief said they measure the pelvis and long bones. I kept asking 'cause they could be wrong. I'm still hoping they're wrong."

"You don't think…?"

"Who the hell else would it be? That's why nobody's heard from him, why he never came home. Gotta be Chet."

"Geez, Dolly. I'm so sorry…"

"Yeah. You know what that makes me, don't you?" Her upper teeth clamped down on her lower lip as if these were words she didn't want to let out.

"Makes you?"

She nodded hard. "Makes me a widow."

"Well, I guess. Sort of."

"A widow. Barely a wife." She shook her head. "Said he was shot in the head, too. Like the other one. Two murders. And something else. They think the first bones were Indian. An Indian girl. Pathologist's sure about it. They got ways to figure that out."

"Old? Maybe it's all a mistake. Nothing to do with Chet."

"Not new—with all the flesh gone. But not fossilized either. I'll bet they come up with about thirteen years."

"If she was Indian, the tribe will want her back."

"One of the Odawa was there to see Lucky already. Says they want her immediately. Has to be reburied right away according to their religion."

"But if it's murder...?"

"He told 'im. They won't get anything back until the investigation is over."

"Lucky say if they had any idea who did this?"

She made a noise and looked out her window. "No. Course not. He doesn't even know it could be Chet."

"Geez, Dolly, it's time."

She snapped her head around to look directly at me. Her eyes flashed something I hadn't seen there before. Maybe this one day had finally extracted more than she could tolerate; maybe it was more of Dolly's "family" thing; whatever she was shooting at me, I had the feeling we were back in deep shit together.

"I've got to think it out first. Oh God, I'll have to call his sister. We'll have to bury him."

"You don't know anything for sure," I said. "Anyway, he walked out on you, Dolly. Let his sister and mother handle the funeral. They'll want him buried down by them."

Dolly tucked her chin into her neck. "Chet was my husband, Emily. I'll see to him in death the way I did in life. And I'm not going to let some murdering creep get away with killing my very own husband in my very own town."

When she sniffed I knew she was crying.

"You just watch and see if I do," she muttered, then sniffed again. "I've got things to figure out first. Like who she was. Wish I'd noticed more when I saw 'em together at The Skunk. All I did was see the dog tags and get so mad I stormed out. In the morning he was gone. Clothes gone. Spurs gone. Truck gone. Hunting rifle—gone. Nothing

71

left of him at all. Like he never existed. Just swept right out of my life. Without my dog tags, well, there was nothing but a dirty coffee cup of his in the kitchen and some hairs in the bathroom sink. Still got the coffee cup. Just the way it was. Had to wash out the bathroom sink but I kept some of those whiskers in an envelope.

"Guess we gotta know who she was," she said, talking to herself, words half staying in her mouth. She dug a Kleenex out of her pocket and blew her nose. "Find her family. Find out if anybody knows anything. Start with missing persons from back thirteen years. That's it. Start there."

"Check with the Odawa. They want her back so bad, they must know who she is," I said.

"Can't contact the Indians. They're gonna be all over me—when they hear for sure it's Indian bones. Their religion's big on burying people fast." She took another swipe at her nose then tucked the crumpled Kleenex into my glove compartment. "Why don't you check your newspaper morgue. Just in case something shows up from another town that looks like it could be her. We don't even know if she's from around Leetsville. Maybe see about Peshawbestown, the reservation. I mean just go asking about missing girls. Nothing else. Hmm ... Got any other ideas?"

I shook my head and prayed for the trip to end. Whatever Dolly was going to get herself involved in, she meant we were in it together. I made a face toward the windshield and wondered what I'd ever done to make this feisty little policewoman light on me as her compatriot in crime fighting. I'd come up north for the solitude, for the quiet to write, for peace from trouble and anger and stress. What I needed most right then was to get back home, kiss Sorrow, get Deputy Dolly Wakowski out of my car, and get lost in my new book.

Or better yet, get lost in the spring woods for a while. Maybe I'd take Crazy Harry up on his offer to help me find edibles growing out there. I could learn to tell a false morel from a real one. He'd teach me the names of all those flowers lighting open spaces under the just filling out trees. The thought of it made me feel cleaner. I didn't want to be involved with old bones, cheating husbands, murderers, awful foster mothers who didn't remember a child who had nobody else to love. There were better places to be and I wanted, desperately, to be there.

"You don't have to help me with anything," Dolly said in a small voice after I'd been quiet all the way around Grayling. "If that's what's bothering you, I can do it alone."

I made a noise, something like agreement but also something like: got my own work to do. She took my noncommittal sound to have another meaning.

"Thanks, Emily. I knew you'd want to be there for me."

I made another noise, aimed at me. Too late to disagree. I sat straight and still, visions of my writing, my quiet, my garden, the woods leaping out of my head like those rats that are supposed to be the first to leave a sinking ship.

"I'll go see the chief. Tell him everything. Then I'll go through old missing persons' records. You wanna see Eugenia? Ask if she ever heard about Chet and some Indian girl? If anybody knows anything, you know it will be Eugenia."

"Tomorrow, Dolly. I'm tired. I want to get back to my house and forget dead people for a few hours."

"Great reporter you are. When you gonna call your paper?"

"Let me handle my own business, all right?"

She shrugged. "Can't drag your feet." The eyes she turned on me were red-rimmed. She lowered her head fast, as if she had no right to pain.

"I need time to … heal from all of this." I made a gesture encompassing I didn't know what.

"Yeah, well, healing's one thing. Getting on with life—that's another. I'm getting on."

One blunt hand went up and Dolly began ticking off things to do on her fingers.

Thumb: "I'll go over to The Skunk and see if anybody remembers back that far."

First finger: "Then—let me see—I'll try the gun shop and the barber shop. Wish he'd been a churchgoer. No chance there."

Middle finger: "I'll go through all our missing persons from back awhile. Don't expect her to be there though. I've been over the old cases before.

"More than anything I wish I'd raised a fuss when I saw 'em together. Be forever sorry now. Just too shocked at the sight of his dog tags around her neck. Might have saved them both if I'd raised a stink when I should've."

"Yup, all your fault, Dolly."

She turned my way. One eye wandered just far enough off center to give her a disoriented look. "Shut up," she said, and fell to thinking and muttering all the way back to my house, and her car. She grabbed her backpack and was gone.

It was a relief to see that Sorrow had been a good boy. Only one screen busted out on the porch, one rope chewed through, one pile of poop, one water dish overturned onto the bare boards, and only one garden clog chewed to a mass of rubber worms.

I rewarded him with kisses for all that good behavior.

# ELEVEN

I WASN'T HAPPY WHEN we got home from Detroit. I was made no happier by a call from Jackson, wondering how far I'd gotten on the chapters of his book. Going through the mail did nothing to lift my spirits: house insurance due, huge electric bill. Double because I hadn't paid the last one. And the phone bill. The Sears bill for the tires the Jeep had required. Two more rejections of *Dead Dancing Women*.

I gave myself an hour away from everything, first going down to the lake to throw a stick for Sorrow, who joyously leaped and loped until he lay wet and exhausted at my feet with his long pink tongue hanging out. Not once, in sixty minutes, did I let myself think about the awful Dolly business. Then, with a sigh, I went back in the house and got to work. I called the Michigan State Police post at Gaylord. When I had what they would tell me, I wrote the story of the second skeleton and e-mailed it to Bill. After that I figured I had done my duty. I was going over to Crazy Harry's to see if he wanted to play in the woods, chasing mushrooms and other edibles. I dug my mesh mushroom bag out of the pantry, put on an old denim jacket, and left, leaving Sorrow home. I was afraid Harry's weird dogs might attack him. His indignant barking followed me up the drive to Willow Lake Road.

Harry was in the middle of skinning another of those raccoons he told me walked up to his door and died of old age. Not a pretty sight.

"Give me a couple minutes, Emily," he said, sticking his long knife into the tall tree stump where he worked and wiping his hands carefully on the rag sticking from his pocket. He went into the house while I kept my back turned to the dogs throwing their bodies at the chain-link fence around the kennel. In a few minutes Harry came out, unfolding his huge, mesh mushroom bag so it dragged along behind him. It always threw me for a couple of minutes that Harry could wear his burying suit every day and half live in the woods but never get the suit dirty; never lose the crease in the long, skinny pants that skimmed his legs. I had the feeling Harry had more than one suit but it wasn't the kind of thing you came out and asked. There was a dignity, and privacy, about Harry that I knew better than to try and get around. The man had lived alone most of his life. Talking didn't come easy to him, nor telling strangers truths that could come back to haunt him.

———

Last year's leaves didn't crunch under our feet as I followed Harry through the woods. The ground was soft, with an old leather feel, kneaded into decomposition by heavy winter snows. All of it—the thick bed of leaves—going to feed the earth. This stuff still amazed me. Cycles. Cycles. Cycles. *Big wheel keeps on turning.* I ran it through my head, like clearing out old cobwebs. So good to be where things were dependable.

I'd never had a clue about nature before coming to live in the woods. Never saw the huge canvas around me. How could I know that such a wondrous, slow-moving security existed back when I ran too fast day after day, rarely lifted my head as I hurried to the next story, the next dinner party, or faced the next infidelity from Jackson Rinaldi. Like everyone, I'd wondered what life was about, why I was here, but I never wondered deeply enough to think there might be answers, or at least tiny signposts pointing toward what the amazing earth and I had in common.

Harry and I walked carefully. A little rain fell; a fine mist leaving my skin moist, my hair damp. I could feel and taste the wet west wind. Overhead, the trees dripped sluggish drops as we passed beneath, working our way through thickets of last year's sumac and new stands of aspens as spindly as colt legs. We searched for fallen trees where the elusive morel liked to grow.

Every few yards Harry stopped. He would bend over in his old suit, shiny with rain, and put a finger to his grizzled lips as he studied the ground ahead—swinging his body left, then right, searching for mushrooms. I never spotted one of them. Harry would extend his arm and point—almost at my feet—to a wide circle of wrinkled, brain-like fungi blending into the brown shades of the old leaf bed. We would pick them gleefully, stuffing the mushrooms into our bags.

"Mesh drops the spores behind us," Harry'd said once, when I'd offered plastic bags and he'd shaken his head at me. "That's how ya get a new crop next year. Plastic kills everything it touches."

When Harry pointed next, I crouched and pinched two fingers at the base of one spongy mushroom after another. I squeezed until the mushroom popped off, then sniffed it before putting it into my bag. Everything was caught in that smell—the woods, the soil, old trees, dead trees, tiny insects, rain … everything I loved about this place.

Celebration in a single mushroom. No real ugliness in nature. No sorrow. Even the few deer corpses I'd come upon in my walks hadn't been sad. Something about the inevitability of it all—no futile dream of immortality. Bones were bones. Soon to be a part of everything around them. Not at all like Dolly's bones—with pain and suspicion and horror ...

During the two days I'd spent with Dolly I'd been reminded that life, for human beings, wasn't always fair. Maybe hardly ever fair, and that good people kept getting hurt, and good people tried to rationalize away all the crap that landed on them. It wasn't right for me to get mad at Dolly's past. But how did I not get mad at a woman who pretended to love a child who never knew love?

"Did you know Chet, Dolly's husband?" I asked Harry as he brought a handful of mushrooms over to my bag. His old man's arthritic hands were sweetly cupped so as not to bruise the morels. One by one he lifted a mushroom by the base and set it, with his careful, brown, ridged fingers, in on top of the others.

He looked up at me when I asked about Chet. His pale eyes, surrounded with deep wrinkles, were confused, as if he couldn't switch so fast from mushrooms to people.

He stepped away from me, sniffed, and took a swipe at his nose with the damp, white handkerchief he pulled from a back pocket. "Why you asking?" he asked suspiciously, folding his handkerchief carefully before putting it away.

"I think they might have found his bones out in Sandy Lake."

"The hell, you say. Thought he took off with a woman." Harry frowned and turned his body away as if avoiding a blow.

"Maybe he did. Two skeletons in the lake."

Harry shook his head and thought awhile, toeing the leaves at his feet with his old black shoe. When he looked back at me, his nose was aimed into the wind, sniffing. He looked slowly right then left. "Didn't hear about no skeletons."

"You will. They brought up the second one early this morning."

"Then why you calling one of 'em 'Chet'? How'd they find out so fast?"

"Dolly thinks it's him. She found something by the body… er …bodies."

"Ah." He sniffed again, white and black eyebrows going up and down. "So, you want to know about him?"

I nodded.

"Won't go saying nothing to the deputy, will you? I don't like to get in the middle of things." He toed the earth, then scoured the sky where patches of blue broke up the heavy clouds.

I shook my head, assuring him.

"Well now, Chet wasn't what you'd call one of the sharpest pencils in the box. Grown boy when he came up here. From somewhere down near Detroit, I hear. Wasn't a kid but still he acted like one. Used to get in trouble doing silly teenage stuff. Stupid things like piling a row of rocks in the street on Halloween and covering them with leaves so cars hit 'em and screeched their brakes. One time he and a few of his buddies from The Skunk made a stuffed scarecrow and dropped it down right in front of a car. Driver thought he'd hit a human being. Got in trouble for that, too. But I never knew Chet to do any real damage. Don't think he never went to jail for anything, though I did hear one time he got caught stuffing a roll of toilet paper down his pants at the IGA. Think he just paid for it and that was that. People still laugh about it. That's what we're like around here. Some things're funny. Some things not so funny."

"Ever hear of him having a girlfriend?"

Harry thought awhile. "Just Dolly. There was somebody told me once they thought Chet was cutting out on her, but I never knew another thing about it until I heard he took off with some Indian girl. Came as a surprise. Felt sorry for Dolly then. Until she went and wrote me a ticket for no license on my car when, hell's sakes, it's not even registered. I stick to the back roads now. People flash their headlights at me if they see her car hanging around."

Harry chewed over that last insult.

"Been a long time ago. I'll still feel sorry for her if something bad happened to Chet. Be a shame, too, if that's as far as he got with his girl friend—only out to Sandy Lake. Maybe they was having a picnic. Maybe went for a swim; didn't come up."

"They found him tied to a cement block. Both of them were shot through the head."

Harry pursed his lips, shook himself a few times, and made a serious face. "A fella can't do that to himself, you know."

I agreed. "That's what I thought, too."

"So you think somebody killed Chet? And his girlfriend?"

"That's what Dolly's thinking. Hoped maybe you'd heard something. Anything at all about Chet and that Indian girl. Seems the Indians got interested awfully fast."

"Yeah, well, usually they like to keep to their own. No Indian man's going to stand still for one of his women going with a white man."

"You think one of them might have killed them both?"

"Hard to say. Could be Dolly found out and did 'em in herself." He bent again and put a finger to his lips. He pointed straight ahead. Dozens of morels peeking up through the leaves. A treasure trove of lovely small cones.

"Say, speaking of Indians, I forgot to tell you something." He put an arm out to stop me before I trod on the mushrooms. "One of 'em came to see you while you was gone. I went over to your place, taking care of yer dog. There was a big, dark man standing in your driveway, looking down at yer house. Older guy, he was. I asked him what he was doing there, and he said he needed to talk to you about something he saw you do. I didn't ask what that might've been 'cause it's none of my business. But he was a real serious-looking fellow. One of those straight, dark faces. You know, like there was something big to talk about, like a peace treaty, or a pipe to smoke, or maybe you owe some money at the casino."

"He didn't give you his name?"

Harry shook his head and took a slow step forward. "Never saw him in Leetsville. Maybe not from around here. Say, did I ever tell you about the logging camp right down in that gully over there?"

Whatever the Indian had said to Harry, it must have made him nervous. He was in a hurry to change the subject and get back to what he knew best—the woods, mushrooms. That left me with an uneasy feeling and a lot less interest in searching for food.

I was ready to start for home but Harry motioned me forward, pointing down the steep embankment we stood on, into a thick stand of maple. It was hard to concentrate on Harry's history lesson. I was worried about that man who'd come to see me. If it was the same guy from the lake...I told Dolly he saw what she did. But Harry said "older guy." I was in the middle of something I didn't understand. Darn her. Darn me. Right there in the woods I began looking over my shoulder to see if I could catch sight of a figure with dark hair blowing in the wind, following along behind.

"White man's camp right over there." Harry pointed ahead then turned and pointed behind us, down the other side of the embankment to where the maples weren't as thick. "Indian lumberjack's camp back there. No love lost between the two camps. One night one of the

Indians went over and murdered a man who'd been picking on his brother, then he up and disappeared. They know how to do that, ya see. Know these woods like somebody else might know their own backyard. But that brother wasn't so lucky. Somebody from the white man's camp found him, done him in, and all the Indians left. But not before they got their revenge—in the white man's terms. They turned over one of them railroad engines that was waiting to take a load of logs down to Graying. Track ran right through these woods. Men cut trees in the summer. Pulled out the logs by horse in the winter, when the logs could be skidded over the snow. Took 'em to the log dump— just through those trees there, where the train was waiting. Indians turned that engine over and dumped 'er off the trestle we're standing on. Maybe a hundred years ago. Last I heard the engine was still down there somewhere. Couldn't right it and get it back up, so they buried it. Time's covered it over. That's what time does—just like with your skeletons. Wouldn't think of digging that engine up 'cause some things are best left buried, you know. Best left buried."

I couldn't tell if Harry was just talking or if he was warning me to stay away from old murders. I followed along behind him as we made our way home. We stopped and dug wild garlic, pungent, but not as pungent as it would get later in summer. We came on a patch of milk-weed, young pods about an inch or so long.

"Wash 'em off," Harry told me as he picked the pods. He hurriedly slipped small pods clumsily into the pocket of my jacket. I got the feeling he'd had enough of me for one day. Probably more talking than Harry did in a week. Body bent forward, he walked on ahead, stopping only to hold low-hanging branches so I didn't get whacked.

"Boil 'em in three different waters," he said over his shoulder. "Dry 'em. Cook 'em in butter. Best thing ever."

When we went through an abandoned garden, behind a ruin of a house with only one wall left standing (and the ubiquitous lilac bush), he pointed at what he called purslane. Without stopping he gave me the same cooking direction, ending with "Fry 'em up with butter. Best thing you ever ate."

When we got back to his little crooked house where the dogs went into paroxysms of joy at the sight of him, Harry said, "One day I'll take you collecting cattail roots. Grind 'em and get the same as flour."

After we divided our spoils, I took the long way home. The woods were bright with swaths of the three-leafed white trillium. Clusters of the snobby Jack-in-the-pulpit stood beside the barely discernible deer path I followed. Jack-in-the-pulpits reminded me of gossiping monks with their high cowls, faces turned to each other as they stood above every other flower.

I recognized tiny spring beauties at my feet. And even knew a May apple when I saw one. The bloated pink lady's slipper grew in the woods just behind my studio, along with Dutchman's breeches. There was wild bleeding heart, and squawroot, bunches of them growing near a dead oak. Yellow trout lilies lined the edge of the path. And then the flowers I didn't know by name. I couldn't tell a foamflower from a starflower. Nor an honesty from a pipsissewa. Harry knew them all. He had names for everything and talked about them as friends. The wildflowers weren't weeds to him, nor anonymous plants. Everything had its rightful place in Harry's world. I didn't imagine I could live long enough to know all that Harry knew.

I felt safe in the woods, but was seriously bothered by the Indian who knew where I lived, who'd come to see me, and would probably be back. What would I tell him? How did I defend Dolly but get to the truth about those watery skeletons? I walked very slow, approaching my house, in its small valley, obliquely. I hoped to see him first—if he was there—and not be surprised.

I stepped carefully and quietly from the deep woods into my garden. No man. No car in the drive, but I still didn't feel safe. My heart pounded. He could be anywhere. Maybe following me. Who did I think I was, trying to outsmart an Indian in the forest where his ancestors had lived and hunted for thousands of years?

The cedar cottage I loved didn't look as sweetly benign today. I slipped between my flowering crabs and sprinted up garden paths to my house. I went from window to window, peeking in to see if anyone sat inside. Sorrow spotted me and went into a frenzy of greeting, leaping from room to room, barking his loud, complaining bark. He was mad that I'd gone off into the woods without him. This game of hide-and-seek drove him crazy.

I feared for my furniture as he leaped at first one window, then the next. Not a vase of violets would be left. Not a lamp. I ran around to the side door, praying no tall man with flowing black hair waited on my porch. Everything was empty: porch, garden, drive, but with a feeling of disturbed air, the feeling there had recently been a presence there. Imagination or not, I knew this was one man I couldn't avoid.

# TWELVE

"It's Chet all right," Dolly said without preamble. Her voice, over the library phone, unemotional and flat.

I thought I would be safe at the college library. There had been the hope that for a few hours I'd be left alone, unreachable, and I could search the back issues of the newspaper on microfilm the way I used to do research at the University of Michigan libraries, with no one watching me, everyone intent on their own thing. I had looked forward to this morning. Just me. Alone.

But I was wrong. As if I'd been fitted with a tracking device, she had found me where I'd told no one I was going. At least, no one I remembered telling. But maybe I had been seen in Traverse City, seen entering the library of the college campus on Front Street. Maybe some Leetsvillian had followed my yellow Jeep into town. Had I mentioned to Crazy Harry, as we'd planted pumpkin seeds in little hills that morning, that I was going to the college library to look up girls who had disappeared thirteen years ago?

"Brent found an old silver belt buckle, like clasped hands. Parts of a cowboy boot with a spur on it. Chet loved how he jingled everywhere he went, got looked at. His pride and joy—that belt buckle and those boots."

"I'm so sorry…"

"Yeah. Well. What I expected."

"Still…"

"I know. Can't say it doesn't hurt. Guess I was hoping somebody else ran off with that girl. Somebody who stole Chet's dog tags."

"I don't suppose there's still a…"

"Not with that buckle and those boots to top it off."

"Guess not." I had run out of condolences. "If you need to talk or… anything…"

"Nope. Just need to find the son of a bitch who did this. Now it's really personal. Even Detective Brent's feeling bad. Said we should go on ahead, find any missing girls from that time; start following up; look for Chet's friends. I got a dog bite I gotta get to right now. After that I'm going over to the wood products place where he worked. See if anybody remembers anything from back then. Maybe get some names. I don't know. Whatever. How about EATS tonight? We'll figure out what we got to do and divide up the work."

"I have the old newspapers on microfilm now. Should have a list by then."

"Me, too. Went through the records. Found only one possible. But he was a guy. Let's take a look at what you got."

I agreed we had a plan for later. "Hey, by the way, how did you find me here?" I asked.

"Eugenia told me."

"I didn't tell anyone but Bill, my editor at the paper."

"You know how they are in Leetsville. I think Harry was in. Oh, and Eugenia said to tell you that Annie really needs to talk to you."

"Forgot."

"She's got some big plan to make money for new library books. Guess she figures on you to help her out."

"Oh." I felt the lack of enthusiasm in my voice.

"Won't kill you to do something for Leetsville once in ..."

"Yeah. Yeah. Yeah. You talk to Eugenia about Chet?"

"Yup. She's going to ask around but she didn't remember anything from back then. Not him and any certain woman."

"OK. Brent wants us to go on looking into the murders? What happened to make him so nice all of a sudden? Is he going soft?"

"Nope. What I heard was there's a big trial in Midland. A couple of his investigators had to go down to testify. Gonna take about a week. He's shorthanded." She hesitated a minute. "And I think he's feeling sorry for me."

"Good man," I answered, oddly happy that somebody treated Dolly with respect.

"I just started here," I said. "Shouldn't be too long." I smiled at the librarian who tapped her watch pointedly. "I've been to the magazines, drumming up work. *Northern Pines* assigned me a story on the bones, and one on Indian cemeteries. One of them, up near Alba, sounds interesting. Dark Forest Cemetery."

"You talk to Bill about full time?"

"Not yet, but I'm going back there when I finish here. Might pick his brain—where else to look for missing girls."

"Don't forget to ask about that job." She thought a minute. "You know, I've been thinking. There's always Avon. You could sell door to door. Or maybe scrap booking—everybody's into that now. Or, you

87

know what? I hear there's home parties where they sell sexy lingerie, things like chocolate underpants."

"Hmm." I pushed the phone tight against my ear so the librarian couldn't make out what Dolly, in her strident voice, was saying. "You want to be my first customer?"

"Me? What the heck would I do with chocolate underpants? Sounds messy. I sweat too much."

"I get the picture, Dolly. Think I'll keep hunting for a writing job."

"There's real estate. You're good with people."

"I'll keep it in mind," I said. "Oh, can I run Chet's name in my next story? As one of the murder victims?"

There was a long pause. For a minute I thought she'd hung up on me. "Dolly?"

"Not yet, Emily. You never know. Brent wants to see if forensics can get DNA from bone marrow, or from his teeth."

"They'll need something of his..."

"Hairs. I kept those whiskers of his out of the sink. And I called his sister. She's finding dental records. When they're positive about a match...I'll let you know."

"OK. I'll wait until then."

"'Preciate it. See you about six?"

"Sure. And Dolly, I'm really very sorry that Chet ended...well ...the way he did."

"I know. Me, too." No cool voice this time. Dolly choked.

———

Back at the microfilm machine, I found that back in 1994 and 1995 the newspaper ran a regular police blotter. Three counties reported. I went through issue after issue. A couple of men disappeared while out hunting. Another, a Matthew Conklin in Alba, had gone out for a quart of milk one evening and never returned to his wife and nine kids.

A Jarvis Wargin left work at Crispin Tool and Die, said to be off to a poker game, and was never seen again.

Another man. Nobody really knew his name but he'd just disappeared. He'd been staying with a Jonas family in Leetsville and then was gone. Report stated the social worker who reported him missing said he was a wanderer and probably just left for southern Michigan.

There were six women. Two were elderly. I skipped over them.

Four were young girls:

Lisa Valient, age sixteen, five foot two, blond—short hair, blue eyes. Last seen on Front Street in Traverse City talking to an unidentified male. The report came from her mother, Fern Valient, of Washington Street.

Tricia Robbins of Kalkaska. Eighteen. Five-seven. Brown hair and eyes. She went missing in April 1994. Her father said she'd run off before but never for this long.

Bambi Lincoln of Mancelona. Seventeen. Five-six. Brown hair. Blue eyes. Last seen on her way to school. Reported missing after a week by her sister, Tanya Lincoln, of Elk Rapids.

June 1994: Mary Naquma. Nineteen. Five foot two. Long, dark hair. Dark eyes. Reported missing by a friend: Lena Smith, of Peshawbestown. Last seen at the Tracy Beauty School in Traverse City where both girls were enrolled. Mary never came back to school. Never called anybody. Her friend said it was not like her. All Lena Smith knew about Mary was that she'd once said she lived out on a lake beyond Leetsville.

I went back to the general news for April, May, June, July, and August. There were no stories about any of the missing people. No follow-ups. No bodies found. As if they'd simply fallen in some huge cosmic crack, they were all gone.

It gave me the shivers. Like most disappearances, they had to be somewhere. And it wasn't a distant planet. I once did a story on early disappearances in the Ann Arbor area—back when Michigan was founded. Eighteen hundreds. Kids disappeared. Indians were blamed, but knowing what we know now, there had to be perverts around even back then, or really sick parents.

Today girls got abducted. They ran away. They went to live with another parent. And men still ran from responsibilities. The old "out for a pack of cigarettes and never came back" still held. People left their lives for all sorts of reasons. What Dolly and I would have to find out was what happened to this group of young women. My money was on Mary Naquma, but I'd been a reporter long enough to know that what looked like a sure thing rarely was.

# THIRTEEN

THE LIBRARIAN POINTED TO a shelf of phone books when I asked. I wanted not only Traverse City Area but Kalkaska, Leetsville, and Mancelona. One girl was a Lisa Valient. Her mother was Fern Valient of Washington Street, right there in Traverse City.

I found Fern Valient, still on Washington Street, and wrote down the address and phone number. It seemed a good thing to simply call her. But this matter felt too delicate. I didn't have the right, or the necessary power, to go snooping back into the woman's life. I'd need Dolly with me. Her little gold badge could open doors. A reporter was different from a cop. The cop could scare the heck out of people. A reporter only irritated. But then, I told myself, this might make a good story: girls missing all these years. What happened to them? Where were the investigations? I'd have to call Bill first and make sure he wanted the story. I didn't want to misrepresent myself, or the paper. It didn't do to get a reputation for sneakiness up here where stories spread like wildfire and reputations got ruined by stupidity.

I found two Robbins in Kalkaska. I wrote down both addresses and numbers and wondered how we could go about finding the right Robbins; the family that belonged to Tricia.

There was no Lincoln in Mancelona. I looked up Bambi's sister, Tanya Lincoln of Elk Rapids, and made note of the address and phone number

There were no Naqumas in Leetsville. None in Mancelona. None in Kalkaska. None in Traverse City. There was no Lena Smith in Peshawbestown. I left the library, got my Jeep out of the college parking lot, and drove back to Front Street, passing knots of students enjoying the spring day playing wild games of Frisbee or leaning on trees and dreamily watching the bright sky. A few were obviously involved in that old spring game of hooking up, young girls and guys leaning into each other, laughing at something only they understood. As I drove off campus and over to Garfield, where I made a left turn, I took note of who passed me and who looked my way. Leetsvillians, with their uncanny power to know things they shouldn't know, were spooking me. Then I had that mysterious Indian man looking for me. It felt like the beginnings of paranoia, I scoffed at myself. Still, I couldn't shake the deep-down uneasiness triggering fear.

Everything looked normal around me. The white-haired guy in the Mercedes at the light didn't turn my way. The lady with two kids strapped into their seats in back of the SUV talked busily over her shoulder. Teenage girls out hoping to be seen in Daddy's Ford—they certainly ignored me. Traverse City was gearing up for summer. More traffic, more people on the streets. Even in the little park near Garfield, where I'd turned to go to the newspaper office, people flew kites and chased each other like the swooping robins coming at my car back on Willow Lake Road. Summer, in this northern town, took on a thick overlay of crowds coming up to escape the heat and the congestion of the big city. People came for the lake that would soon be littered with white triangles of sails. Little by little, the town shook off the sleepiness of winter and became a "fun" town. The locals might grit their teeth and pray for rain as the Cherry Festival came and went, and as the intellectual crowd showed up for Michael Moore's film festival, but they loved it all.

I had called Bill and told him I was coming. At the newspaper, in its ivy-covered red brick building, the cheerful woman behind the desk called him to say I was there. I waited, reading that day's newspaper, until he walked up the hall, put his hands out to take mine, then put an arm around my back.

"Glad to see you, Emily." He bowed his large, mop-haired head close and grinned as he guided me through the maze of offices and desks to his, at the back of the building. "Good stuff you're getting on those murders."

"Yes, it is going well . . ."

"Detective Brent sent over two photos. Both skeletons. Got anything more on 'em yet?"

I was surprised Brent had been such a help. For a moment I wondered what it would cost me—his cooperation—then told myself I'd been cynical enough for one day. Accept help where help was offered and let it go at that.

"That second one is probably Deputy Dolly Wakowski's husband," I said. "He's been gone for thirteen years. She thought he ran off with another woman."

"Looks as if that could be the case," he said dryly, guiding me gently into his small, littered office and pointing to a low chair in front of his desk.

I took a stack of newspapers off the chair and set them on the floor.

"Do a story on them both. I'd say go talk to the Indians, but they're going to be after those bones. You bring something for me today?"

"The deputy asked me to wait for a positive ID before I got it in the paper that this second skeleton is Dolly's husband."

Bill nodded and began to push papers around on his desk, moving a pile from one side to the other, then back again in a futile attempt to make room to write notes.

The dark oak desk, which looked like something scrounged from a back alley, was overrun with paper and books and buried things peeking out beneath the piles. Stacks of books and newspapers stood close to the walls.

"How long you think it'll take? The Detroit papers are already sniffing around. I'd like to get there first."

"Depends on forensics. Bone marrow. Hair. Dental records. But Dolly's got reason to be pretty sure that's who these latest bones belong to."

"Uh-huh. Uh-huh. Tough for your friend." He nodded that head of shaggy brown hair. It fell over his eyes as he appeared to drop into deep, serious thought. "Well, get me something by tomorrow early. And some other photos, Emily. I'd like to run photos of the lake, if nothing else. You and Dolly looking into any of this yourselves?"

I wasn't sure I should admit to our plans or not. But this was Bill. Big, charming, warm Bill.

"I'm researching lost girls from about that long ago."

He raised his eyebrows, then stuck his middle finger up, and pushed at the heavy glasses sliding down his nose. I knew better than to take it personally. I guessed that was the only finger he had free sometimes. Maybe due to having ink on his hands from all those newspapers he read; or mayo from the sandwiches he ate at his desk.

He reminded me of that guy from Lake Woebegon, a little better looking, but just as hapless.

"I'll run anything you find. It's just that … well … we don't want to go hurting families whose girls never came back … "

"I'll be circumspect," I promised. "Still, it's a good story. Thirteen-year follow-up. Did they come back? Where'd they go? What's happened since? And if they never returned and were never heard from, where is the investigation today? But listen, if I don't need the story I'll drop it." I took a deep breath. "And Dolly will let me know when I can give you her husband's name."

He frowned and looked more like "Lake Woebegon" than ever.

"The more I think about it, let's wait on those disappearance stories. And don't forget you're working for us on this. I mean, if you learn something you think needs to come out and Dolly says 'no,' well, you have an obligation … "

I assured him I knew where my allegiance lay. "And I have an obligation not to lose my source over there. Dolly's really good about keeping me informed."

He sniffed, took a swipe at his nose, and fixed his glasses while he was in the area.

"Just remember, the cops'll always sit on things until they need our help. Then we're OK again."

Caught between the devil and the deep blue sea. I'd get what I could for him, but I knew I'd never betray Dolly. Especially not this time, when things were falling so close to where she lived, and had loved.

"Speaking of being loyal to the paper," I began, smiling widely, "I could really use more work. If something opens up here full-time, well, would you keep me in mind?"

His heavy brows came together, almost hiding his deep-set brown eyes. He steepled his wide hands at his chest and bit at his bottom lip.

"Nothing right now. Paper's cutting back. You know what's happening to newspapers across the country. Internet's stealing ads. But I can promise to give you as much as I can."

I sighed and smiled as wide as I could get my lips to go, which wasn't far since my whole face felt tight. "Thanks," I said.

He sat up straight, the first step to rising from his chair and ushering me out of there.

"Hey, I'm coming to that dinner your ex is giving. You?"

I frowned. "What dinner?"

"Thursday night. He said you'd be there, too. Told me to bring a date." He gave me an odd look.

"Guess I forgot," I lied.

"I'm looking forward to it," Bill said, planting his large hands on the desk and standing, giving the eternal signal that our meeting was finished. "He's an interesting guy, your ex."

I forced a wide smile, and said, between clenched teeth, "Yes, isn't he."

"Been a lot of places. Bright guy."

"Yes, isn't he," I said again, feeling my cheeks begin to ache.

"So," Bill walked around his desk. "I'll bring a bottle of wine and, I guess, we'll see you out there."

That "we'll" bothered me. It was enough that Jackson co-opted one of my friends; one of my professional connections. Now I had to think of Bill as linked to someone, a woman. A date. I had no romantic ideas about him. It was more that I needed him to stand alone, to be at the other end of a phone line when I needed him. There had to be someone I could count on not to be too busy, not to be out on dates, not to be neglecting his work … but to be focused on me when

I needed him. It was tough, learning that Bill wasn't going to be that man.

———

"Damn," I said as I drove back toward Leetsville with my information on missing girls, my disappointment at not getting the job at the paper, and my depression over losing a guy I never had to some faceless female Jackson had forced out of the woodwork.

# FOURTEEN

Sorrow scrambled across the wood floor toward me, nails scraping like iron spikes over the boards. No wonder my floors were so worn. He was going to have to go to the vet for a manicure. I didn't have the guts to trim those nails myself. He was a squirmy dog and big enough to knock me over. I could just imagine the bloodshed if I had a pair of nail scissors in one hand and a big black-and-white, uneasy dog under the other arm. A trip to the vet was in order.

I braced myself against the doorway and let Sorrow leap in the air in front of me. He was getting much better about not jumping on people and, in the seven months I'd had him, had only knocked me over twice. I clung to every sign of improvement in Sorrow's behavior. It hadn't taken long to learn to love this truly ugly animal with fur of all lengths, long head, skinny legs, Raggedy Andy eyes, and an enormous tail that swept anything in its path like a scythe.

When I'd patted and hugged and talked enough baby talk to turn my own stomach, he settled down and gave my hand a couple of sloppy licks. Odd, how I used to look forward to Jackson's practiced kisses and now adored a drooling, lopsided dog.

My answering machine blipped two missed calls. A big day for me: two human beings needing to talk to me.

The first was from Detective Brent.

I dialed the number he left and asked for him.

I thought he sounded pleased to hear my voice. "How ya doing, Emily?"

A big breakthrough: the first time he called me by name and the first time he'd cared how I was. Something had to be wrong.

"I heard you sent Bill, at the paper, a couple of photos of the bones," I jumped right in, keeping my voice pleasant.

"Figured it wouldn't hurt anything at this point. And we need help finding who these two people were. Alerting the general public can only be a good thing. I know what Dolly thinks…"

"Anything else for me? ID that second one?"

"Not yet. Got a pen?"

"Of course," I scoffed. As if a good reporter would make a call to the police for information and not have a pen.

I rummaged quickly through the papers on the desk then looked around on the floor. No pens. My purse was far enough away so I had to stretch to reach it. I pulled the phone cord, then sat on the floor and tried to catch the strap of my purse with one toe. A few inches short. I pulled the phone until it hung over the side of the desk, snagged my purse, and got a pen.

Brent was saying, "I've got everything here that I can give you at this point. If you've got questions, better hold them until I get a full report."

"Ready," I said. And was.

"First set of bones. Female. Native American. Five foot two. About nineteen years old. Bones weren't in the water that long, so no old

Indian burial. Maybe ten years, forensics says. They've gone down to Lansing. Might pinpoint time of death with more accuracy. Could be a couple of years either side of that. What Graying told us, it has something to do with ossification. Doesn't matter, but the pathologist said they were still in good condition. No wave action on Sandy Lake to toss the bones around. That's why they were still together and in pretty good condition. Well, except for the bullet holes."

"Anything on the gun that killed them? Caliber?"

"Hard to tell. Hole's not large. Hand gun. No weapon found on the lake bottom. Nothing else found with her. The guy's another story. Old rotten boots. Belt buckle. Got some nail heads like for decorating a jeans jacket. No jacket found though."

I wrote everything down. I'd take a look at what I had and digest it later.

"Deputy Wakowski seems to think it could be the guy who ran out on her thirteen years ago, as you said. Fits, but we're not sure yet. She brought some hair samples and she called his sister, down near Detroit, for dental records. Sister's checking into a family dentist they used to have. She'll call Dolly back. The bones are male. That much fits. Five foot nine. Dolly says that's about how tall her ex was. Twenties. Dolly said he was a soldier but the army's got nothing on a Chester Wakowski."

"I think the army was a … er … fabrication to impress Dolly. His sister kind of ruled out military service. Dolly's checking all the missing person files around there for the girl." I forged ahead. "I checked the newspaper morgue today."

"You two going to contact the people?" he asked.

I hesitated. He hadn't liked me and Dolly getting involved last time we'd all worked on the same case. But there was something hopeful in his voice.

"As I told Dolly," he went on, "we're shorthanded right now. It would be a help. Just the preliminary information, you understand. We'll take over if you find anything..."

"Sure. As long as I'm free to write up what we find."

"After you run it by me."

This was a deal breaker. I wasn't into censorship. "I find it, I'll bring it to you. But I'm going to give the paper anything that won't mess up the investigation. I'll bet Dolly will be able to tell me what has to stay confidential and what can get out there to the public."

"Deputy Wakowski's not in charge and..."

"Oops, somebody's at my door. Gotta go. I'll call tomorrow to see if you've got a positive ID on the second skeleton."

"Now, just a minute..."

"Bye. Nice talking to you."

I hung up fast. The old "somebody's at the door" thing always worked. Who could challenge it?

Now, to that second call.

Jackson.

"I hear I'm invited to a dinner party at your house this Thursday?" I started with no "hellos" when Jackson answered, giving his usual hurried welcome as if he had been incredibly busy and a little annoyed at being disturbed

"I called this morning but you didn't answer. Thursday. About seven. People up here eat much earlier than I'm used to. I suppose it's all this fresh air. Or maybe a lack of restaurants that stay open later than nine."

"What can I bring?" I cut in before we got tied in knots over people up here doing other than Jackson believed proper. "A date?" I couldn't help the little dig. There was this nagging idea at the back of my mind that Jackson knew full well he was interfering in my life by asking Bill to bring a woman with him. If Bill had said he didn't have anyone to bring, Jackson would know one thing about him. But now he knew another thing. That he wasn't a serious threat. Though to what, I couldn't imagine.

Jackson ignored my dig.

"Hmm, well, let's see. I'll be working all day so there won't be a lot of time to prepare. I think I'll cook out on the barbecue. Steaks? Hamburgers? That way I'll be free until the last minute." He stopped to think. "Could you make the salad?"

"Sure. No trouble."

"And maybe you could pick up something for dessert. It doesn't matter what. Ice cream would be all right, though a pie from Grand Traverse Pie Company would be splendid. Simply splendid."

"That all?"

"If you're going to be in town, how about a good bread? Would you be going by the Bay Bakery? Whole grain, I suppose."

I was silent long enough to make him think I was writing everything down. I wrote nothing.

"And yes, a bottle of white wine. Maybe a red, if you feel like it." He went on, enumerating my gifts.

"Uh-huh." I rolled my eyes and waited.

"I think I'll grill some asparagus, too. If you're going by Cherry Street Market, could you pick some up? They've got the best and I rarely get over that far."

"And the meat? Do you think you'll have time to pick that up?" I asked, wanting to laugh.

"Now that you mention . . ."

"Forget it. If I'd wanted to give a dinner party, I'd have given it here."

"Oh, dear. Sorry. Am I asking too much?" Here was the hurt little boy voice. Nasty me.

"I'll bring everything but the meat. You can drag yourself into town as well as I can."

"Of course, Emily. Didn't mean to make you so angry."

"I'm not angry," I snarled between clenched teeth, then knew how I sounded and that he'd gotten to me again—for all the wrong reasons. "Really, I'm not angry, Jackson. I'm just tired. A lot of work lately. And my new novel ..."

"Yes, well another of those mysteries of yours, I suppose. They do take time, don't they?"

I didn't answer. No more pissing contests over whose work was more important. I'd learned at least that much in the months Jackson had been up here.

"And, Emily. If you have my chapters done ..."

"Sure," I said. "I'll bring what I have."

"But I need all of them."

"Certainly," I said, "I'll bring what I have. See you Thursday. I'll get there a little early. 'Bout six thirty."

I hung up before he could protest again how he needed all his work run off, send me on more errands, or ask for charcoal and lighter. And a match.

There's only one way I knew to get antiseptically clean—inside and out. That was to work at something. I needed to clear my head of all the voices. I needed my studio and anything I could get done out there.

Dark clouds had rolled in over the lake as I'd returned phone calls. A spring rain was on the way. There was no yellow to the clouds so there wouldn't be wind. I didn't hear thunder in the distance. Nothing to fear. I'd get a little wet.

I put on an old yellow slicker and started out to my studio with Sorrow, looking unhappy, dragging along behind. He didn't like rain and would sometimes bite at it, yipping when he couldn't chase it away. Although he was a water dog, leaping high off the dock into the lake to chase a duck or goose or tangle with the beaver, he resented getting wet when it wasn't of his own choosing.

I intended to finish Jackson's work. That's what I had decided. Get him off my back and give him no reason to think badly of me. I was nothing, if not dependable.

The first rain drops fell softly, pattering on the forest floor around me. Then a little harder. I stuck Jackson's manuscript sheets under the thick plastic of my slicker as rain ran down my face and off my shoulders. Sorrow loped in circles, snuffling the ground for his own reasons then turning to look at the sky, highly annoyed. I leaned my head back and opened my mouth to accept the rain. It cooled the insides of my cheeks and ran on my tongue, making me a part of everything again.

The thought struck me that one day I would be the same as those two found in Sandy Lake. Bones. All my frantic needs and small conceits—gone. All those things I'd thought necessary to do for others— so I could think well of myself—they'd be gone, too. What really mattered was this small time in the woods. I wiped my cheeks and looked at my glistening hand covered with dampness that would never come again, never gleam with just these droplets. And I would never be the same person standing out under the newly greening trees, among proud white trilliums, under just this dark sky. Something buried in that fact I hadn't the capacity to grasp. The one thing I did understand was that I was alone. Ultimately, no matter how many friends I made up here, how many men might come into my life—I was alone. At that moment, with no Indian standing in the drive waiting for me, no police detective threatening me, and nobody watching or ordering me to do this or that—it didn't seem to be a bad thing.

I called to Sorrow and went to my studio, shook off the slicker and hung it in my metal cupboard to drip dry, then carefully locked the door behind me. I always locked the door. Not to keep anyone out. More symbolic than that. I was locking myself in with my writing. I was defending my mind against outside intrusions. A locked door was the ultimate barricade.

Sorrow shook himself violently and settled to the rug under the coffee table. He groaned, stretched, and was soon snoring, as the slightly chilly room filled with the smell of wet dog.

I decided that I wasn't going to call anyone. I wasn't going to do work for Jackson after all. I wasn't going to think about bones and missing girls. I was going to write my novel. Maybe it wouldn't be the next great thing, but it would be a way of offering my mind—through my characters. If I was lucky I would take it down into the realm of the unconscious and tap into something meaningful to others. If I wasn't that good after all, at least I could entertain. My form of clowning. Be a court jester. A magician. *"Come here, little girl. Let me show you wonders…"*

I was soon well into moving my elderly lawyer into a new case: *A young man came to the office. The lawyer, too old and slow to avoid the disturbance, agreed to listen to him. It was a hopeless case. Cut and dried. A case that was not winnable. Yet, at his age, what was there left, he'd asked himself, but hopeless causes? He would take the case, he told the man. He would look at all the facts and then defend the young man against a charge of murdering his wife.*

I think I was biting my lip, impressed with my own inventiveness, when I heard a loud knock and then a heavy thud, like a large object thrown at my door. It didn't take more than seconds to scare the hell out of me. I turned, startled and well into the flight or fight response, to find a large, dark man filling the open doorway.

# FIFTEEN

THE MAN TOOK ONE heavy step into the room, his wild dark hair shining with rain, his lined face fierce, black eyes narrowed and fixed on me.

Sorrow sat up under the coffee table, banging his head with a hollow thump. I expected growling, leaping. My protector should have been at this intruder's throat. Instead Sorrow crawled slowly out from beneath the table. He was on all fours, belly dragging. With a cowardly whimper, Sorrow approached the man, who seemed taller than he really was; he seemed like a growing shadow.

It was the dark raincoat. It was the dark hair. And those arms held wide at his sides, as if he might be reaching for a gun. Then there were the eyes, intent on staring me down. With an ungraceful upward push, I was out of my chair and standing behind it so I had something between this man and me. His face was set, lined, and furious. I was afraid this could be the last face I would ever see.

Sorrow whimpered. How shameful. Even with my own gulping fear, I felt disgust for my servile dog.

I looked quickly behind the man, expecting to see splintered boards where my door had been. The door stood open, rain blowing in, but it was intact. I'd locked it. I knew I had. Locked it as I always did because of just this kind of intrusion. Like my worst nightmare, the man hovered in my private, open space, glowering at me.

Sorrow reached one paw out and tapped the man's black boot. He slithered closer and gave the boot a lick. Oh yuck, I thought.

"What do you want!" I screamed from behind my chair. Somebody in there had to have a backbone.

He reached behind and closed the door, trapping me in with him.

I didn't want the door closed. Let the rain come in. Let the wind blow my papers everywhere. There was something too intimate about the two of us in my own space. Not enough air. He soaked it up and left nothing for me to breathe.

"I hear you are a smart woman," he said, his voice deep and hesitant, as if he wasn't used to a lot of words at once. He hunched his shoulders forward, making him even larger than he looked already. "I hear you work for the newspaper. I hear you haven't been up in our country very long. You have things to learn. Stay out of tribal matters. None of what happens to an Odawa has anything to do with you. Do you understand me?"

He glowered, even took a menacing step forward.

"You have no right... I'm calling..."

He put up one brown and very lined hand. "We want our dead woman returned. We want nothing more in the newspaper. Stay out of what you don't understand. And tell your friend, the deputy, we will be watching her."

"I have nothing to do with the... body."

"You have too much to do with it. You don't belong in what is … our business." He shifted his weight. "She will be buried. And you will leave us alone."

He squinted at me. "That will be the end of it."

I quickly sensed that the words were the only threat. I stood straighter, ready to take him on. "Somebody shot her. Don't your people care about murder?"

"We care about our people." He put a hand behind him, on the door knob. "We will do what has to be done. It isn't your business. Nor is it Dolly Wakowski's business."

"Those other bones, that man, is probably Dolly's husband," I said, stepping out from behind my office chair. "She has the same rights you have."

"Let her see to her own. We care … for the woman who was from the Odawa. She must be buried." He took a deep breath.

"I work for the newspaper. This is a story. Does the woman have a name?"

He shook his head. His voice dropped. It was almost a growl. "Stay out of our business … or something you won't like will happen to both of you."

He straightened his back with effort and some pain. A momentary flinch crossed his harsh, incised features. As he spoke, he turned the knob and opened the door a little more, letting rain blow in.

"Are you threatening me?" I demanded, brave now that I saw he was leaving.

He only sighed and shook his head.

"I have a job to do and I damn well intend …," I blustered.

"What's done is done. Don't keep snooping where you have no business … snooping. I came to warn you, that's all. You and the deputy.

She removed something from the water. We saw her and need to know what she took away."

I didn't have to ask which "water" he was talking about. The room grew colder and damper from the partially opened door.

"It can mean big trouble for her ... what she did."

This wasn't something I could deny without digging a deeper hole for both Dolly and for me. I stood motionless, taking in one deep breath after another.

He reached down to tap the whimpering Sorrow's head. "We'll find out. Then we will go to her superior." One of his deeper, chest-clearing breaths. "She'll be charged with removing evidence from a crime scene. Trust what I say, we will have her job."

He stepped toward me, away from the door, his hand out, holding a folded slip of paper. "My number," he said, putting the paper into my reluctant hand. "Dolly Wakowski has to tell us what she took from Sandy Lake. Then it is over. No more stories."

He bent and whispered to Sorrow, then stood, turned, opened the door fully, and went out. The door shut behind him with a soft catch of the latch.

I grabbed on to the brown chair with both hands, folding forward, shaking and feeling sick with fright now that he had left. When I could stand again, I went outside to look up my drive. No one there. I looked down toward my house, lost in clouds of mist and light rays. No one. Not a car. Not a tall man walking.

The lock on the door was intact. I tried it a couple of times—closing and opening. It seemed to work, maybe with a little play in it. I'd have to get Harry Mockerman over to look. There was no feeling safe anywhere now. Whoever the man was, he'd shown he could get to me.

I could drop the whole thing the way the man wanted me too. But I wouldn't. If anything, I had to step up the pressure. Maybe I would write about an elderly tribe member who tried to intimidate the press. Maybe I would write about a tribe of Indians bent on covering up old murders. I was damned angry by that time and ready to take him on.

The only thing I could think to do right then was get into town and find Dolly.

I walked the shamed Sorrow back to the house. He sensed my disgust and anger and followed slowly behind, head hanging low, tail between his legs. There was no answer for how he'd let me down. Something between my dog and the man that I didn't understand. The man was a stranger, and I was the woman who loved and cared for this animal. Another severe case of perfidy in my life.

# SIXTEEN

I TRIED TO CALL Dolly, but I couldn't raise her. Chief Barnard, always affable but business-like, answered at the Leetsville station.

"Not here. Want me to find her?" the chief asked in his deep, brusk voice. I didn't want any red lights going off. No citizens listening to their police radios, wondering what was happening. I told him it wasn't important, that I'd be seeing her in an hour, at EATS.

"This thing with the bones is really growing," he said. "Getting calls from out-of-state newspapers." His tone implied a man with time on his hands to talk. "You heard Dolly thinks the second skeleton found is that husband of hers, who ran off awhile back?"

"I heard," I said, adding nothing. I didn't know what Dolly had told him so far and didn't want to step on any toes. There was still the evidence-tampering issue to get out of the way. She would have to tell the chief soon. Very soon.

"Anyone from the Odawa been in touch?" I asked.

"Had a call. Just asking when the bones would be released. Some guy from their council. No trouble. Nice guy."

"Really?" I said, not sure I should mention my visitor to Chief Barnard before talking to Dolly. I felt out of my depth here. I didn't have a clue who to trust.

"Hmm," the chief said, hesitating. "You having any trouble?"

"No. No." I took the easiest path. I'd tell Dolly, let her take it from there.

"How's Charlie doing?" I asked, getting off the subject of bones and back to small talk about his sick son. In towns the size of Leetsville you didn't want to appear too much in a hurry. That got you a reputation of being impressed with yourself. For a reporter, a rep like that didn't help as I went around asking questions and digging up information. One chief, back in Ann Arbor, could put his feet up on his desk; clasp his hands behind his head; and settle in for an hour's talk about Ann Arbor, the country, and right on out to the state of the world. Experienced reporters learned quickly to smile and back off with a wave, maybe a look of regret. New reporters got stuck listening. The thing was, those new reporters began getting stories from him first, and he was always in to take their calls. So, something to be said for good manners.

"Fine," Lucky said. Charlie had been operated on a few months before, a touch-and-go time for Barnard and his wife, Frances. Dolly took over the station then and did a great job. He wasn't holding the string of police cars she had smashed against her, at the moment. The last one happened when we'd been forced down into Arnold's Swamp near my house. Dolly had been injured and the chief was just happy to get her back in one piece. There'd been a detente between them ever since and Dolly swore she was being extra careful how she drove.

"Well, thanks anyway," I said, and got off the phone.

I had to find her but since she patrolled most of the back roads and could be up any two-track on a poacher call or down a logging road on a marijuana plant hunt, I'd have to wait until she got to EATS.

———

I thought I could go in quietly, make my way through the smoke undetected, and grab a shadowed corner booth to wait for Dolly. What I didn't know was that word had gotten around town that Deputy Dolly's husband was dead, found out to Sandy Lake all these years after he'd disappeared, right along with the bones of his girlfriend.

That was what circled in EATS when I walked in. I heard the whispers and caught the looks. You could almost smell the pity in the air, and the curiosity. If they didn't have Dolly to console, I'd be the substitute until she got there.

I nodded to Flora Coy, the sad bird lady who'd lost most of her childhood friends to a couple of killers last fall. She sat at a round table in the middle of the room, along with John Ripple, who trapped beaver and sold their pelts for a living.

When I'd first arrived in the north, I'd thought it behooved me to get rid of the beaver in Willow Lake. He was taking down the aspen—one by one. I loved the aspen. Especially the quaking variety that turned up their leaves and shook like a hundred rattles.

I'd been introduced to John Ripple at that time. When I told him what I wanted to do—live trap the animal and take him to some other lake—he'd chewed at his white mustache and said he, maybe, had a trap just like that. We met early the next morning. I got the big green trap out of the back of his pickup, into my trunk, got it home, and down to the lake. John hadn't mentioned anything about bait so I figured the beaver would walk on in out of curiosity. I would then remove him to another wild lake, and that would be that.

Day after day and no beaver in the trap. Out at the growing, conical, mud and stick house, the beaver worked steadily, even when I sat on my dock giving him the mean eye. After a while I figured bait was in order so I threw in a couple handfuls of Cheerios. Nothing. I added some peanut butter another morning. Still nothing. After three weeks I gave up and took the trap back to John. He never laughed, though a few days later he told me he had a surefire way to kill off the mosquitoes I complained about.

"Hang a side of beef from a tree," he started, lips dead straight. "Hit 'em with a board when they land, one little bugger at a time." Only the quivering of his shaggy white mustache showed he was having the city girl on.

I nodded to Flora and John. Flora gave me a pleasant, benign smile and blinked her small eyes behind thick lenses in big pink plastic frames.

Seated at another table was Gertie, the town beauty shop owner. Not long ago her shop burned down and all the women in town went into Traverse City to have their hair done. Until the shop got rebuilt and Gertie was back as the arbiter of style in Leetsville, the women had looked almost natural. No big beehives. No "do's" lacquered to remain immobile for at least a week. Now everyone had returned to high style and Gertie sat in the middle of the restaurant talking in whispers to Sullivan Murphy, who owned the newly built funeral home over on the corner of Griffith and Mitchell Streets.

Anna Scovil, the town librarian I'd been avoiding, sat by herself in the first of the line of red Formica booths. I nodded and turned sideways to sneak past her. She caught me, clamping one hand around my wrist, and pulled me down close.

"We all feel so bad about Dolly," she whispered. "These are truly terrible times."

I nodded and tried to wrest my wrist from her hand. The woman was tenacious.

"Before I lose you again…" She looked around to see if anyone was watching. "I'm planning this very special Night at the Library. It'll be a fundraiser, Emily. To buy new books. Now, what I've got in mind is to have readings by local celebrities."

Her breath was warm against my skin, almost moist. She smelled faintly of liver and onions. "I hear you're into a new novel, and I would love to have you come by, share some of your work with an audience. I've kind of built the program around you."

She smiled and poked at her hair. The hair didn't move. Considering how mine flew at the slightest breeze, I thought Gertie's obvious skill almost otherworldly.

"Well," I began, thinking as fast as I could. "I'm no celebrity…"

"Now," Anna patted at my captive hand, "neither are the other writers who'll be reading with you."

Her eyebrows shot up and I got a wide smile. "I've already talked Ronald Williams into reading from his family history. Publishing it himself at some Universal place. He knows all about the Internet. Said he'd come. The only thing I've got to do is give him a limit on how much of it he can read. Man riffles the manuscript at anybody who'll listen—like he was selling French postcards or something." She frowned, then brightened. "Not that it isn't interesting. I'm sure he could draw a crowd all by himself."

I nodded. OK. Me and Ronald Williams. A truly nice guy but one of those gung-ho genealogists, like Eugenia, who kept coming up with one more boring relative after another.

"And," Anna went on, "there is Winnie Lorbach. I haven't asked yet, but she's been putting a book on lady's slippers together for the last fifteen years. I'll bet she's got fascinating information to share.

Probably a lot of pictures, too. You know, you and Winnie might want to have a talk with Ronald, see how to do it. What's the sense of sending your work out and getting it back? He says he knows how to get anybody's book published and it costs almost nothing. Except for the books you have to buy. And, of course, his book will be a little expensive for a paperback. Still, at least you'd have a book in your hand. Think of the postage you'd save. I've heard money's a little tight for you right now so you might want to give it some thought."

I agreed and got away, fuming that somehow my lack of funds was making the rounds of the town gossips. I wasn't used to other people knowing, or caring, about my business.

I got a little farther along when an elderly gentleman stopped me to whisper something about a murder. "Might be you could get a book out of it. Saw it last night on *Matlock*. Thought of you right away. Bet you could sell this one and get yourself some money."

I thanked him, put my head down, and made for a shadowed booth in the far corner. I slid across the red plastic, and buried my face in a menu.

The talk around me moved from whispers to the usual low level of conversation and laughter. Gloria, who was also my mailman's girlfriend, hurried over to slide a cup of tea across the table at me then kneel on the opposite banquette, settling herself in for a talk.

"Figured you'd want something fast," she said. Her pretty face drew into a frown as she nodded at the white tea cup and silver pot of hot water. "We're all so sorry about poor Dolly. You know anything about the ... eh ... arrangements?"

"Arrangements for what?"

"The funeral, of course. We're a little afraid of asking Dolly. You know, because of how she is about her privacy."

"Nothing planned yet, Gloria. The pathologist in Lansing's got the … eh … body. I'm sure you'll know as soon as something's taken care of."

Gloria looked behind her, at the table where Sullivan Murphy sat watching us. "It's just that Sullivan has to make arrangements. You understand. Dolly maybe should at least go talk to him."

I nodded. "When the time is right, Gloria. Please tell Sullivan some things can't be rushed."

"Oh, and Sullivan told me to tell you that he's looking for somebody to keep the books at the funeral parlor. Now that his mom's passed and his brother's in prison, he could use some help. Might be a job in it for you."

I stared at her. Was I being bribed by Sullivan Murphy to make sure he got Dolly's business? I looked over at him, a big man with a gruff face. He raised a paw of a hand in the air and waved. The smile he gave me wasn't pretty. More feral.

"I don't know bookkeeping," I said from somewhere deep in my throat.

"Doesn't matter. Just add some stuff up and send out bills. I guess that's about all Sullivan would expect."

I felt anger bubbling in my chest. "Why does everybody think I need money?"

Gloria colored at my tone. "Now Emily. Just some things said, I guess. You know how we are, kind of watch and pick up on our neighbor's troubles."

"I don't have any troubles, Gloria. I'm fine."

She seemed about to argue, then gave a little cough into her balled fist, stood, and straightened her short blue uniform skirt. "Just passing on news of a job, Emily. Hope I didn't make you mad or anything."

Next to pick her way over through the miasma of the nonsmoking section was Eugenia. At first she had a look of sadness on her wide face. When she got to my booth and slid in, she put a hand over her mouth as she leaned across to taunt me. "Didn't find her, did ya? Old Etta out there. Knew you wouldn't. Real proud I am of that old auntie."

"Old auntie, my foot. Ellen Liddy Watson. Hung for running her own ranch. Men didn't like a woman sticking her nose into their cattle business. She was no outlaw, just a woman who got in the way. Certainly she's no relation to you. And her husband was named 'Pickell.' I found it all, Eugenia. Nothing's that hard to find anymore. It's all there on the Internet."

"Where the hell you think I get them from?" she hissed across the table, her multiplicity of chins bobbing just above the table.

"Probably everybody knows those outlaws aren't related to you. People here are just too nice to say anything."

"Unlike you, you mean. Nobody else in Leetsville ugly enough to point it out." She settled back in the booth, her hands thumping a loud bump on the table. "Guess I should give it up. Still, I like doing that kind of genealogical research. Fun to poke around in the past."

"Start on somebody else."

She shrugged. "Who? Most of us in town known each other and our families from as far back as people go. I mean, we all grew up here."

"Except me. You'd do me a big favor if you got it spread around that I'm doing just fine. I don't need them looking for jobs and I don't need plots for books. I don't mean to be ungracious..."

"Yes, you do. And let me say right here, not everything's about you, Emily." Eugenia got up slowly, bending in close to make sure I heard her. There were things I knew Eugenia might help me with and

I didn't want her pissed off at me, like the rest of the town would soon be. I put my hand on one of hers.

"Please, I'm sorry if I seem ... well ... huffy."

"Hmph." Eugenia shook off my hand and looked around at the others watching us.

"There's been a lot happening," I went on. "I had a visitor, out at my house. He kind of upset me."

Her face settled into kinder wrinkles. "When this happen?" she demanded, still not smiling.

"Little while ago."

"Who was it?"

"I don't know. Definitely a Native American."

"Scare you?"

I nodded.

"Hmph," she said again. "They're good people. If they get upset with any of us from time to time, well, you can't blame 'em, can you? I mean, every time I go to one of the casinos and lose, I don't even get mad. Just a way of paying reparations for this land we're all sitting on that was theirs before we got here. What'd this guy say he wanted?"

"It's about the other set of bones. They're Indian. Female. They want them back for burial."

Eugenia shrugged and stood. "Only ones I ever knew from around here was an old guy and his kids, lived out of town somewhere. Long time ago, that was. Didn't like him much. Didn't see the kids hardly ever."

"Lived where?"

Eugenia shrugged. "Somewhere out in the woods. He wasn't the kind you got friendly with. Still, they never bothered anybody here in town. Got along, as far as I heard. So, what's this man think you can do? Tell him to go see that Brent guy in Gaylord. More luck with him.

He want you to write something in the paper? That what it was about?"

I shook my head, sorry I'd mentioned him.

She got up and walked away only to turn abruptly and lean back toward me. "What do you think about me doing Dolly's family?"

"Doing what to them?"

"You know, doing some genealogical research on 'em."

"She doesn't have anybody, remember."

"Heard she's got a sister-in-law now."

"Chet's family," I said.

"Feel bad for her. There's got to be somebody. She didn't pop out of a pumpkin."

"Better ask Dolly," I said, then held my breath along with everybody else in EATS as Dolly walked in, head down, and made directly for me.

# SEVENTEEN

THE HUSH IN THE place felt thick as a quilt. A few people mumbled condolences toward Dolly as she knocked her way through the tables. Nobody dared to stop her. She slid in across from me, took off her hat and settled it on the seat beside her. She plumped up her striped hair and fixed me with a sour look.

"They know about Chet, don't they?"

"How long did you think it would stay a secret?"

She made a derisive noise. "What're they saying? They think I deserve it, you know, because of all the tickets I give out."

I shook my head and sipped at my tea which had finally cooled below a hundred and fifty degrees. "Everybody's sorry. Every one of them. You'll have to talk to people sooner or later. If nothing else, you should let them get it off their chest or they'll burst wide open."

"Yes," she said, and grunted "coffee" from the side of her mouth when Gloria sidled up to our table. "Talked to his sister. She's coming up when Lansing's through with 'im. Gonna stay with me. We'll plan a funeral."

"Dolly, I've got to warn you…" I took a deep breath and halfway covered my mouth. "A man from the Odawa came to my house."

She grimaced. "Same one from out to the lake?"

I shook my head. "Different. Older. But he's determined." I swallowed hard. "And Dolly, he said they know you took something from the crime scene. He's going to Chief Barnard about it, and maybe even the state police."

"Damn," Dolly swore.

"What are you going to do?" I asked.

She shook her head. "I don't know. Looks bad for me. Actually, the chief could relieve me of duty. Put me on administrative leave until it's all cleared up."

"That's not going to help anybody."

"I know, I know…" Dolly rubbed at her chin with the back of her right hand, then bit at her lip a few times. "Only thing is for me to tell the chief myself."

"That's what I was thinking. If you need me, I'll go with you. You know, back up what you did and why you did it…"

"I don't need a babysitter."

"You did when we went out to Sandy Lake."

All I got was a nasty look. I felt in the pocket of my denim jacket and handed her the folded paper the man had left with me.

"What's this?"

"That's the Indian's number," I said. "He didn't give me a name."

Dolly thought a minute. "I'd better get over to the Council. See if I can talk to them. Explain what I took and why. Can't hurt."

I shook my head. "The chief first. You owe him. If he hears from somebody else, it will only be worse for you."

At first she protested, then settled down and sat thinking, her watery eyes on me. "OK. So, what'd you find on missing girls or women?"

"Four that year."

She nodded. "Anybody a possible?"

"Only one sounds Indian."

Gloria came to take our order. She mumbled a few words of condolence toward Dolly. Dolly took it pretty well. She even reached out to touch one of Gloria's hands and thank her. The special was liver and onions. I ordered a cheeseburger. Dolly had the salad bar and a bowl of leek soup.

"One from Traverse City." I read from my notes after our food came. "Lisa Valient, age sixteen, five foot two, blond—short hair, blue eyes. Last seen on Front Street in Traverse City talking to an unidentified male. The report came from her mother, Fern Valient, of Washington Street."

Dolly made her own notes in a tiny notebook.

"There was a Tricia Robbins of Kalkaska," I went on. "Eighteen. Five-seven. Brown hair and eyes. She went missing in April 1994. Her father said she'd run off before but never for this long."

"Un-huh."

"Bambi Lincoln of Mancelona. Seventeen. Five-six. Brown hair. Blue eyes. Last seen on her way to school. Reported missing after a week by her sister, Tanya Lincoln, of Elk Rapids.

"Then there's this next one: June 1994: Mary Naquma. Nineteen. Five foot two. Long, dark hair. Dark eyes. Reported missing by a friend: Lena Smith, of Peshawbestown. Last seen at the Tracy Beauty School in Traverse City, where both girls studied. Mary never came back to school. Never called anybody. Her friend said it was not like her. All Lena Smith knew about Mary was that she'd once said she lived out on a lake beyond Leetsville."

Dolly's eyes popped open. "She's the only one sounds Native American. Naquma—got to be an Indian name."

"So? Who do we contact? This Lena Smith?"

"Think so. We gotta get out there. I'm talking to the chief tonight. Could be a private citizen tomorrow."

"Well, maybe I could go in the morning…"

"Can't. I'm talking to the kindergarten about stranger safety. Have to go in the afternoon."

We settled into our food just as Eugenia came bearing down on us.

"Dolly." Eugenia pushed Dolly over with her ample behind and sat next to her. "Everybody in this whole darn place wants to tell you how sorry they are for your loss, and you're blowing everybody off."

"Nobody said nothing and all I did was come in and sit down," Dolly said through a mouthful of cheese ball and crackers.

"You know how you are. What they all want to say…," Eugenia swept one arm wide, taking in all those staring at us, "… is that if you need anything at all, why, we're all here for you."

Dolly lowered her head and kept chewing hard at those crackers. I smiled and made a face at Eugenia, who got it right away. She changed the subject.

"And you know what else, Dolly?"

Curious this time, Dolly looked up and kind of sideways at Eugenia.

"I know how important family is to you and now you've gone and lost Chet."

Dolly nodded and added pickled beets to the cheese in her mouth.

"I think I've reached the end of my own family, with that poor soul hanging out in my foyer, so I thought I'd start looking up some of your people."

Dolly's face remained still. She chewed, then stared off beyond me. It seemed there was a tug of war going on in her head. Maybe it was just the word "family" that got to her.

"I got family still," she said, talking down to her plate. "My sister-in-law's coming up soon. We got to plan Chet's funeral."

"I'm talking about your own people, Dolly. You must've had a mother and a father. Who knows who else is out there? People find relatives all the time on the Internet. What you got to do is know how to look. Well, I know how to look."

Dolly frowned over at me. I couldn't tell if she needed my help getting rid of Eugenia or if she was thinking over the idea.

"Not much to go on."

"As I was saying to Emily, you didn't pop out of a pumpkin."

Dolly considered the possibility.

"Want to give me your birth name?"

"All I know is Delores Flynn. Not even sure that's real or something one of those foster mothers stuck on me."

"I can start with that. You know your mother's name?"

Dolly made a noise. "I don't know a thing about that woman. Nobody ever could tell me who she was, why she left me, nothing."

Eugenia nodded. "There's a lot in that boat with you. What about your father?"

"You kidding?" Dolly looked at Eugenia as if she suspected madness. "Well, maybe he was called Harold. Seems somebody at one of the homes told me that much. She had papers on me, or something from social services."

"Brothers? Sisters? Aunts? Uncles?"

Dolly's face got red. She had had about enough of Eugenia's prying. "Nobody, I told you. And, you know what, Eugenia? I like it that way. I wish you wouldn't go rooting around looking for people who never gave a damn about me and who I don't care about either. Got enough family with Chet, now his sister, maybe someday I'll meet his mother."

"Don't go getting overexcited. I said I'd try. If I find anything, I'll hang it right up out there with my folks. If I don't find anything you won't see nothing of yours there."

Dolly gave Eugenia a slight push, to prod her up and out. "Go ahead. If I see anything hanging I don't like I'll take it right back down. If that's all right with you, well, OK."

Eugenia shrugged. "Ya never know, Dolly. Look at the long line of fine people I come from."

Dolly gave Eugenia a harder shove, forcing her to the end of the seat and then up to stand beside our booth.

"Yours were all hung, Eugenia. Is that what you're going to come up with for me?"

Eugenia smiled and waved a hand at Dolly. "Not all of 'em. A couple were just tarred and feathered. I think that's kind of interesting, don't you?"

Dolly felt in her pants pocket, drew out a ten dollar bill, and headed for the cash register.

I hurried after her. I thought she needed somebody with her for a while. And I sure wasn't going to leave her swinging in the wind at this point.

# EIGHTEEN

WE HAD AN ARGUMENT in the parking lot. My car or hers. I insisted I was going with her to tell Chief Barnard. She growled that she didn't need me. I growled back that she certainly did and that I'd been out there with her and could attest to what she took and why. After a few minutes of that, I got in the patrol car and rode over to the station with her. Anyway, facing down the pleasant Chief Barnard was better than going back to my place.

Chief Barnard was just slipping on a light jacket, getting ready to go home for the night, when we got there. Emergency calls that might come in after he left were sent directly to his house. Most of the time calling the police in Leetsville got you the chief himself, even if he was in his pajamas.

"See you found her," Lucky greeted me.

I nodded.

Dolly said nothing. She'd removed her hat as a mark of respect and held it over her heart. If I'd ever seen a little kid in trouble, this was that little kid.

The chief looked from me to Dolly and back. He frowned, took off his jacket, and went back into his office. We followed and sat on the two armchairs across the desk from him. Dolly gave a huge sigh as she settled back, crossing her legs then uncrossing them.

"I take it something's going on here," the chief finally said after a few minutes of silence.

Dolly nodded.

I nodded.

"You want to tell me, Deputy Wakowski?"

She cleared her throat, squirmed on the hard chair, and settled her shoulders into a true slump. "I've done something I gotta tell you about, Chief."

He nodded. Waited.

"Well, it's about the bones, out to Sandy Lake."

He nodded again, his long face very serious.

"I did something I shouldn't have done out there."

The kind man's face drew into a scowl. He was smart enough to know that whatever was coming at him was a thing he didn't want to hear. "What'd you do, Dolly?"

She looked around at me, then back at the chief. "I took something from the crime scene."

"What'd you take?"

"I took something that could have been considered evidence."

"What?" He said again, impatient now.

"I stole ID tags from the lake."

"Whose tags?"

"Chet's."

"So, why'd it take a couple of days to ID him? What was the point in hiding the tags?"

"I wasn't hiding … exactly. It was that they were my wedding present from him and …"

"And what?"

"Well, the last time I saw them they were around the neck of a woman Chet was with over at The Skunk."

"This is serious, Dolly. You better come straight with me."

"I know. I know." She shook her head as if trying to get thoughts to line up right.

"There was this …." She put her hand into a back pocket of her pants and drew out the corroded chain with tags and that red beer stein. "You see, I was afraid maybe Chet killed her and dumped her body out there." She sat forward. "Not that he was violent. Never violent with me, I can promise you that."

"Well," Lucky shook his head and scowled harder. "That's not what I was worried about. Somehow you thought he could be violent enough to kill a woman. That says something."

"All it says, Chief, is that I was stupid. I wanted to find him before the state police got on his trail."

"Planning on warning him, were you?" His thick eyebrows were up, his face more serious than I'd ever seen it. "You going to aid and abet a felon? Doesn't sound like the Dolly I know. Never once in the fifteen years you been on the force with me, Dolly, did I ever know you to …"

Dolly shook her head, interrupting him because once started it was difficult to stop Lucky. "I just wanted to talk to him. Get him back up here with me."

"Still, you tampered with evidence that could have been very important to the case. I don't know how we're going to resolve this."

"I know. I don't blame you—whatever you have to do to me. The dog tags aren't even real. Don't have his name on them. I found out from his sister that Chet wasn't ever in the army."

Lucky shook his head at her.

I leaned forward, having seen Dolly crawl as low as she could crawl. "I was out there with her," I said.

"You too, Emily? I'm surprised you had anything to do with this. One of you should have known better. Seems to me that you two weren't using your heads and ..."

"She's telling the truth. She only took them so she could talk to him first. After all, Chet was her husband."

"More than that, if he murdered the woman."

"But he didn't. He's dead, too."

"Yeah, well, we know that now."

"And something else ..." I looked at Dolly, who avoided my eyes. "A man from the Odawa was out there. He saw Dolly take the chain and put it in her pocket. A friend of his came to my house and threatened to tell you about it. Maybe even go to the state police."

The chief nodded. "When's he gonna do all this?" He swung his chair right then left. He thought awhile, sat forward, and put his hand on the phone in front of him. "Got a name?"

I shook my head. "He left a number."

"Let's call the guy. See what he wants from us."

Dolly pulled the slip of paper from her pocket and passed it over. The chief dialed, leaned back, and looked hard at both of us. "After this, we're gonna have a talk about duty."

Dolly, miserable now, shrank back in her chair to await her fate.

The phone must have been answered right away. Maybe the guy had been waiting to hear from us. The chief identified himself and went on to tell the man that his deputy had been in and told him

131

quite a story. We could hear noise on the other end, but the chief interrupted to say he knew all about what she'd done.

"I'd like to come out and talk to you, if that's all right," the chief said finally. "I think we can clear up this part of the problem in a hurry, if you're willing to listen."

He waited, his face drawn and nervous. "OK, my deputy's coming with me."

The chief gave Dolly a tough look. She stopped the feeble protest she'd been about to make and folded her hands in her lap.

In a moment the conversation ended. The chief hung up, stood, straightened his shoulders and his gun on his hip. "We're going out there now, Dolly. He's meeting us at the tribal offices. His name's Lewis George. He's a tribal chief."

She stood awkwardly, half falling over one arm of her chair. "If you think that's necessary..."

"Hell yes, I do," he said, coming around the corner of his desk. "We're going to get this straightened out, and then we'll talk about what has to happen to you."

"Could I copy that phone number?" I asked. "I want to know who I'm dealing with."

He held out the slip of paper for me to copy. The paper went back into his pocket.

I got up and followed them out of the office. The chief locked the door to the station and headed toward Dolly's patrol car.

"You're not going, Emily," he turned back to me, putting a hand up like a crossing guard. "Deputy Wakowski needs to start concentrating on her job. I'm not a hard-nose. There are what you might call extenuating circumstances at work here, but we've got to get this evidence business cleared away first."

Before Dolly got in on the passenger side, letting the chief drive, she lifted her saddened eyes to me. "If everything's OK, we'll go back to Peshawbestown tomorrow evening to see that woman about the Naquma girl."

"Can't tomorrow night, Dolly. I'm having dinner at Jackson's." I backed away from the car. Nobody'd mentioned giving me a lift to the restaurant. I was just as happy to walk the six blocks. I needed the exercise to clear my head.

"What the heck do you mean you're having dinner at Jackson's?" Dolly hissed at me. "We've got work to do here, Emily. He's only taking advantage of you, and God knows where it will lead, you over there. We both know what kind of man ..."

"Well ..." I turned and walked off as fast as I could down toward US131. "That's what I'm doing," I called over my shoulder. "If you can't go in the morning it will have to wait until Friday."

"Yeah," was all she said, and slammed the car door.

# NINETEEN

I SPENT THE NEXT morning in the woods hunting for morels and hunting for a center in me. There was the money thing. I did my best to resolve that, coming up with ideas as I walked over spring windfalls and past alluring red and black toadstools of all shapes, toadstools that could have killed me with one bite. Odd, how things could be lovely and deadly at the same time.

Each time I worked with Deputy Dolly Wakowski, it seemed I was set at further odds with the people and things around me. Maybe I had no business staying where I obviously didn't belong. I could go back to Ann Arbor, get another job on a newspaper, find a condo, and pick up with old friends. I'd be safe there, one among many.

It took a certain sensibility I didn't have to accept faults the way northern people accepted fault in others. It took a lack of my kind of outrage. Maybe they could take in anybody who needed help—the way Eugenia did. Maybe they could gossip and pass judgment on each other's lives and then go on to the next bit of scandal, the next bit of juicy information, without ever demanding justice. I couldn't. Even

Dolly circumventing the law still left me with a load of guilt that really wasn't mine.

Everything I'd learned up here seemed to be drifting away. Where was the magic and healing power in the forest and in the water? What had happened to my deep and true belief in the simplicity of a slow-paced life? I'd even begun to dislike my own dog, my Sorrow, for what I took as his cowardice in the face of an intruder. How the hell did I know what went on between dog and man? How did I know anything?

I stepped carefully from dead elm to dead elm, stopping to squat and examine the terrain ahead of me. The wind warmed enough for me to take off my sweater and tie it around my waist. The sun emerged from a sky piled with gold-lit clouds.

I would find a job, I told myself again as I walked. I had to believe in possibility, and in serendipity. If I stayed still long enough and didn't worry; if I gave into a day-by-day life and stopped trying to manage things—something would appear. I'd get a job. I'd sell a book. I'd find a way to make money and stay in my little golden home on my little bluest lake.

I walked, forgetting for the moment that I could be surprised out here. When I came on a group of three lady's slippers, I laid down on my stomach to give them a good once over. Silly-looking things. An ant crawled out of one blossom and gave me a puzzled look then went back to his business. Ugly flowers. Bloated and spotted, like badly designed purses. Such overblown press about the beauty of these spongy-looking things. And to think, I'd be on the program at the library with a woman who had taken fifteen years to write a book about them. Maybe she'd convert me. I hoped so.

Ahead, I could see, from my prone position, a group of ten of the late morels. Gnarled heads peeked through the leaves. A few hadn't even broken through, but pushed up into small hillocks—giving away their hiding places. I scrambled to my feet, picked the mushrooms carefully, and laid them at the bottom of my bag. I would dry them for a winter stew, or a soup, or to fry in butter, as Harry recommended.

"Emily!" It was Harry's voice, coming through the trees off to my right. He sauntered slowly toward me, head down, the huge mesh bag dragging, filled, on the ground behind him.

"Thought that was you," he said, stepping carefully into the clearing.

"See you got a few morels." I enjoyed the sarcasm. "No wonder I can't find any."

"It's not me," he said. "You just ain't good at it."

He pointed to a group of about twenty morels I'd walked right through.

"Don't you worry. I'll share. Got plenty to sell and save, both."

I smiled, grateful for kindness.

"You get those vegetables in yet?" he asked as we picked.

"You said not to put the rest of the seeds in until danger of frost passed."

"Think you can go ahead. Frost's all gone for this year. Get 'em in before Memorial Day so they'll have time to ripen. Corn and beans in the same hill. That's the way to do it. Indian style."

"Guess I've got another job ahead of me then."

"I could come help."

"Can't afford to pay you anything right now."

He shrugged. "Don't always have to pay for neighborliness. When you got it, pay me something. When you don't, pay me nothing but a nice smile."

"Got plenty of those," I said, and gave him one.

"That Indian fella come back, eh?"

I nodded. "At least once. He wants those bones we found."

"How does he know they're theirs?"

Hmm, I thought: the obvious question I didn't even think to ask.

"I have no idea, but he scared the crap out of me. He came right into the studio even though I had the door locked. He opened it and Sorrow didn't bark."

"I'll have a look at that lock. Probably sticks. Doesn't close exactly right. And as to Sorrow, well, there are people who know animals so well they're welcomed anywhere in the woods. Some people just give off the kind of trust animals sniff out. Nothing bad about your dog, Emily. He's a creature of his nature and his kind's history. Guess you don't understand how much you learn, living where other things want to kill you."

"Maybe I am learning," I said. "That was how I felt when he zeroed in on me. Sure makes me feel less secure now. I keep thinking I see him out my windows. Or up my drive. I sense eyes on me. Sleep hasn't been easy since he came to see me."

Harry nodded. "Everybody makes haunts of stuff we're afraid of. Me too. I fear Deputy Dolly and that ticket book 'a hers. I'm afraid of those tax people who come sniffing around and send me bigger bills. And those DNR guys—looking for my traps. Lived my way all my life, now I got one after another coming to tell me I can't do this, I can't do that. I see plenty of eyes in the woods, just like you. Once in a while I take a shot at 'em."

Harry always made me feel better. I went back to my house without even checking to see if anyone stood on the porch, or hung around the drive. I let Sorrow out after planting a big kiss on top of his spotted head. He had been punished for being a traitor by not being allowed out on walks with me. That was over. Every mean and vindictive bone in my body melted away. I had plenty to keep my mind busy. It didn't have to center on a poor dog's confusion.

I strung my meager number of mushrooms on a doubled thread and hung them from nails out on the porch. When they were completely dry I would store them and enjoy them next winter, when the snow was five feet deep and the tall trees nothing but black brush strokes etched with white.

Out in my studio, I worked on the bones story for *Northern Pines* most of the afternoon. I made a few phone calls to a forensics expert I knew back in Ann Arbor, getting information on bones in water: how long it took the flesh to be eaten off by fish and water action; what happens to the hair; how bones are identified; how marrow and teeth can still provide DNA for identification. All very nice tea-time talk. I'd planned the story around identification of both victims so I still needed to find out who the woman was. But I had a structure, a kind of outline, and a list of what I needed to know before the story could be e-mailed in.

When I'd pushed "Bones: Up From a Watery Grave" as far as I could take it, I pulled out my notes on the missing girls. We would have to visit all of them. We had to be sure of our suspicion that Mary Naquma was the one we were looking for.

I put the names and numbers and my story aside. I had other things to see to. First an hour with my novel: *A Hard Case of Murder*. I wanted to get the elderly attorney immersed in the facts in a hurry, get him mired down, believing this scamp of a client didn't really kill his wife. And he'd be wrong, of course. A witness would come forward. A woman giving him an air-tight alibi. She might be a married woman who didn't want her husband to find out about her affair with this great-looking creep. But that had been done so many times. Still, everything old is new again—if you know how to put a creative spin on it. So, a married woman having an affair with him ... or so she says. But something else ... hmm ... it would take a great deal of thought and a lot of walking beside the lake to get the plot laid out right.

Later, the fact that Dolly hadn't phoned finally sank in. Either she was in big trouble and didn't want to call, or she was mad at me. If she was mad, that was too bad. The one place I couldn't let her into my life concerned Jackson. She didn't trust him and didn't like him. All I got from her on the subject was that he was a moocher and a user. Since I wanted to get along with him, and since I needed him—in my own way—I didn't want her sticking her nose in my business.

By four o'clock, when I still hadn't heard, I called the station. A new woman on the board was taking calls. One I hadn't met before. The chief's wife, Frances, used to man the board from nine to five, until their boy got so sick. Now this new one, Mandy, covered most days, she said. Mandy, in a high, friendly voice, said she didn't know where Dolly was but would pass along the message.

I had an hour before heading to Kalkaska and Cherry Street Market. Then on to Traverse City and the Blue Goat for wine, Bay Bakery for bread, Grand Traverse Pie Company for a cherry pie. If I got lucky I'd have fifteen minutes to stop for a cannoli at Eurostop in the old train station. That woman knew how to make soups and sandwiches like I hadn't tasted since Italy.

I called Detective Brent only to find out what I already knew: the second set of bones belonged to Chester Allen Wakowski, Dolly Wakowski's husband—as suspected. The first set of bones, the female, American Indian, hadn't been identified as yet. They were working on it, tracing missing girls over the last fifteen years, and hoped to have the case solved as soon as both skeletons were identified. Brent's tone softened when he got around to asking how Dolly and I were coming at our end. I went into my laconic, know-nothing voice, and told him we were checking out the same missing people he was, probably. Just hadn't gotten around to making personal calls as yet.

"Anything else? Dolly know anyone who wanted to kill Chester? I'm going to have to ask her to come on in and talk with me."

"She doesn't remember any trouble he had, just that he ran off with that woman. Probably the skeleton we found."

"She been asking questions? Like at the place he worked? Maybe places he hung out?"

I didn't want to tell him she was having other troubles. My dance around the truth was a sad one. He couldn't have believed my evasions, but he didn't press on any of it.

"You will share whatever you find with me?" He was insistent.

"Of course. Oh, and by the way, the Odawa are getting a little nervous about that skeleton that belongs to their tribe."

"We don't know that for sure, that she's one of them. Just that she's Native American."

"I think they're assuming."

"They shouldn't assume anything. When we know who she was and where she lived and what happened—maybe then we'll have something to go on. You can tell whoever it is over there that we're holding on to the bones until we know for sure. Last thing we want is to give them to one tribe only to find she came from somewhere else and wasn't Odawa at all."

Detective Brent, like Harry, had come up with what hadn't passed through my mind. Why the heck didn't I challenge that man over the dead woman's tribal connection? What made him so certain she was one of theirs? Had to be he knew more than he was telling anyone. I hated the thought of bearding a lion as tough as he was in his own den, but something didn't smell right here. I would toss it to Dolly.

Let her face those fierce eyes and that almost magical power over animals—and that power over me.

After I changed into a blue silk shirt, black pants, and black heels—my regulation dress-up clothes—Dolly finally called. She reminded me that she'd been giving a program on Stranger Danger at the elementary school. She'd been invited to have lunch with the kids, seated on one of those tiny chairs drawn up to a tiny table. After that she'd had mailbox vandalism to deal with.

"I sat there at lunch like a munchkin," she growled. "No place for my gun."

"You shouldn't have had it with you. Not at an elementary school," I said, and moved right on. "So, what happened? You and the chief find that man?"

"Yup. Sure did. One of the chiefs of the tribe. I guess he's in charge of personnel or something like that at the casino."

"You tell him why you picked up Chet's dog tags?"

"We told him and he understood. Seemed relieved, as if he thought it could be something else. He didn't give in on much, though. Said he might still go see the state police, if we don't help him get the bones released. They sure are hot on burying that woman. I don't blame them, I guess. I feel a little the same about getting Chet buried. His sister's coming up in a few days. We're with Sullivan."

"What did Lucky say? Is he doing anything to you over the evidence tampering?"

"Putting a letter in my file, is all. Says he's got to do that but he can keep it kind of vague so maybe it won't be clear to anybody looking in there. Says he might have to tell Detective Brent, what with the Indian threatening us if we don't help him get what he wants. I hope not. That Brent can be such a strait-laced prude."

"Did you give him the dog tags?"

"Lucky? Sure did. But I'm going to get 'em back when all of this is over. Only right. I explained that they were my wedding present and all. The chief is a good man. He understood."

"Then you're out of the woods on this."

"Looks like. Pretty much."

I told her I had phone numbers for the families of the missing girls, all except Lena Smith.

"Let's get busy tracking them down. We'll go back out to Peshawbestown, call on some of those Smiths." I heard her yawn over the phone. Rough morning with the little people, I guessed. "Somebody will know who Lena Smith is. They keep track of each other. I'm going over to The Skunk now. See if anybody remembers Chet and the woman he was with. Maybe they got a name. Or something."

"Brent suggested talking to people at that mill where Chet worked."

"Yeah. I'm planning on that."

"I've got that dinner at Jackson's tonight. We can start first thing in the morning."

"Why don't we meet at your house? The earlier the better. Then we'll head out to Peshawbestown. And I've got some other things I want to talk over with you. What time you getting home tonight?"

I shook my head. This was kind of nosy. "I have no idea. Depends on how much fun we have."

"So, that Bill from the paper's going to be there, too? And a girlfriend. Good. I'm glad you won't be alone with what's his name. Don't trust him as far as I can sling him."

"Don't worry. I'll be fine."

"Well, don't get talked into anything."

"Like what?"

"You know what I'm talking about."

"Oh, for God's sakes, Dolly. I'm not sixteen."

"Yeah? Well, sometimes you act about twelve. Keep your pants on and you won't get your heart broken all over again."

With that last bit of motherly advice, Dolly hung up.

I slammed my phone down, muttered the things I'd been ready to tell her, picked up my salad bowl, my salad tongs, my purse, my keys, and took off for the dinner party.

# TWENTY

Heavy black clouds swept in from the west by the time I got to the Cherry Street Market in Kalkaska. A storm coming. I picked bright red tomatoes, arugula, and tiny green onions from the outside bins under striped umbrellas. Asparagus wasn't in season yet, but what they had wasn't heavy or woody. It would grill up fine, I thought, and picked through the basket for the straightest and greenest spears.

Inside, as I maneuvered my way through the other people with baskets, into the tiny space leading to two cash registers, I couldn't help but buy myself a white chocolate cookie for the road. Cherry Street Market is one of my favorite places, though they closed at the beginning of December each year and didn't reopen until April. That's when the flowers began to come in, at least a few pansies, and then on to Mother's Day with the flats and pots of flowers I coveted—every one of them. Between December and April I felt bereft. Like Emily Dickinson's "hill of April," when the Dickinson larder had gone empty, I thought of winter as my own personal time of drought.

In Traverse City, I hit the Blue Goat first, buying a bottle of red from Château Chantal and a bottle of white from the Leelanau Cellars. After that I was off to the Grand Traverse Pie Company for a cherry pie still warm from the oven. Then over to Bay Bakery where I walked up the steps of the old building and into the smells of childhood. Maybe not *my* childhood—my dad never went to real bakeries. He bought off the shelf at Kroger's. But those smells came from somebody's childhood. The smell of baking bread had to be buried deep in the human genetic code.

I walked out with one loaf of bread for Jackson and one for me; one banana-nut bread for Jackson, and a scone for me. No time for Eurostop. It was already a quarter to seven.

Between the cookie and the scone, I felt full before I got to Jackson's. I pulled up the sand drive under the tall pines just as the rains came. I parked beside the log cottage on a high bank of Spider Lake. Other legs of the spider led off around bends and into deep coves. The lake ran up to wild banks where old cottages settled into the earth behind walls of reeds and tag alder.

Jackson's place sat spread out under long-needled pines. The front porch faced the lake. Inside, his ceiling soared up two stories and had high windows across the front. There were two bedrooms upstairs. The larger one, at the front, was his. The smaller, he used as a study.

I had visited twice before, to pick up work when he didn't have time to deliver it. He was pleased with his temporary house: plenty of room with space to entertain, and the lake for swimming and boating. I wasn't crazy about it. Too big and too open. Too filled with the nondescript stuff people left in rentals. Always that ubiquitous jar of Florida shells having nothing to do with Michigan.

I lugged my grocery bags and the finished manuscript chapters in the door and yelled that I had arrived.

Jackson clumped down the log staircase from his study and grabbed me up in his arms, bags and all.

"I don't know how to thank you. I had the whole morning to work." He half whirled me once, then let me go. He stood back to admire my silk shirt and the old gold necklace I'd found at a resale shop.

"Lovely, lovely, lovely," he enthused.

"Pay me," I growled and handed him the bills for the food.

He looked down at the bills, smiled at me, and stuck them in his pocket. I'd get paid later, if he figured out what the wadded paper was when he took his pants out of the dryer, after he washed them.

It didn't take long to set the white wine in the fridge, open the red to breathe, line up the vegetables on the counter, make my salad, set the table, and help Jackson flatten patties out of the hamburger he'd bought. We were almost ready when, at seven thirty, Bill called through the open door and hurried in with a small pretty redhead beside him. Together they held a wet newspaper above their heads, protection from the soft rain still falling. Bill set a bottle of wine on the counter.

As Jackson got them settled in the living room, I poured the wine: white for Ramona Sheffield and me. Red for the men. I couldn't help but take in everything about Bill's date. Fashionable glasses that seemed to fit, unlike Bill's. Her nose was off center enough, green eyes too far apart, mouth a little wide. She wasn't beautiful, maybe not really pretty. She was somewhere close to my age, thirty-four, and about in my league. I liked to think that women like us would be called striking, if not beautiful.

Phooey, I told myself, using one of my Dad's terms for a peculiar situation. Bill meant nothing to me. I had no right sizing up his date. And no right to the niggling jealousy I felt.

We sat and talked until the rain stopped and Jackson could light his grill. The men cooked the hamburgers and asparagus. I heard them laughing as I stood behind the counter dressing the salad while smiling tightly at Ramona, who insisted on resetting the table. I'd forgotten napkins. I'd forgotten water glasses. I'd forgotten salt and pepper. I'd forgotten ... oh, who cared what else I'd forgotten. This wasn't my party.

The food was good. Ordinary. I mean, what can you do with a burger? The asparagus tasted great, grilled in a little olive oil. My salad was ... a salad. The bread was a hit. By the time we got to dessert, everybody dug into the pie as if it were the first course.

I sat across from Bill, trying not to notice how comfortably his big bear of a body fit into the armchair, and trying not to laugh out loud as I got the finger again and again when his glasses slipped down his nose.

We talked about town politics—a new mayor had recently been sworn in. Jackson soon grew bored with local stuff and changed the conversation to an upcoming national election, quickly offending Ramona.

"What an elitist attitude," she said, putting her fork down and sitting up in her cane-backed chair.

"Not at all," Jackson leaned back in his chair too, the way he did when settling down for a good fight. "You're looking at events with a populist eye. Being soft is all right, as long as you don't do any real harm..."

Now Bill joined in. I stayed out of the discussion because I agreed with Bill and Ramona, but didn't like thinking of the two of them as a team I might join.

Eventually they all agreed to disagree and laughed that constricted laugh people give when they are slightly angry but know they shouldn't be. Soon they discussed Ramona's job with the Dennos Museum and an upcoming exhibit of Inuit art.

I watched, adding little. Something wouldn't allow me to enjoy this pleasant dinner with pleasant company. When I tried to smile or joke, I ended like a balloon poked with a stick: deflated. I didn't like seeing Bill with a woman. I liked picturing him in that messy office at the newspaper. I liked hearing his deep voice over the phone. And if he was going to be anybody's friend, I wanted him to be mine, not Jackson's and not this Ramona's. Whoever this woman was, they didn't appear close. You can tell if people are sleeping together by how they touch and lean when they are standing. They kept their distance and seemed to simply enjoy being in each other's company. Still, though I had made myself feel better, I wasn't happy.

Jackson was interested in her. He gave Ramona his attentive look after their small political tiff. Knowing him, he would pour on the charm, get her on his side, maybe even go after her, and then drop her as punishment for disagreeing with him.

Not a pretty side of Jackson.

I decided not to like Ramona, and to make fun of her as soon as she and Bill left. Or not make fun—Jackson would catch on to what I was doing—but at least make her unimportant.

We all agreed finally that it had been a very nice evening and that we must do it again. Jackson and I stood in the doorway waving them off and pointing to the glorious sunset—all those wild reds and mauves and pinks of a spring sky.

"Why don't we take a swim?" Jackson suggested when they were gone. His arm lay across my shoulder, his good-looking face smiled down into mine.

"No bathing suit," I said, shrugging off his arm and turning back into the house.

"I wouldn't mind," he called after me.

"Your neighbors would."

There were dishes to scrape and pile into the dishwasher, food to put away, a table to clear. Jackson stopped me, told me not to worry about the mess—he had a woman coming in the next day. We'd get the food cleared and that was enough.

"And we can do all of that later," he smiled, looking down at me.

I gave in, sat down in the living room, and accepted the glass of wine he brought me.

"Thanks for the pages. I have more—if you think you'll have the time."

I was going to ask to be paid from then on. He must have an allowance for secretarial services. I was even going to suggest that without payment for my services I couldn't keep on working as hard as I had been for him.

I was going to do many things for myself.

I sat still, sipping the wine, listening to Jackson's low voice as he told me how he appreciated my help and how he felt so comfortable—the two of us the way we used to be.

As if something wormed into my brain, I found myself agreeing, laughing lightly about other dinners we'd given—some that went well, some that were disasters, where guests got into snarling arguments and stormed out.

Soon he took the glass from my hand, pulled me close, and kissed me.

It was all so easy and familiar. As if I hadn't a worry in the world, I leaned my head against his shoulder and took in a few deep breaths. We watched as the dying sun played off the lake in skittering diamonds. If anyone had asked me right then what I'd been so desperate about a few hours before, I couldn't have come up with a thing. Here, with Jackson's lean body against mine, I hadn't a worry. There I was, in a past life in Ann Arbor. Nice house, nice furniture, nice garden, nice friends, nice job. No money worries. No unsold novels. No perfidious dog. No Indians after me. And on and on…

I sighed heavily as Jackson kissed me. It wouldn't be bad, I thought, looking up and smiling, to be back with him. Maybe he had changed. Maybe there would be no other women. Maybe we could be the couple we'd pretended to be—loving, faithful. The kind of people who go on year after year, contented simply to be together.

I snuggled against him.

When he led me upstairs to the bedroom there was no pushing or pulling. I was as eager as he was. It had been a long time for me. No sex. No love. Three years. Not a good life for a woman in her thirties. Just the smell of him was so good. And the warmth of his arms, and then his whole body.

Maybe this wasn't a step backward, I told myself, as Jackson unbuttoned my silk shirt and pushed it back off my shoulders to fall to the floor. Maybe this was where we were supposed to go next. At that moment I stopped thinking and let myself simply be.

# TWENTY-ONE

NOTHING LIKE A MOOD-KILLING angry face waiting on my side porch to bring me back to earth with a ground-shaking thud.

All morning Jackson and I had been the way we used to be: touching each other, laughing together, no old animosity or manipulation. Just a man and a woman. A couple who looked, to outsiders, as if they were very much in love. I liked the feeling. I liked daring to draw in a deep breath and not hurting inside. I welcomed touching his cheek over coffee, making love a last time before leaving, taking one of his well-manicured hands in my rather rough hand and bringing it to my lips, looking up at him, seeing him contented and pleased with me.

Driving home I thought about what it could be like if we married again. I'd have to leave my house on Willow Lake. The real estate market wasn't very good in Michigan; maybe I would hang on to it for a while. Why not? I asked myself. We could come up here to write. Nothing stopping us from having a second home. I wouldn't have to give up my place entirely, just be ready to share a little. Lots of couples did exactly that. Or they had time apart at their summer home. Maybe

I couldn't keep the garden, but then I could hire Crazy Harry to weed for me, maybe spray on deer repellant. There was no reason to go on in such turmoil, not with a perfectly good marriage as an alternative.

I drove down my drive, happy with myself, but guilty that I'd left Sorrow on the porch alone all night. I thought, with a thud, I might have to get rid of Sorrow. Really no place for him back in Ann Arbor. He was too big, too clumsy, too unmanageable. And he was used to freedom. I could see him leaping on a leash, tied to a post outside of Zingerman's, straining to get away. No, I would just have to harden my heart and find him a good home. Maybe Dolly would take him. She didn't have much in the way of entertainment. A dog would be good for her.

Or Crazy Harry. He could add Sorrow to his kennel of dogs. I even told myself Sorrow would like that, having his own kind for company.

The Leetsville patrol car sat in my drive. Sorrow, who had escaped, leaped in place beside my squat, angry friend, standing with her fists jammed at her waist, watching me pull down the hill. Eleven thirty. We'd said early, but I'd forgotten.

I parked beside Dolly's car, got out, and waved, happily calling out, "Hi! Beautiful morning."

"Where the hell you been?" Dolly growled.

Sorrow leapt in wild circles around me. He had learned not to throw his body at a human being, but had not learned how to stay on the ground. I grabbed a couple of fistfuls of his thick hair and forced him to calm down. He lapped at me, his long pink tongue reaching for a bare arm, a leg, anything he could get to. I patted his head and bent close, whispering an apology.

"We were supposed to get going early. Remember what you said yesterday?"

I murmured something and nodded.

"You stay in town?"

I grabbed my purse, salad bowl, and tongs out of the car and started toward the house with Sorrow leaning his big black-and-white body into mine.

"Looks like it," I answered Dolly over my shoulder, opening the door, and nudging Sorrow to sit.

The two of them followed me inside. I hurried to feed Sorrow, still feeling guilty that he'd probably been out all night, and hadn't been fed. Water he could get down at the lake.

"You sleep with Jackson?" she demanded.

I turned an astonished, and innocent, face to her.

"None of your business," I said, and slipped off my shoes. I needed a shower, my hair washed, a change of clothes. Maybe an hour. Dolly had been there almost two hours already I probably wouldn't have time for a shower. No time to wash my hair. But I was at least going to change out of the silk shirt and pants into something more suitable for hunting down missing women.

"Are you nuts?" She took a seat at the kitchen island, wiggling around so her gun found a place for itself over the side of the chair. "You know what that guy's like. He'll use you again. You're already typing up his stuff, sending it to the publisher for him. Now he'll have all the sex he wants, too. Sounds like some damned geisha to me. Never thought you'd be that kind of woman."

I gave a disgusted snort and headed back to my bedroom to change. When I came out, dressed more for the day ahead in jeans and yellow cotton sweater, she was still talking.

"You think you'll marry him again? Start all that over—finding underwear in the glove box of his car?"

I decided I'd told Dolly too much and was sorry. I had needed a place to go with my misery when I first knew her, but I should have kept it to myself.

I shrugged. "Might. Things aren't working that well up here."

"You mean your crappy books?"

"Well, yes," I sat on a stool and changed into tennis shoes. "My crappy books. No decent jobs. Being alone too much. Talking to a dog like some old lady."

"What about the *Dead Dancing Women* thing? The one about us?"

"No takers."

"Thought you were sure about that one. Didn't like it myself—made me look kind of like an odd person—but I thought, 'cause it was based on those murders here last year, well, that it should sell. If that happens you should be OK."

I nodded. "If that happens," I echoed.

"Doesn't take a lot to live up here."

"Takes some."

"You said you still got money from your dad."

"But it's running out. Probably by next year..."

"Geez." She looked away, disgusted. "Anything can happen between then and now. If I was you I'd get my real estate license, just in case. You could make enough off that."

I nodded. An idea I'd been kicking around. A week of schooling. Have to pass a test. Find an office that would take me...

Thinking about Jackson and Ann Arbor was easier.

"I thought you loved it up here." She sniffed and picked at the skin on her left hand.

"I do," I said. "But..." I couldn't finish the sentence.

Sorrow had to be put on the porch, though I promised him a long walk when I got back.

A woman has to be practical, I told myself as we headed out to my car. Maybe it was time to move on. Still, as I turned to lock my door, I felt the solid brass knob in my hand, put a palm against the warm and firm wood, and turned away from the house I loved with a frisson of sadness.

# TWENTY-TWO

"OK, SO HERE'S THE deal." Dolly sat on a bench at the Trout Town Grill making notes in her small notebook. "Let's go see these Robbins families."

Trout Town Grill, in Kalkaska, had good food, especially their Cobb salad. The restaurant was crowded but we got a booth at the back in five minutes. I ordered my salad and Dolly went for the fried chicken. She dug her notebook out again and laid it on the table.

She frowned over her notes. "Then we'll head out to Elk Rapids. That Tanya Lincoln, sister of the missing girl from Mancelona. She's out there."

I nodded and dug into my salad as soon as it got there. If Dolly decided we'd better hurry, there would be no time to finish my food. She could bolt down a plateful of anything in nothing flat.

"Then we'll make a stop in Traverse City. See this Fern Valient. Then out to Peshawbestown and Lena Smith. That's going to be the hard one. We'll have to go door to door."

"Or to the casino. Somebody there might know her."

Dolly nodded and bit into a piece of chicken as a man in his mid-thirties with shoulder-length brown hair, dirty jeans, and a clean checkered sport shirt walked over and stood beside our table.

"Heard you was looking into that bone thing, from out to Sandy Lake," he said, smiling and nodding at me then turning his attention to Dolly.

She leaned back and frowned up at him. "Billy Kramer?"

He nodded.

"When you get out?"

"Long time ago. I was a kid, Dolly. I'm married now. Me and Cassandra got us a little boy."

She smiled. "I'm really happy to hear that. I never thought you was bad."

"Thanks," he said, and lowered his head shyly.

"Why are you asking about Sandy Lake? Just curious?"

He shook his head and looked at people in the other booths. "Heard it might be Chet, your husband."

Dolly nodded, scrunched up her face, and waited.

Billy leaned close to Dolly's ear and told her something I couldn't hear. She looked up and demanded, "You sure?"

Billy nodded, waited a minute, then walked back to a table near the far wall where a young girl sat holding a baby dressed in a blue onesy. He kicked his feet and made happy noises. She looked over at us and nodded her head.

"What'd he say?" I asked.

"Said he'd seen Chet with a woman once. He said it was an Indian girl, and he knew she had a brother because he knew the brother. Maybe another girl in the family, too. Said they lived somewhere around Leetsville back awhile. The brother's name is Alfred. Had a little run-in with Alfred when Billy was about twenty. Didn't know the last name but he heard the brother works at one of the casinos; maybe is high up in the business end of things."

"Should have asked for a description."

She shrugged. "What good is that going to do? Billy's got to be thirty-six now. So, thirteen years ago?"

"He say what the run-in was about?"

"You mean with Alfred?" She shook her head then thought awhile. "Billy was a mean guy when he was young. Had something to do with his dad. He got some awful beatings out there on Crawford Lake. Got into a lot of scrapes with people he saw as different. His dad was maybe a Klan member, something like that. Wouldn't be surprised if Billy called this Alfred names. Insulted him. You know what boys do."

"Some guy," I muttered and glanced back at what looked like a nice young couple, and at the baby the woman dandled on her lap.

"Don't glare, Emily. Billy's a different man since marrying Cassandra. Up here, we keep tabs on the bad guys. Happy when they get turned around. I think Billy's one of the turnarounds. And his dad died. That was a big help."

She finished her chicken while I was only halfway through my salad. I could see she was getting fidgety, so I had the waitress box up what was left. We headed out to Third Street, to call on the first of the Robbins.

The house was small, white, and set back on a lot between two huge Victorians.

A woman came to the door wiping her hands on a dish towel and frowning through the screen at us. "Yes?" she said, looking over Dolly's blue summer uniform, then me. I didn't think we looked like a menacing duo. Had to be Dolly with that gold badge pinned way up over her left breast.

"Ma'am," Dolly said hesitantly. "I'm Deputy Wakowski with the Leetsville Police. This is Emily Kincaid, with the *Northern Statesman*. We're getting information on disappearances from a ways back. Can you tell us if you're related to Tricia Robbins?"

She frowned harder. "She's my daughter." One of her hands went up to hold on to the door. "Oh my God—she's not ..."

"No, Ma'am," Dolly hurriedly pulled the screen door open and reached in to grab the woman's shoulder, supporting her. "It's nothing like that."

The woman backed into her living room and sat down on a brown checked sofa.

"Did your daughter ever come home?" I asked.

She nodded, but looked disgusted. "Back when my husband reported her missing she'd already run off maybe three times. That last one seemed longer than the others."

"She come back or did you just get a phone call or something?" Dolly said.

She made a motion with her hand. "She came back, then ran off again in a few months. Next thing she was gone, and we finally heard she was living with some man down in Grand Rapids. Pregnant. After we heard that, well Tim and I decided we didn't want anything to do with her." She gave a decisive shake of her head. Her lips pulled in tight, forming a halo of tiny wrinkles around her mouth. This was a woman still angry with the child she'd borne, yet something in her eyes said different.

"You got scared when you thought she might be dead ..." Dolly always stepped in where angels knew better than to tread. "Seems you love her."

The woman made a noise and got up from the sofa. "Natural enough. I'd feel bad about any Christian soul coming to a bad end."

Dolly was about to say something else—I thought it had to do with that "Christian soul" stuff—and I grabbed on to her arm. It didn't do to get into religious arguments and our time was limited. We could mark Tricia Robbins off our list and go on to the next, though even I was hoping Tricia'd found a happier home down in Grand Rapids.

———

Tanya Lincoln, of Elk Rapids, lived in a second-floor condo looking out on Lake Michigan. We pushed the doorbell but no one answered. We tried the next-door condo and the elderly man who answered said Tanya worked at the insurance agency right downtown.

That was our next stop. The overly made-up receptionist in the small lobby of the vine-covered brick building smiled a lot and went to get Tanya Lincoln from the lunch room. The receptionist came back with a short and wide woman who smiled as much as the receptionist and stuck out her hand as she walked purposefully forward.

Dolly introduced us, and asked if we could talk in her office.

We sat in two blue and chrome chairs across from her desk in what was a very spare office. Tanya folded her hands on the desktop, showing us she had all the time in the world to listen to our insurance needs.

"It's about your sister," Dolly began.

Tanya frowned.

"What about her?"

"I'm talking about Bambi."

"Yes?"

"You reported her missing thirteen years ago."

The woman looked surprised at first. She finally smiled, her broad face widening, her deep brown eyes looking amused.

"And what do you want to know about her?"

"Did she ever come back?"

Tanya laughed. "She sure did. Married a man from Mancelona. They've got four kids and she helps out here in the agency. You want to meet her?"

Before we could say that wasn't necessary, she got up and motioned us back to the lobby.

"Bambi," she called to the smiling receptionist, who sat leafing through an *Elle* magazine. "These two are here to find out if you ever returned when you ran away."

Bambi's chin dropped. She stared up at her sister. "You are kidding me."

"No," I said, feeling a little embarrassed but not knowing why. "We're checking on all girls who came up missing about thirteen years ago."

"And you're with the newspaper?" she asked, looking at me. She'd overheard the introductions. "I hope this won't be in the paper again. That was a long time ago."

I shook my head. "I'm working with Deputy Wakowski, here. Something to do with a current case she's on. Just covering it for the paper."

"Probably that Sandy Lake thing," Tanya said toward Bambi, and leaned back on her heels. "I read about it. Awful."

"Well, you can take my name off your list," Bambi said. "And I sure don't want to see my name in the paper connected to anything like that. First place, I don't want my kids to know I ran away like that. Trouble enough, with four boys."

I put my hands up as if surrendering. "No need to bring you into anything."

Bambi's smile was gone. Those bright red lips were pursed tight. "That is so right. And I'll be watching the paper. If I see my name you'll be talking to Tanya's lawyer..."

Tanya rolled her eyes. Dolly and I backed toward the door.

We thanked them and left the office. Behind us, I heard the women arguing.

# TWENTY-THREE

TRAVERSE CITY, ON THIS bright May afternoon, resembled Disney-
land waiting to open. The clean streets and bright blue bay looked
ready for happy characters to come bouncing down the sidewalks, zip
by on motor boats, glide overhead in balloons, and wave stiff hands in
the many parades to come. There is something about a waking resort
town. The locals walked Front Street smiling, nodding to each other,
and calling out as if about to break into song.

Washington Street was in the downtown area. A block over from
Front. Between two of the houses we passed stood an old signal tree,
severely bent out of shape by Indians making their way from winter to
summer hunting grounds. Once they had tied young saplings at an
angle to mark their trail through this place of the grand traverse.

Fern Valient's house, one of the smaller homes, was nestled in between larger homes with wraparound porches and tall trees. A black
SUV was parked at the curb in front of the Valient house. We knocked
and waited. No answer. Dolly walked to the backyard to see if Mrs.
Valient might be out working in her garden.

"Nobody back there," she said, coming around front.

"We'll call later," I suggested and started down the front steps.

"Guess we'll have to." Dolly headed out the front walk to where my yellow Jeep was parked at the curb. "Too bad. Could have all these loose ends tied up."

I figured it didn't matter. My money was on the Naquma girl. I did wonder, though, why she hadn't lived on the reservation at Peshawbestown. Maybe that wasn't so unusual now, but thirteen years ago the Odawa weren't doing quite so well. Would this one family have had the money or the self-confidence to live away from the tribe? Maybe leaving the reservation was more common than I thought. I guessed I didn't know a lot about the Odawa.

The bay, awake after a long winter of ice and snow, reflected a brilliant blue and cloudless sky. A few fishing boats worked the middle of the bay. One sailboat and many speed boats dotted the water's surface. Memorial Day would be the official kickoff. The marinas we passed already teemed with boats coming out of storage.

Along the way toward Sutton's Bay, a flock of returning swans circled and chased, making spring fools of themselves near shore. Dolly sat with her elbow resting on the window ledge and her fist jammed into her chin.

"What are you thinking about?" I asked after too long a time of quiet.

She turned and gave me a wan smile. "Oh, just Chet and that girl. I wonder if there was another boyfriend in the picture. You know, somebody really jealous. Soon as we know who she was for sure, let's start asking about boyfriends."

"This Lena Smith might know."

Dolly shook her head. "Didn't seem she knew a whole lot. Paper said they were only friends at the beauty school. She didn't even know where Mary Naquma lived."

"What about the school? Shouldn't we go there and see if anybody remembers her?"

"Out of business. Already tried to call."

It didn't take long to get to Peshawbestown, still an Indian Reservation, but now one sprawling along M22 and back into the forest. A casino, hotel, and conference area were the town centers. I remembered coming up here quite awhile ago, before I married Jackson, and driving through on my way to Northport. The houses were mostly trailers then. Run-down, rusty places. Unemployment among the Indians had been high. Alcoholism destroyed lives. Now the houses were neat, many of the homes new. They'd created their own jobs, and all shared the money made from gambling. There were no ego-swollen Donald Trumps among the Odawa. The money they made gave every member of the tribe a better life. Their children got college educations, and the tribe was building its own colleges. Everybody got a piece of the pie, like the true meaning of democracy—not simply consumerism.

Dolly tapped me on the arm and pointed to one of the houses set back in the woods. The place was very small, but neat, with a perfectly square, newly tilled, and planted garden off to one side.

"One of the Smiths you found," Dolly whispered as if anyone could hear. She pointed to a mailbox.

I turned in, pulled between garden and house, and parked. I looked with longing at the perfect rows of the garden, hilled, and, I'd heard, probably planted with fish heads and other parts for fertilizer. I thought longingly of spending spring and summer days in my garden until my skin was brown and my garden luxuriant. Maybe taking on a Native American life was what I was after. Complete peace and nature. No TV.

Maybe no electricity at all. I could live in a teepee and keep a wood fire going at the center all winter. I'd heard of a woman in Traverse City who'd lived like that, close to the park along M72. The thought of baking my skin over a fire all winter, and maybe freezing to death anyway, cooled my rustic dreams.

We knocked at the many-times-painted white front door. No answer. Again. No answer. Dolly stepped off the small square of cement and looked up at the house. I was making my way to the car when a woman came from the woods. As she got closer, she put a hand in the air, hailing us with a "Yoo-hoo, there. Can I help you?"

The woman was too young to be Lena Smith. In her early twenties, with straight black hair cut in bangs and left to hang around her face, she was slim and pretty, with a timid smile.

"Are you looking for Tobias?" she asked when she got up to us.

"Looking for Lena Smith. She one of the Smiths who live here?"

"No. Tobias Smith," the young woman said. "Why do you want to talk to Lena?"

The way she said it made me suspect this woman knew Lena.

"Actually," Dolly said, "We're looking for a Mary Naquma. Do you know her?"

The woman's face changed from open and halfway friendly to dark. Her eyes went cold. She took a few steps from us, backing off the way she'd come. She shook her head.

"How about a man named Alfred?" I stepped in, trying to close the gap between us.

She glanced over her shoulder at the woods, as if she was going to bolt at any minute.

"Lena Smith reported Mary missing back a few years and we're doing a follow-up," Dolly went on. You couldn't miss the instant reluctance we were getting. There might even have been a big dose of fear.

"Can I have your name?" Dolly moved up beside me.

"You got a card?" The woman ignored Dolly's question.

Dolly felt in her pockets, took out the punch card they'd given her at Trout City, and a pen. She scribbled her name, address, and number then handed it to the woman. The woman looked down at the card and then at us.

"You both from Leetsville?" she asked.

We nodded. "I'm with the *Northern Statesman*," I said. "We're following a series of disappearances that happened awhile ago."

"What about this 'Alfred'?" Dolly asked. "Probably Alfred Naquma."

"Never heard of him." She snapped her mouth shut.

"If you hear where this Lena Smith lives now, will you have her call me?"

The woman barely nodded.

"And if anybody out here admits to knowing 'Alfred,' give me a call on that one too, OK?"

"Yeah. Sure." She nodded, turned, and hurried off through the woods the way she'd come.

Dolly and I exchanged glances. "What do you make of that?" she asked, climbing back into my car and slamming the door.

"No idea. But obviously those names meant something to her. Guess we wait."

"Casino?"

"There are other Smiths out here we could look up first."

She shook her head, lifted her hat, and repositioned it on her sweating hair. "Give you ten to one we hear pretty soon."

I backed out the drive to M22 and drove south. "OK, but let's ask for 'Alfred' at the casino. See what happens."

For a late afternoon, the parking lot of the casino was surprisingly full. The bells and clanking began as soon as we opened the door. I had this thing about gambling. I knew I had an addictive personality, and those sounds made my blood bubble and my brain stop working. I immediately began calculating how much money I had in my purse.

"No gambling," Dolly leaned in close and whispered.

"Maybe just a Triple Diamond machine."

She shook her head and scowled at me. "We're on duty, Emily. You don't drink and you don't gamble on duty."

"I'm not a cop." I pouted and blamed her for losing me the fortune that was waiting here, among the flashing lights and loud voices and old people dragging oxygen machines through the cigarette smoke, from machine to machine.

"You're with one," she said, and headed off to the line for the customer service area where I could have gotten a personalized casino card that would have paid big dividends. If it weren't for Dolly Wakowski.

When we got to the counter Dolly asked where the main offices were. We were sent back out of the casino and down the next road to the hotel/conference center and tribal offices.

A pleasant Odawa woman sat behind a modern oak desk in the lobby of the tribal offices. Dolly didn't ask directly for this "Alfred" guy but instead asked for a member of the council. The girl went through a set of double doors behind her desk and came back with a tall man who looked like any other white man. So many Odawa were of mixed blood. The names could be American. The faces American. And yet they could be close to full-blooded, the white genes winning out in the big lottery.

"May I help you?" the man stepped over. His manner was stiff, business like, and guardedly friendly.

Dolly introduced us. "We're looking for a Lena Smith. Does she still live around here?"

He thought awhile. "Many Smiths. I don't recall a Lena."

His head dipped, as if bowing.

"What about Mary Naquma?"

There was a small intake of breath. I knew what to look for now. That name brought response. Not the one we were looking for, but still a response.

He shook his head slowly.

"Are you sure? She disappeared about thirteen years ago."

"Not from here," he said with conviction.

"No, not from here. But she was an Odawa."

"Many Odawa."

Dolly put out a hand to me. "You got some notepaper?"

"You've got your own notebook," I hissed back.

"Forgot." She patted her pant's pocket and pulled out her notebook.

After writing down her name and number again, she tore the paper off and handed it to the man. He took it, folded it neatly, and put it in his shirt pocket.

"And your name is ..." Dolly put out her hand to shake his.

"Nicholas Adajawa. I'm manager of the casino."

Dolly nodded. "If you hear anything about Lena Smith, or about Mary Naquma, you'll give me a call, OK?"

He said nothing. He put his hands deep into his pockets and stood there waiting for us to leave.

Outside Dolly was spitting mad. "They know something."

I nodded, as frustrated as Dolly.

"Let's go back to the casino."

I gulped. I'd made it out intact once. I didn't know if I could go back in there and not fall from grace.

"I got a couple of bucks," she said. "We'll play your nickel machine. I just want to see who hangs around us now that the word's out. I've got a feeling something's going to happen."

It wasn't at the nickel machine that something was going to happen. After losing the ten dollars I'd confidently fed into the machine, an almost physical sadness set in. The few times I hit were only tiny blips in the constant gobbling of my nickels. At first I played the full shot—seventy-five cents a pull. Soon I was down to twenty-five cents a pull. Then a dime. Then I fed it one nickel at a time, meaning one line. Of course, that time the machine hit big on a line that wasn't covered so I had my sense of stupidity to deal with at the same time as my deep regret at losing. One thing I learned about myself I didn't know—I was cheap, as well as poor.

Dolly did better. She made small wins and kept playing even though she missed a lot of the plays due to looking around the huge room where we sat against the wall.

When my ten dollars was gone, I waited for her to finish, turning my chair back and forth, scanning the room, the people, the workers.

Just as Dolly hit triple diamonds on a line she'd covered and the machine went into its deep rumbling and flashing, I saw him standing inside the archway to the restaurant. He was talking to another man with long dark hair. They spoke in urgent conversation. It was the man from Sandy Lake.

I grabbed Dolly's arm, which wasn't easy. She was leaping in her chair. Her other arm flailed over her head. With a whoop, Dolly did a dance as the machine celebrated. People looked over, pointed, and came to stand nearby. Everyone congratulated her as if she'd done something wonderful. Dolly basked in it.

I shook the arm I held.

"It's him," I had to shout over the noise and the merriment around us.

"Who?" Dolly yelled back at me.

"The guy from the lake. It's him. Over there," I pointed to where the man stood.

"God!" Dolly looked from the man to her machine and back again. "I can't leave it now," she groaned. "I just can't."

I nodded, got up, and headed toward the restaurant. He was gone but had to be at a table inside or somewhere close by.

I stood at the hostess's station and waited for a bent woman with long, dark braids to make her way back toward me.

"A man was just here," I said. "Maybe you seated him. Young. Long black hair."

The elderly woman narrowed her eyes at me and shook her head. "No man here."

"Sure he was. I saw him."

She shook her head, harder.

"I know him. It's all right. His name is Alfred."

She opened her mouth to give me another "no," but stopped. "You know Alfred? You sure?"

I smiled a Cheshire Cat smile and told her he used to be a friend of my husband's.

"He went out in the parking lot. Gone now. If you leave your name and number I'll pass it on."

I figured no name and phone number would get me a response from Alfred Naquma. He was a man used to disappearing. I nodded at the woman, turned, and ran out the door to the parking lot.

The sunlight blinded me after the dark of the casino. I blinked a few times and hurried down the steps to look both ways, out over the parked cars. One old couple came slowly from the far lot. There wasn't another person in sight.

So, it was "Alfred" we were hunting for. I'd taken a shot in the dark, using the brother's name. He probably worked for the casino the way Billy Kramer said. Maybe it would be as easy as calling and asking for him, I thought. Maybe not.

I went back inside, told the hostess I'd missed him after all, and gave her my name and my number for him to call as soon as he could. I told her it was urgent, though I figured my chances of hearing from him ran the gamut of nil to none.

It wasn't easy getting Dolly out of the casino. Now that she'd won eighty dollars she figured she could go on playing awhile. I was just as determined to get her to leave with a few extra dollars in her pocket.

"You buy dinner," I said, tugging at her arm, dragging her to the cashier then out to the Jeep.

# TWENTY-FOUR

IN THE MORNING, THERE were nine calls on my answering machine. An overflow. A bounty of phone calls. A veritable inundation. Nine people wanting me. I was almost afraid to press the play button, hating to have my bubble burst, to find they were all calls from the electric company, all sweet voices enquiring about a payment because they still didn't believe that I'd lost the envelope in transit from my purse to the mailbox.

OK. The first two were hang-ups. The next was Jackson. He needed to see me, he said in that deep voice he affected when he wanted something from a woman. "Let's get together for dinner. Tonight? Tomorrow? My place, or yours. And if you've got that work ready for me ... terrific. You are a gem, Emily. I'm so lucky." His voice swelled with emotion. I caught my breath. He sounded the way he used to when we first fell in love. Maybe, I told myself, this could work again. The two of us. People change. If I'd learned anything in life, it was that: change happened, for good or ill. Why not Jackson? Why couldn't he have worn out the coed chase and be ready, at last, to settle down with me? It would be easy to go back to my old life. No money woes. Be with old friends. Possibly get my job back at the paper. I'd be in a familiar world instead of living up here where I didn't belong, and probably never would.

There are times, I told myself, leaning hard on the phone, when a woman has to get practical, accept her limitations, and run for cover.

Jackson's would be the first call I returned.

The next message was another hang-up—number three.

There was a call from Jan Romanoff of *Northern Pines Magazine*: "I'd like to schedule that bones story," she said, her voice distracted by noises behind her there at the office. "Oh, um, Emily, please call me. Oh, oh, yeah, and the other one—about the Indian cemetery—let's do that as a separate story. OK? Think I'll do an all Native American issue. Maybe get somebody from the Odawa to write a short story, or a history piece. Well, call me."

Another hang-up. This one wasn't immediate. There was someone there, listening, breathing into the phone, and then came the click.

Next: ah, that sweet voice from the electric company. Why the heck didn't I just pay the bill and get it over with? I asked myself. I had the money. I wasn't indigent—yet. Something about hanging onto my bank account like a squirrel dreading winter. I vowed to stop playing games and pay all my bills on time.

Next: a call from a charity wanting me to collect money from my neighbors, with a phone number to call them back—which I wouldn't do.

The last call. For a few seconds no one spoke. Then a man's voice came on. "Emily Kincaid. You have been warned enough. Stay out of our business or …"

The call ended.

I shivered and listened again. The voice was hesitant, the words slow, almost as if from someone who didn't speak English well. I hit the button. A threat? I should call Detective Brent, I thought. I would play it for him, let him decide if I'd been threatened. Probably he'd want the tape, maybe for voice recognition sometime in the future when, or if, we caught the man who'd murdered Chet and the Indian woman.

I played the call one more time. I knew the voice. The man who'd come to my studio. The man Dolly and Lucky met in Peshawbestown. Same hesitations. Lewis George.

I called Dolly. Had to go through the office. It was good to keep my mind on the mechanics of action and off the fact I felt vulnerable.

Dolly came right on the phone. She was going home. I played the call for her. It must have shocked her, too. She fell silent for a long time.

"Recognize the voice?" she asked.

"That Lewis George you went over to the casino to meet. The guy who was here."

"I think you're right. Don't understand why he's after you. I can see them wanting to get the bones back, but that's not up to us. Geez, there's so much about this whole business that frustrates me. And what's that 'or' mean? 'Or' I'll report you to the state police for overstepping your bounds? 'Or' you'll never be allowed inside another casino if you keep it up? 'Or' I'll stop my subscription to your newspaper? I don't get it. Can't be anything worse—like 'or' I'll kill you. You don't think he means to hurt you ... ?"

"How do I know? Let's take a look at what we've got. The girl murdered out there was Native American. She's probably Mary Naquma. The guy at the lake was Alfred Naquma, her brother. I'm pretty sure of that though I didn't put the Naquma part to the Alfred part. If he was the dead woman's brother, why doesn't he come forward instead of hiding? Maybe offer himself for DNA testing. They were sure worried about what you found out at the lake. What else could be out there?"

"How about the gun?" Dolly asked.

"But after thirteen years? And they want us to stop looking into the murders. There's got to be something they're afraid of."

"Would they protect a murderer?" Dolly asked. "Could it be Lewis George? Maybe it's not Alfred and him together, but him alone. He could be the one who murdered Chet and Mary. He's the one doing the intimidating. Seems a little old to have been a jealous boyfriend."

"Divers checked the lake bottom and didn't find anything. What else could be out there?"

"Look, before you break out in hives, call Brent. Ask him what you should do with the tape. He has to know about it, and have a copy made, in case you come up missing, or in case they find your lumpy body in a ditch somewhere."

"What do you mean, lumpy?" I came right back at her. "Look who's talking, you sack of ... And if anybody's going to meet an untimely end here, it should be you. I get suckered into going along to protect your sorry ..."

"Yeah, yeah. Well, nice talking to you."

She was gone.

I fumed. When I called Detective Brent in Gaylord, my voice must not have sounded properly afraid. Brent didn't believe me until I played the tape for him. Then he asked for a copy. "Look," he said, seeming worried, "maybe you and Dolly better lay low on this. I'll get an investigator over there. Pull somebody from another case. I gotta have a talk with this Lewis George."

I didn't like the sound of that. There was still Dolly's breach of police ethics. Brent didn't know about the dog tags and maybe never would. There was also the fact we'd invested a lot of time in this. And the fact I'd been threatened. I felt the way Dolly would feel when she heard we'd been pulled. Not that I was overly brave, or stupid, or out to prove anything. This was my job, what I did for a living. I had a story to finish and I meant to finish it completely.

"I'll get the tape to you," I said. "But we're not backing down. I'm sure I can speak for Dolly, too. This is personal now. You'll be hearing when we've got something for you."

I hung up on a protesting Detective Brent, who would either call Chief Barnard and get us off the case, or would think it over and let us go. He was in a pinch for investigators and he wasn't dumb.

# TWENTY-FIVE

JACKSON WANTED TO COME for dinner. He would bring the wine, he said. Something in his voice felt good; that old familiar lilt of sexuality and eagerness. I liked hearing him fall from his usual lofty, academic plane and come back to where we'd been human beings in love.

But I was tired. A lot of running around and a lot of stories left to do. I had phone calls to make for that Indian cemetery story and my own novel to work on. I had to have something I was happy about to read at Anna Scovil's Writers Night at the library, for which I'd seen flyers hanging at EATS and the gas station.

"Maybe tomorrow, Jackson," I said reluctantly. "I've got so much to do."

"That include getting my pages into the computer? My editor is eager to see more of the book, if you could send them along once you've put in the changes."

"I'll try. So much going on right now."

"Emily. I hope it's not more of this bone stuff I've been reading about in the paper."

"Well, some."

"Hardly up to your standards."

"Whoops!" I said. "I've got a lot to do."

"Then tomorrow. What time do you want me there?" His voice slipped back to the personal. "Shall I plan on staying the night?"

Yuck. Sounded oily to me. He had a right to ask, I guessed. We'd slept together.

"Let's talk tomorrow. I've got to get to work. I'll see how much I get done today..."

"I'll call in the morning and..." He hesitated. "It was great to be...eh...that we..."

"I know, Jackson," I said, stopping him in his fumble for words. "Me, too."

Sorrow had been alone a lot lately and though he still wasn't perfect—one pile of poop and two large wet spots on the wooden floor of the porch—I decided we'd take a short walk through the woods before heading to the studio for a few hours of writing.

Out in the woods, though I kept my eyes open for morels, I saw nothing. Probably too late in the spring, or too many of those mushroomers up from Ohio. But I did pick a bouquet of wildflowers. No trilliums, since they're protected. And Sorrow did stir up a skunk from a windfall. Luckily the skunk just eyed Sorrow, who put his scruffy tail between his legs and slunk back to cower by my side. I backed off from the fallen trees and headed to the studio, my clutch of wilting flowers in my hand, sulking dog at my side.

My novel was finally shifting from a halting forward thrust to a place where I could see ahead of me. I knew what my elderly lawyer had to do, who he had to face, and where the book was going. A lot of writing is simply thinking out the plot line. That's the kind of thing I did while walking in the woods, or eating alone, or on waking. I could put myself in the attorney's place, walk the streets he walked—in Philadelphia—and go to his club with him, listen in on conversations with old friends, listen to his thoughts, and see the man he was defending in the murder charge and the people who were beginning to gather around him. I was thinking of an old woman who knew the defendant. A motley character—elderly, sexy. I didn't have her fixed in my head yet—but I would. Soon.

Sorrow, feet flying in a dream—probably running from the skunk again—leapt to his feet when the phone rang. He stood blinking, mouth open, tongue hanging. Did I have a dopey dog? I asked myself and picked up the phone.

Dolly, not bothering with hello. "Hey, I got ahold of that woman in TC. You know, Washington Street. That one. Her daughter came back right after she reported her missing. Lives down near Midland. Husband works for Dow Chemical. She said we could call her daughter if we needed to, but I told her no, it wouldn't be necessary."

"Good. Another one down."

"Any more phone calls?"

"Nothing."

"Guess who called *me*?" she asked.

"Who?"

"No. Guess."

"Tom Hanks."

"Who?"

"Just tell me, Dolly, or I'm hanging up."

"Lena Smith. You know, the one we went looking for in Peshawbestown. Told you they'd get word to her. Sounded really nervous. I asked her to meet us. Told her about you. She said OK, but nothing about her can go into the paper. I promised. She'll be at the Shell station in Kalkaska in about an hour. You want to come along?"

I groaned. "I turned down dinner with Jackson in order to get some writing done."

Dolly made a disgusted sound. "Hope you don't plan on hopping into bed with him again. You want a boyfriend, how about Bill, at the newspaper? He's a nice guy."

"He's got a girlfriend."

"Oh. OK, there's a lot of guys out there ..."

"Haven't seen you with many of them."

"That's just me. I'm particular. You shouldn't have any trouble."

I hung up. I had forty-five minutes, but writing time was over. I'd been knocked out of that place in my head where dreams—and novels—begin. Time to take a shower. Time to check the vegetable garden, see if anything was up yet. Probably not. Just a week since Harry and I put in the early seeds. But I was anxious, and maybe seeds could sense if you were eager to greet them and they would hurry...

The one thing I really knew about gardening was that nothing hurried along because you wanted them to bloom, or germinate, or live. Gardens, like most other things in life, took their own time and had their own pace. On the way back to the house, I checked our neat rows of hilled dirt. Nothing yet, though I was sure I saw a tiny thread of green in one row; a row Sorrow investigated with me, stomping on my one green shoot and leaving it flat. I hollered at him and he looked over his shoulder at me, hurt that I was angry because he shared my avid interest in gardening.

The phone rang as I entered the house. I figured it had to be Dolly again, or maybe Jackson, offering to bring a salad for our dinner, or a loaf of bread from Stonehouse Bakery in Leland, or a Santa Margherita Pinot Grigio, just because I loved it so much.

I had a warm greeting ready. After all, if I expected him to change I'd better be ready to forget the caustic cynicism I doled out.

"Hi," I said. Not a loving greeting, but upbeat. Short.

No answer.

Someone was there. That absence of air on a dead line isn't hard to miss. Then there was breathing.

"Hello."

I waited. Nothing. The phone went dead. Whatever it was he wanted, this guy was scaring me. Maybe it was the absence of threat that was so alarming. I put the phone down, wrapped my arms across my chest, and shivered. For a millisecond I considered calling Dolly and removing myself from the whole investigation. But what good was that, at this point? How did I know for sure backing off would protect me? Maybe he'd come after me anyway. The only way to get out from under all of the things falling on my head was to get it over with. That meant learning what happened out there at Sandy Lake thirteen years ago.

What I did was shower and dress. I hadn't done laundry in a while so I dug out an old purple thong and picked the cleanest from among the pile of jeans at the bottom of my closet. I had a washed and neatly folded blue tee shirt. Good enough.

I put Sorrow on the porch with a stack of dog bones as bribe for good behavior. After checking the drive, the garden, the woods, everywhere around me—I jumped into the Jeep and headed to Kalkaska to meet Dolly and the elusive Lena Smith at the Shell station at the corner of M72 and 131.

# TWENTY-SIX

THE TALL INDIAN WOMAN waiting at the Shell station was my age, early to mid thirties. She had long black hair and a round, soft face. Her thin, athletic body, in tank top and jeans, was taut and narrow. She leaned against the hood of her blue Caprice, arms crossed, long legs out in front of her. Dolly stood next to her. I parked, got out, and took the hand Lena held out to me. We went through the usual first meeting stuff: how are you, glad to meet you, happy you could give us some time...

"Can't stay long," the dark-eyed woman said, glancing around at the empty pumps and a log hauler stopped at the light on M72. "I gotta get on the road."

"Where you headed?" Dolly smiled. She was at her most affable self.

Lena looked away and bit at her lip. "Just out of town for a while." Dolly nodded.

"I wouldn't have stopped to meet you... I mean, if I didn't want what happened to Mary to come out..."

"What do you mean 'what happened to Mary to come out'? You know something about her murder?"

Lena worked one hand over the other nervously and looked away from us. "I don't know anything. It's just that Mary was a friend. I mean, we were in beauty school together and I liked her. She really wanted to make something of herself. We even talked about maybe working in the same salon after graduation."

"You reported her missing."

Lena nodded. "She didn't have a phone, so I couldn't call her. People at the school didn't know what happened to her but she was paid up to the end of the semester. Mary didn't have money to throw away. I knew she'd be there if she could."

I asked, "Do you know where she lived? The school have an address?"

"Didn't ask. School's closed now. Don't know how you'd find out. But it could have been that Sandy Lake they mentioned in the paper." She shrugged, then pulled her tank top down over a bare belly with a gold circlet pierced into her belly button.

"But she never said?" Dolly asked.

Lena shook her head, a slow, uncertain shake. "We only saw each other at school. I did ask her why she'd moved off the reservation. Long time ago she lived in Peshawbestown. Maybe just when she was little. She said it wasn't her idea—moving. But that's all."

"What about boyfriends?" Dolly asked, glancing, like Lena, around the station as if expecting to find someone watching us.

Lena took a minute. "One guy. That's all I heard about. I remember we were at Burger King for lunch one day and she whispered that she was seeing a married man." Lena rolled her eyes and folded her arms, leaning back against the car again. "I gave it to her. I told her how stupid that was, that she would never be happy, and so on and so on. She only said she loved him."

Dolly winced. I expected her to tell Lena the married man had been her own husband, but she said nothing.

I watched Lena lick her lips. Her eyes moved back and forth, looking hard at every car turning in for gas. I watched a tic at the corner of one of her eyes. She was beyond the kind of nervousness that comes from talking to the police. This fear had nothing to do with me and Dolly.

"You OK?" I asked, keeping my voice low, and kind.

She made a face.

"No, I mean it. You're not in trouble or anything?"

She hesitated a minute. "I don't like murder, and Mary was a friend…"

"Who called to tell you we were there yesterday, looking for you?" I asked.

Lena made an impatient noise. "A neighbor. My family lives down the road."

"Nobody else? Nobody threatened you if you got mixed up in this?" Dolly said.

"Why would anybody threaten me?" Her face tightened. A tiny scar near her mouth bunched up and curled with the lip.

"We've had run-ins with members of your tribe. You know anything about that?"

She shrugged and bowed her head. "It's just … the bones. You know. We've got our ways. Our leaders don't like when white people get in the…"

"We're trying to find out who killed Mary. That's not butting in."

"Yeah. Yeah." She looked straight at me. "But the tribe can take care of their own business. They don't like when others get in the middle of things they don't understand."

"You mean like murder?" Dolly asked, surprised.

Lena shook her head. "No. No. But like when it is our business, we have our own laws."

"I don't get it," I said, and didn't.

Lena shrugged. "If you were Odawa you would."

"I think I'm being threatened over this. Somebody keeps calling my house. You know who would do that? Anybody from the tribe?"

She shook her head. "Nobody would threaten. But we protect our own."

"You mean Mary? Or somebody else? Would the tribe protect a murderer?"

She shook her head again, very slowly. "We don't protect people who murder."

Dolly moved from foot to foot, as if ready to leave. I thought of one more thing.

"Mary ever talk about brothers? Anybody named Alfred?"

Lena scowled at me fast. Too fast. She pushed herself away from the car and reached in the pocket of her jeans, pulling out car keys. She dropped them, then bent fast to pick them up. "She had a sister. She talked about her. Christine, her name was."

She straightened slowly, avoiding my eyes. "But nobody named Alfred. Hey look, I gotta go. I gotta be someplace before six o'clock."

She opened her car door. "We never got too close. I just know I liked her. I hope somebody finds out what happened. Honest to God, what I want most is to have Mary sleep peacefully. That's all I can do for her. I wish ..."

Obviously there was something she wanted from us and we weren't giving it to her. I couldn't figure out why Lena had agreed to meet us in the first place. We surely hadn't gotten all the truth out of her. She was afraid of somebody, or maybe it was fear of doing something forbidden.

Dolly and I thanked her for helping. She nodded and slammed the car door shut. In seconds she was pulling out of the station. Beside me, Dolly raised her arm and yelled. "Hey Lena. How about a phone number where we can reach you? Hey... Lena..."

The blue car turned at the corner and was gone.

Dolly pulled the little notebook from her breast pocket, wrote down the license number of the Caprice, closed the notebook, put it back in her pocket, and buttoned the pocket shut.

# TWENTY-SEVEN

I FOLLOWED DOLLY'S PATROL car up 131 toward Leetsville, thinking about Lena Smith and food. I couldn't figure out Lena. If she was scared, why did she agree to meet us? Then meet us and not tell us things she obviously knew? Maybe, I thought, it had something to do with the ways of the tribe coming up against her caring for a friend. It wasn't always easy to understand a different culture. Just coming here from Ann Arbor had been a form of culture shock for me. Some of the values of the people up here seemed better, more human, than I'd known. Some of the things were maybe not as good—like not reading books much and making fun of new people.

Still, people here cared for each other; got involved in each other's lives; stood by during times of trouble. Even I, living alone back in the woods on my little lake, didn't feel as isolated up here as I had after Jackson and I split up.

I drove past Sorrow's vet on my way into town, reminding me he needed a manicure. I passed The Skunk Saloon, the gas station, a church, and a few stores. My mind quickly switched to food. I saw the lighted EATS downward arrow ahead and began to salivate. Like one of Pavlov's dogs, just the thought of food made my stomach rumble. Tuesday night. Meatloaf night. The rumble changed to anticipatory flops. Yuck!

But maybe Eugenia would surprise me. Summer was coming. In peak season Eugenia could really put herself out and offer things like beef stew, or roast chicken. Maybe, just this once, she would have something spectacular on the menu. Maybe—just this once—the service would be slower and the food cooked individually, with thought and careful preparation. Maybe just this once I wouldn't think of Alpo when the meatloaf arrived.

Dolly was inside by the time I parked between the pickups. She sat in a corner booth, menu propped in front of her. I waved to people I knew as I cut through the tables. Anna stopped me to remind me of the library readings.

"Next Tuesday," she said, and smiled a wide smile. "I'm getting flyers up all over town. Cate, the librarian from Kalkaska, is coming. Lots of people from Mancelona and Elk Rapids and other places will be there to support us. It will be a very good night for you, Emily. Get your name out. People will be looking for your books after this."

I gave her a skeptical half smile and pushed on toward Dolly. A few others waved and inquired, "How's it going, Emily?" I knew they would like it if I stopped and discussed bones with them, but I wanted to get some food and figure out what we were going to do next.

I slid in across from Dolly and looked at the specials, handwritten on typing paper and shoved in the little metal holders on each table. Even my brain wanted to groan when I read: Meatloaf, Mashed Potatoes, Gravy, Corn, and Jell-O.

"Glad it's meatloaf," Dolly murmured at me. "Meatloaf's my favorite thing."

Gloria stood with her pad ready, not asking questions though I could tell by her tightened face she was dying to. We ordered and talked a little about Lena Smith. I wasn't the only one wondering what made her so nervous, and why she met us if she'd been warned away. Dolly didn't have any better answers than I had.

The meatloaf came in four minutes though the corn looked a little shriveled and cold. Not that it made any difference to the taste. I was hungry. Sometimes life gets that simple: got to eat something; might as well be half-frozen corn.

Over red Jell-O, I told Dolly about calling Brent in Gaylord and getting the feeling he wanted us off the case.

"Yeah, sure, like we'll be scared away when it's my own husband who was murdered," she said, scraping the bottom of her Jell-O dish, then licking the spoon. "I talked to him after you did. He's worried. That phone call you got. He doesn't want us getting in over our heads. That's all. Standard stuff. He's got his hands full and this is a tough case. Dealing with old bones. I get the feeling Brent would be really grateful if we came up with anything at all."

"I'm worried, too."

"Don't be a baby. Nothing's going to happen to you."

"Why aren't you getting the phone calls? I have nothing to do with releasing the bones. They should be calling Brent."

"You think maybe it's because you're a reporter?" she asked. "I'll bet they don't want anything in the paper. You know, keep it private. Or maybe it's just that somebody's afraid of the law. That's what I represent here and that can be intimidating."

I looked hard at her open and eager plain face, at the flat striped hair. I looked in her trusting blue eyes, and wondered who the devil would be intimidated by Dolly.

"All the way back here I was thinking about what Lena Smith told us." She leaned in closer and put a hand up to cover her mouth. Protection from the lip-reading Leetsvillians.

"If this Mary Naquma lived out at the lake, there should be a house somewhere close by. I called Eloise, the county assessor, but she couldn't find any property under that name. Even going back, nothing around Sandy Lake showed under Naquma. Eloise said the oil company owns all of the property out there, including the lake. Nobody else on the tax roles."

"Had to've been a house, a shack. Something."

"You want to go look?"

"Wouldn't hurt. See what we can find. When do you want to go?" I asked.

"Morning, I guess. I've got to fill in at the station tonight. The chief and his wife got a retirement party in Traverse City so somebody's got to hang around."

I made a face, thinking of Jackson and his manuscript. I'd slacked off, probably out of boredom. The only one of that group on their way to Canterbury that I liked was the Wife of Bath and Jackson had moved on beyond her. The other pilgrims didn't have the spirit or the personality of the Wife. Most were sanctimonious and dull—as they probably should have been on a pilgrimage. Still, though the work was tedious, I wanted to get it done. And I had to go over what I would read at the library event. "Can it wait until Thursday? I've got so much…"

"You want to drag this out? Maybe give whoever's after you more time to get mad?"

"OK. OK," I agreed. "Do I need to bring anything with me? I mean, to go hunting for a house on Sandy Lake?"

"What do you mean? Like a Geiger counter or something?" I thought she was sneering.

I sighed. "No. I meant, like a bathing suit. Are we looking for anything in the lake? Or ... ?"

She laughed at me. "Just bring yourself, and shoes for walking in sand."

Gloria brought us separate bills as Dolly counted out quarters for a tip from her small-mouthed change purse.

"You enjoy the meatloaf, Emily?" Eugenia demanded of me, her face screwed up into one of those "don't you dare" looks.

I smacked my lips.

She turned to Dolly who she didn't need to ask. It was Eugenia's home cooking, like the meatloaf, that kept Dolly coming back year after year.

"You know," Eugenia came around to stand at the side of the counter, "I'm going to keep looking for somebody in your family. I'm doing a search of the Flynns all around Detroit. That's where you're from, right?"

"You're not putting anybody from my family up on that wall, Eugenia." Dolly cocked her head toward the vestibule. "Everybody knows that family of yours ain't all your family. Don't go pulling tricks like that on me."

"No, no," Eugenia looked contrite. "I wouldn't do that. It's just that, who knows, I might really find something."

Dolly gave her a disbelieving look, a threatening sniff, and turned on her heel, stomping out of the restaurant.

# TWENTY-EIGHT

DOLLY MARCHED AHEAD OF me through the deep, yellow sand. The morning sky, reflected on the still surface of Sandy Lake, was streaked blood red and mauve. One of those "sailor take warning" skies, which always seemed to prove true. Probably rain by evening. I looked up at the clouds, their overhead direction and speed. Maybe a woods-cleaning, spring storm out of the west coming. The kind that brought old trees crashing down and wiped out my electricity for days. Everything part of that gigantic cycle, I had learned. Ebbs and flows. Nothing personal in the storm that took out my electricity. Just the old cosmic swing; events working toward a bigger goal than I would ever understand.

Dolly muttered over her shoulder at me, complaining that I was too slow. "Stop all that thinking and move," she ordered. "Got to get around to the other side. We'll comb the woods up the slope. Look hard at the shore. If anybody lived out here there's gotta be something left of 'em."

"Probably had the wrong lake. Nobody knew where this Mary really lived."

"Yeah, well, all signs point to this one. Otherwise why sink 'em here?" She stopped, turned back, and let me get within ten feet of her before taking off again, throwing little bursts of sand back at me as the heels of her boots lifted and fell.

"What about a boyfriend of Mary's?" I called after her. "If we're looking for someone mad at both of them, makes sense it would be a jealous man."

"Sounded like Chet was her one true love, from what Lena said." Dolly shook her head as she went around the first cove, then moved beyond where we'd found the skeletons, toward an area of deep woods.

I trudged along at a slower pace. If she wanted help searching the woods on the other side of the lake, she'd have to let me go at my own speed. The one thing Dolly Wakowski would have to learn is not to push the unpaid help too far. Still, the distance between us grew as she marched on, head down, arms swinging, shoulders bent forward. She looked like a blue-backed gnome on a mission. I glanced at my own feet, in sandals, and wondered what the heck I was doing out here. Maybe I'd get a story—if we found anything. More than likely it was another of Dolly's wild goose chases—like that abortive trip to Detroit.

The air cooled fast. My sandals filled with damp sand. I had to stop every so often to take them off, bang them together, slip back into them, and be off again.

It took half an hour to reach the wilder side of the lake where hummocks of grasses grew, and the thick trees blocked the uphill slope. I looked at the lake, a deeper mauve and purple mix of storm warning.

I caught up with Dolly where the trees grew thickest. The forest must have stretched for miles, out from the sand's edge to I had no idea where. This was typical of land the oil companies owned up here. Hundreds of miles of forest crisscrossed by two tracks. Every once in a while there would be a pumping station or shed filled with equipment. At times men manned the various stations. Most were self-operated, the thick arm of a pump going up and down, throbbing, sucking oil and sending it along pipelines to the next station.

Dolly scanned the ground, walking slower. Her hands were caught together behind her back as she took small steps up into the woods, then down, leaving no area unsearched. I moved ahead of her, into the thick woods, and assumed her stance: hands at my back, head bent forward, feet shuffling through weeds and broken tree limbs.

In an open space among the trees, I came on what looked to be a cement pad for a garage or a shed. The grasses growing around it and through the large, crooked cracks were dull, almost blue in color. Everything looked much drier and sandier here. Beyond the cement pad, milkweed grew, and here and there a browned trillium. I thought about collecting the young milkweed pods and sticking them into my jacket pocket. I ran my fingers over one of the small, silky feeling pods and decided: no, I wasn't a backwoods girl after all. I bent and more closely surveyed the ground around me.

"Hey, over here!" Dolly called from up the rise, a little ahead of where I stood. "Found something."

"Me, too," I yelled back. "A cement pad. Like maybe it was a garage …"

"Saw that." Her voice, coming from among the trees, bounced off tree trunks, and got lost in the slight soughing of the pine boughs. "Got something up here."

She stood next to a long row of vine-covered cinder blocks half buried in the ground. I could follow the line to where it turned a corner, then disappeared underground. We walked the course of blocks, turning with it, following where they disappeared, possibly covered over with sand years before.

"There," Dolly pointed to a place farther into the trees. It was difficult to make out anything beyond a pile of charred timbers covered with dead vegetation, all dropped into what had once been a rough hole in the ground. I reached in among the burned beams and drew out the rusted remains of a lawn chair. Dolly tugged at what looked like a badly rusted pot. There were other things among the ruins, but nothing truly identifiable.

"This has got to be it. You bring your camera?" Dolly nudged me.

I pulled my digital Nikon out of my jacket pocket and snapped pictures from all angles, though I figured I'd have to come back to get good shots. The sky had already darkened so there was little contrast between trees and ground. And no shadow to differentiate the walls of the foundation from the burned wood. I pushed at a growth of fiddleheads and crouched as low as I could, to get perspective on the ruin. One darkened beam, sticking up from among the others, gave form to what had once been a house. But what did it mean that the place had been destroyed?

Dolly said she'd go to Gaylord and talk to Detective Brent. I handed over my answering machine tape for her to give him. "How about you go to a pumping station and see if you can find anyone who remembers this place, and who lived here?" she said.

I agreed to do that, but not until the morning. There was a storm on the way and I had Jackson coming for dinner. Maybe Dolly didn't believe in having a life outside her police work, but I did.

# TWENTY-NINE

How COULD I MESS things up so badly? I wanted everything perfect when Jackson came to dinner. A wild, atavistic urge to feed a man came over me. Must've been straight down from a grandmother I'd never met; from back in the times when a woman caught herself a productive male or perished. My dinner would be spectacular. A mating dance to end all mating dances. Intimate, with candles and wildflowers and wine. It would fill him, satiate him, make him mellow and tranquil and putty in my hands. I'd decided this was the evening I would mention moving back to Ann Arbor.

The storm, when it hit, was wild, but brief, the air crystalline clear afterward. The evening promised to be one of those May times when the world smells like every flower in the whole spectrum of flowers, and when the late golden sun is thick enough to roll in. There wasn't a cloud left in the sky by dinnertime; a great evening for eating on the deck. But I was conflicted—eat inside or out? Inside would be cozier. Outside restful—but with too much demanding our attention: the lake, the birds, the beaver out there mocking me.

So … inside. I spread a yellow striped cloth on the little table in my kitchen nook. Blue tapers in crystal holders … well … maybe not real crystal. Blue cloth napkins beside my burgundy plates. Colorful. Lovely. I planned to serve tomatoes with mozzarella I'd picked up at Cherry Street Market; fresh basil and olive oil on top of the luscious little beauties. I prepared bruschetta with bits of garlic and roasted red pepper. There would be a risotto with freshly grated pecorino cheese, peas, and morels. And tiny lamb chops with a salad of arugula, ceci beans, and blue cheese. I felt like Martha Stewart on steroids, dashing about in my kitchen, gathering my wares, weaving my web. I could feel the bluebirds sitting on my shoulders, singing. There are days when you know nothing could possibly go wrong—until it does.

The tomatoes and basil were fine. The bruschetta burned in the oven. But what could that matter, with the pleasures yet to come? The risotto didn't absorb the chicken broth—it remained a kind of soup. I let it rest until Jackson got there, thinking it was sure to set up. It only needed time to be perfect.

Jackson arrived with his arms filled with more of his manuscript—pages and pages of handwritten notes. I put Sorrow out on the screened porch with a mammoth stack of dog bones, hoping he would eat and go to sleep.

My hair was done—as well as I ever do it: left long and wild and thick. I had swiped color on my cheeks, pink lipstick over my mouth, and added a smudge of gray to my eyelids. I had dressed in a deep pink silk shirt and slinky black pants. I even wore low backless heels. At my neck I draped silver chains, and stuck silver hoops in my ears. If I said so myself, I looked more Ann Arbor than northern Michigan.

In the doorway Jackson bent to peck at both my cheeks. I hugged him awkwardly—all that paper between us.

"Something's burning," he said after dumping his paper on the living room desk and turning to stick his nose in the air.

I assured him it was only the bread and that I had a wonderful dinner planned for us.

"I'm assuming you've got my work done? What I gave you before?"

I nodded and pointed to a stack of sheets on the counter, with a freshly burned disk sitting on top.

"Good." He fingered the sheets of his manuscript then lifted the first page and began to read to me.

Since I'd already read it once, I only half listened as I stirred my risotto and put the lamb chops into a pan to sear along with garlic, olive oil, and pepper. Jackson settled into a living room chair as I poured the white wine—not Santa Margherita—and brought a glass to him. He waved for me to set the glass on the table and continued to read, stopping only to give a cluck of admiration from time to time.

The manuscript came with him as he followed me around in the kitchen. He read on until I took the stack of papers from his hands and set it on the counter. For that I got a pained look, his dark eyes accusing me of ingratitude.

"Dinner," I said, and led him to the table, where I'd put him next to me, not across.

The tomatoes were wonderful.

"Any bread?" he asked and I had to shake my head, not bringing up the bruschetta I'd burned.

"Remember that time you forgot to pick up the roast beef at the butcher's when we were having all those people over?" He snickered and shook a finger at me. "God, but that was funny. How you scrounged up a vegetarian dinner only to discover most of that Indian delegation weren't meat eaters anyway. Very, very lucky."

I nodded.

"And the time when you cooked your first turkey and forgot to take the giblets bag out?" He took another tomato from the pretty Chinese plate I'd set them on. "But you came around—eventually. We had some wonderful meals. I like to think I had something to do with your education." His lips smacked together.

I smiled and took a deep breath. "I've been thinking about our life in Ann Arbor."

"It wasn't all bad, was it?" He smiled indulgently and patted my hand. "Now be honest. We made a good couple."

"Yes, well . . ." A little irritation settled deep in my brain.

I poured the rice out onto his plate. It spread and then it spread some more. It reached the edge of his dish and kept going as he tried to catch it with his fingers. Fortunately, he laughed.

We ate the rice with spoons. The salad was flat. Lamp chops were inedible—tough and cooked all the way through. I had no dessert.

I suggested we take our wine out to the deck after the meal. He looked longingly over at his manuscript and then at me, but my scowl stopped him.

We set our deck chairs to face the lake. There was no breeze. It was the quiet time of evening when the birds settled into their nests with a last weak riffle of sound. The sun made long horns of gold across the surface of the water.

"I brought my things," Jackson said quietly and turned his head slowly to give me an anticipatory look.

I smiled, then launched into the subject sitting like a lump between us.

"You know, Jackson, I've been thinking about moving back to Ann Arbor," I said.

He shrugged and said nothing.

"I mean," I went on, "I've been up here for over three years now. I think I miss working at the newspaper. All of that urgency every day."

"I can see where you'd miss it. Still, it is beautiful here. Quiet. Perfect for a writing getaway. I think I've envied you this."

"Yeah, well, I was thinking I could keep this place. A weekend retreat. Or if one of us has to write…"

"Nice of you to include me."

"What I was suggesting…"

"Could I have more wine?" He held his glass in the air. I hesitated then went in and brought the bottle out with me.

I didn't know why I was tongue-tied. Maybe because I felt I was doing too much of the work and he just wasn't getting it.

"This would be a great place for me to come work on my next book," he said, glass turning in his hands. "I'd pay you rent, of course."

"No, what I meant…"

"Give you a little income. You'd need an apartment. Maybe a condo. Could you swing it without selling this place?"

I shook my head hard. "I don't…"

"But of course you could rent in AA."

I stopped trying. He wasn't getting it or he didn't want to understand. Maybe I was pushing too hard; scaring him. Jackson could be a timid and frightened man when cornered. He needed time to adjust to the changes between us. I looked over at his slightly worn profile and felt a rush of love.

When I got up to bend and kiss him, he put his arms out and held me. It didn't take long to find our way back to my bedroom and spend the rest of the night without talking.

After we'd made love, I slept as I hadn't slept in days. Some old admonition from dead family women made me feel safer, having a man in the house; a knight in shining armor, who would leap up and fight off all intruders with his trusty lance.

# THIRTY

IT WAS A MORNING of confusion. And, I'd have to say, embarrassment, in the careful way Jackson and I smiled at each other. I dressing furtively, hurrying into jeans and shirt as if not wanting to be caught unclothed. I dashed on makeup: lipstick and blush, as I wouldn't have on any other morning. I brushed my hair back and caught it on top of my head with a tortoiseshell clip.

Jackson sat in an easy chair in my living room, looking over his manuscript. Unlike me, he was at ease in his blue boxer shorts and no shirt. I made coffee for him—espresso—and tea for me. I brought the coffee to his chair, arranged a napkin beneath the cup, and asked if there was anything else I could get him. It felt like pandering, like I'd slipped a notch or two in my own estimation: *here, let me wait on you, my darling man* ...

The sex was like an old ritual we'd fallen into, a place where all other irritations between us disappeared. I would name it a safe place, but that wasn't what I wanted to think about myself: that I ran to the safety of illusions.

The talk over breakfast stayed general, careful, and light. Jackson wondered when I could get this last bunch of pages into the computer and when he could see them. I talked about my garden and my plans, adding, "Unless I decide I'm going back to Ann Arbor. Then I guess I'll have to let it all go."

He murmured something unintelligible at me and stared out at the lake. The beaver was busy—swimming in circles with a log in his mouth. The trees swayed. The lake was a soft painting, with the light and shade of Monet's garden. For just a moment I felt an ache inside me, as if I'd already given this away—sold it to someone who would rarely see it for what it was. The disconnect didn't last long. There were practicalities to be considered here. This new burst of feeling for Jackson meant I would have to choose between my life up here and my life with him.

Dolly called as he was about to walk out the door. She launched into her plan to go back to the tribal council and ask about the Naquma family. She wanted me to get out to that oil pumping station and see if there was anyone who remembered the old Indian and his family squatting by Sandy Lake. Jackson came to kiss my cheek and whisper good-bye while she talked on. He left, but Dolly had heard his voice.

"He's still there?" she demanded, as if she had a right.

"Dolly, watch the boundaries, OK? What I do or don't do isn't really any of your..."

"You're nuts. You're doing it for money and 'money's the root of all evil,' you know."

"'The *love* of money is the root of all evil,'" I corrected, though she ignored me.

"You are not a city woman, Emily. I don't care what lies you're telling yourself or what airs you put on. You belong in the woods..."

"Well, thanks a lot but I think I'll make my own de—"

"Yeah, dumb ones."

I hung up on her.

———

I needed to be away from all of them for at least that day. I wasn't up to facing Dolly or talking to oil men. After Jackson left with his completed sheets in his hands, I decided this was the perfect day to get out to the cemetery beyond Alba, get my photos, and write the story for *Northern Pines Magazine*.

I packed my bag with a sandwich, a Diet Coke, tape recorder, notebook, lots of pens, and my camera. The cemetery was only twenty-five miles out past Alba, on 131, but I hoped to make a day of it. Dark Forest first and then maybe a stop at Dead Man's Hill to hike down the steep slope into the Jordan Valley, with Sorrow. He'd be great company on the hike. I stuck a couple of dog bones in my bag, along with my lunch, and got his leash. The moment the red leash came out he leaped in the air around me, careful not to knock me over, but yipping in his silly baby voice and ready to go.

Sorrow sat in the back. I lowered his window so he could ride happily along with his head hanging out, long red tongue dopily flapping from the side of his mouth, and button eyes half closed against the wind.

Another soft May day. I kept my window rolled down too, feeling as free as Sorrow. I drove through Leetsville, then through Mancelona, then out past the potato farms lining both sides of the road. When I drew near the sign to the Jordan Valley, I was half tempted to take the hike and save the cemetery for later but decided work came first. I had to get out to Dark Forest, which was supposed to be an isolated and meaningful place. Cemeteries weren't high on my list of "meaningful" places, death not being one of my favorite pursuits, but it would be good to work on my own story and not something Dolly or Bill had decided I needed to follow.

The roadside sign for the cemetery was almost indecipherable. I drove past without seeing it and had to turn around at the next side road. The gravel lane was dusty, and little more than a two-track. If a car came from the opposite direction, I'd be hard pressed to find a spot to pull over. Trees met overhead, making the drive beneath dark and dappled with flashes of bright sunlight. The road went on for a little over a mile, then opened out into a field. I drove in, parked beneath an ancient oak, grabbed my bag with my gear, and got out to stretch in the sun like a happy cat. Sorrow had to stay in the car. His face, through the window, was long and astounded—that I would bring him this far and leave him behind. He had a finely tuned sense of doggie justice, and this wasn't it.

There were no other cars. No people. To my right was the newer cemetery where I walked among rows of markers and white crosses. Vases of flowers stood in front of some of the graves. On others, rocks had been left, and circles of papier-mâché—some disintegrating. The saddest were the tiny graves with a toy boat or a small, weathered doll laid near the base of the white cross. Many colored ribbons fluttered. There were American flags on the graves of veterans. The feel of the cemetery, under wide trees, was of shade and love and care. Not an unhappy place. I made notes of grave decorations and names as I walked through. I took photos. When I'd finished, I hurried back over the road to where a sign pointed to "Old Cemetery."

I followed the pointing arrows into a very different place, a quiet land of nameless white crosses meandering here and there as they disappeared down a hill, up another hill, and out of sight. Between the crosses, wild flowers grew, along with vines, mints—all things of nature. Even the plain crosses seemed to have grown in place, stitches holding the earth together. I'd never been anywhere like this before. Nothing eerie about it. I walked along checking the few graves with markers sinking into the earth, beneath their white crosses. I looked at the names, not expecting to see a Naquma. I didn't. I took photograph after photograph—white, white crosses against the darkness of the surrounding forest; white, white crosses gleaming at the top of the far hill. I meandered from place to place—marveling at the equal care the simple crosses were given. No ostentation here.

The only sound around me was the wind sighing through the pines. I moved slowly down and then up the narrow path bordered with wild greenery. The path curved on around another hill. I followed, almost mesmerized by the soothing sound in the trees, the softness of tall vegetation bowing between graves, the hard places where rocks anchored graves. So much more appealing than *ashes to ashes, dust to dust*...

"Emily Kincaid." A deep voice came from nowhere.

I hadn't heard anyone coming down the path behind me. I'd been too preoccupied with thoughts of death as not ugly, but inevitable.

"Emily Kincaid." The voice rang out behind me.

Startled, I wasn't certain my name was real. The voice had to be in my head. Maybe an ancestor. Maybe I had a connection here. I looked down at a crooked cross near my feet, above a large stratified rock where erratic quartz layers shone in rainbows as a sunbeam fell across them.

"Emily Kincaid!"

The deep voice was real. I looked up and around me, feeling my heart catch.

Two men stood on the hill I'd just walked. Two men, more silhouette than real against the bright sun. I held my breath. My heart beat furiously. One of the men had long black hair blowing softly about his head. The other was as dark, but older. I recognized Lewis George, the man who'd burst into my studio. He raised a slow hand to hail me. The other man simply stood, as I'd seen him standing out at Sandy Lake.

*Think,* I told myself. One of these guys could be a killer. Maybe both. They had to have followed me out here. No other reason for them to be the only ones in the cemetery with me. What did they want? And why two of them? Too many questions to stand there and become a target.

I searched quickly around me. No place to run. Survival mode took only a moment to kick in. I hugged my gear bag close. There was nothing but trees, undergrowth, and crosses everywhere. The only real way out was back up the path, toward the men walking slowly toward me. Otherwise...I looked around, then took off running straight uphill. I dodged between crosses, feeling my feet pulled by vines covering the ground.

"No!" The deep voice shouted.

I glanced hurriedly over my shoulder. They stood where they'd been on the path, not coming after me. Yet. Or maybe they were waiting for me to get entangled in the undergrowth and thrown to the ground. I had to concentrate, stay on my feet, keep going—one foot after another, up the hill between crosses, through places where the graves were sunken, the ground uneven. I ran hard.

When I got to my car I pulled the door open and pushed Sorrow's wet, inquisitive nose away as I dug my car keys out of my pocket, locked everything, and started my car.

I wheeled in a wild circle as the two men came loping up from the cemetery and into the road. There was a red pickup parked beyond where I'd parked my car, off to the side. They'd come in after me. That was certain. This was no coincidental meeting in a cemetery.

I sped out the two track, up the gravel road, and onto 131, heading south in a matter of seconds. As I drove, I kept my eyes on the rearview mirror. Could I outrun them if they came after me? So little traffic. Nobody anywhere. Nowhere to run for help.

I headed toward the police station in Leetsville. If those men were truly after me I couldn't think of a single truly safe place left to go. I had to get ahold of myself. I had to plan. Most of all, I knew I had to go after them fast now, before they came after me again.

# THIRTY-ONE

DOLLY WAS OUT ON a domestic violence call when I got to the station. Lucky Barnard was in Gaylord. I didn't know the girl at the front desk so I left a message for Dolly to call me at home later and went back outside to my Jeep.

I sat there, in one of the police station's diagonal parking spaces, and tried to calm my brain. Sorrow was no help, leaping over the seat at me, dripping dog spit down my back. He probably had to pee. So did I, but there were only the choices of EATS (and I wasn't up to being questioned there) or the BP station in town. I chose the BP for me and a field behind The Church of the Contented Flock for Sorrow. As he circled, hunting for the perfect spot, I figured what I had to do next.

I had to keep going—and even faster than we had been working. I would get right out to a pumping station and see if anyone remembered the man and his family. Then back to Peshawbestown and some real answers.

After sitting awhile, I found I wasn't as scared, or mad, as I had been. The older man frightened me, that time he came to my studio.

The other man—I'd only seen him those two times, neither had been really threatening, nor very friendly either. Probably it was the cemetery, I decided. They belonged there. I didn't. I'd felt that all too keenly. I figured I was my own worst enemy, and if I ran into the men again I'd go right up to them and ask what they wanted...

But not in an Indian cemetery. Not in the dark. Not when there were no other people around...

———

The pumping station was down a grassy track, up a dusty back road, off a pot-holed county road. A large green-armed pump chug-a-chugged in a wide, weedy clearing. The place wasn't easy to find, but I was lucky enough to catch two men checking gauges, hard hats on their heads, tool belts dipping around their waists, and big brown boots on their feet. Both in their mid-thirties, I figured they might be too young to help, but perhaps they knew someone who could. I let Sorrow run, since we had never made it to Dead Man's Hill. He took off at one of his gallops, straight for the two men, leaping in the air around them, and woofing a hello.

"Emily Kincaid." I stuck my hand out to first one of the disconcerted men and then the other before grabbing Sorrow's collar and settling him down until I could let him go quietly sniff the earth and trees and any hole in the ground he could find. They had been surprised to find a woman driving in, the older man said. One who didn't work for the company.

"I'm a reporter with the *Northern Statesman*..." I fudged my position a little and squinted up at the men in unrelenting sunlight. "Following up on a recent story. Maybe you heard about the bones found over in Sandy Lake?"

They nodded. One, with black hair sticking out from under his hard hat, deeply tanned skin, and sharp blue eyes said, "Awful thing. I used to go out there swimming. Gave me the creeps to think those dead folks might have been down there and me floating over them."

"Yeah," I agreed, "not a pleasant thought. What I'm looking for is anyone who was with the company about thirteen years ago. Somebody who might remember a family—Native Americans, I think—who lived out by the lake. Guess they would've been squatters—since the property belongs to the oil company."

The men exchanged looks. I wiped perspiration from my upper lip. For May, the day was getting abysmally warm.

"Not me," the blue-eyed one said, shaking his head. "Just got hired on a month ago."

I turned to the other man with a bad complexion and a tiny mouth. He nodded. "Think Willy Shimmers would've been around back then. I'll give him a call for you, see if he can help."

I wrote my name and number on a paper I found jammed in my jeans pocket and handed it to the man, thanking him for any help he could give. I called Sorrow and left with a wave to the two men's backs. They had already returned to checking gauges.

The one thing I didn't want to do was go directly home. What I did was park up on Willow Lake Road, in behind some tall bushes. I made my way down the hill obliquely, moving from tree to tree, sneaking up on my own house, as if I could sneak up on anything with my exuberant dog running on ahead. I got to the door, got inside, with Sorrow bashing the back of my legs to get ahead of me, and locked the door behind us. I locked every window, and when the phone rang I waited until the answering machine picked up and I heard Dolly's voice before I grabbed the receiver.

"What's going on?" Dolly demanded. "I heard you was in here looking for me."

I told her about my trip to Dark Forest Cemetery and who'd been there, calling my name and chasing me.

She was quiet for a time. "Maybe you better get out of this, Emily. I don't get why they're after you, but that's what it looks like."

"Yeah, well you tell me how to get the word around that I'm not involved. What we need to do is move faster. I went out to the pumping station. There were two guys there but they weren't with the company back when the family lived at the lake. They know someone who was and are calling him for me. I should hear soon."

"I didn't go back to Peshawbestown yet either. I still want to see if I can flush out those guys—or get more information on the Naquma family. Maybe we'd better ..." She hesitated. "You want me to come out there? Are you scared they'll come after you?"

"I was. But now ... I'd just like to finish this. I don't like being intimidated. That's not who I am ... I don't think."

She made a noise. "Last thing you are is a coward. Don't let 'em get to you."

"Let's give it an hour," I said. "If I don't hear I'll call the oil company offices and see if I can get ahold of this Willy Shimmers the men told me about, OK?"

"Then what?"

"If he can tell us, for sure, who the people were out there we'll have something to go to the tribe with."

"What about getting back out to Sandy Lake? We didn't go through much of that burned-out house. Maybe there's something ..."

"Didn't Brent send investigators?"

"I didn't tell him yet. There wasn't anything to connect the ruin to the Naqumas."

We agreed to meet in an hour and a half, back at Sandy Lake. If she wasn't there, she didn't want me parking anywhere nearby, in case the men were out there too.

"Why don't you just drive in and out until I get there? Don't make a sitting duck out of yourself. Think I'll bring Lucky with me. Wouldn't hurt."

———

After an hour without hearing from Willy Shimmers, I called the main office. The woman who answered said Willy wasn't in but she would page him and give him the message. I gave her my name and number and made myself a pot of tea to pass the time while I waited. The water hadn't even boiled when the phone rang. I let it ring, the way I had when Dolly called, then picked up immediately when a deep, male voice said he was Willy Shimmers, returning my call.

"Mr. Shimmers. This is Emily Kincaid. I'm with the newspaper and am following the story of the bones found at the edge of Sandy Lake."

"Yeah," he said, his voice deep and slow. "Read about that."

"Were you with the company thirteen years ago?"

"Been with 'em almost twenty years now."

"Were you ever out around Sandy Lake back about thirteen years?"

He took his time answering.

"You don't mean this has something to do with that Indian guide who built himself a shack out there, do you?"

I caught my breath. Here was a connection at last. "Was his name Naquma?"

"Never called him anything but Orly. Could've been Naquma. Lived out there for maybe ten years. The company never bothered him. Fig-

ured he kept other trespassers away, and there's a lot of territory to police. We're not into policing unless there's reason."

"Did he have a family?"

The man's voice hesitated. He coughed. "Well now," he started in
that way of northern men who don't want to pass along gossip, "I
never saw a woman there, if that's what you mean."

"How about children?"

"Saw a few. Older ones."

"Two?"

"Maybe three."

"Girls? Boys?" This was another case of pulling teeth to get the
story.

"A couple girls. One boy, that I remember."

"Do you know what happened to them?"

I could almost feel him shaking his head. "Never did hear. One
day I went out there and the shack Orly'd built was burned to the
ground. The family was gone. I figured they moved on someplace else
where he could get work taking out hunters and fishermen."

"That's what he did? A hunting and fishing guide?"

"Well now, that's what he called himself. I talked to a couple of
guys who hired him, and they said they'd never hire him again. Guess
the guy drank a lot. Not very dependable, I heard." He stopped talking
and took a deep breath. "To tell you the truth, I felt sorry for those
kids. That wasn't a way for anybody to grow up. Couldn't imagine
how they got out to school—maybe hiking back to the road, but that
wouldn't have been easy in winter. The boy seemed smart and real
quiet. Both girls were pretty. But they were like most Indians are. You
know, kept to themselves. And probably old Orly was afraid of getting
run off the property, so he never was too friendly. At least not with
me."

215

I thanked Willy Shimmers, got off the phone, put Sorrow out on the porch where we both pretended he wouldn't be sailing through the taped-up screen and down to the lake in five minutes, and left to meet Dolly at Sandy Lake.

# THIRTY-TWO

DOLLY AND LUCKY BARNARD were there ahead of me, parked in the wide clearing behind the trees. They leaned against Dolly's patrol car, stepping forward to wave when they saw my Jeep drive in.

Lucky said he'd heard I'd been followed by a couple of men from over to Peshawbestown. "You better be careful 'til we find out what's going on. Nothing says that the men you saw out to Dark Forest are dangerous, but I wouldn't say they aren't either. Not with this double-murder investigation going on and you in the middle of it. I'd say, Emily, that you maybe should back off a little and let me and Dolly handle things from here on in. And if your paper wants a story about where we're getting on the investigation, why we will be happy to fill you in 'cause we know you need the money and we know how hard you've been working to make it up here. Those books of yours not selling." He shook his head, took a deep breath, and put a hand to his chest.

" … Or, as I was saying to Dolly before you got here, if you two want to keep working on this together, well, I guess I can't stop you and maybe the faster you keep going, the faster it will be over with."

So, that established—or not established—we made our way down the sand path and through the trees to the lake. We walked around the lake again, since there was no road or path on the other side. Dolly pointed to where the house had been. She and Lucky squatted, poking at the charred beams and the few burned pieces of furniture, while I moved off to the other side of the hole in the ground that had been Orly's cabin. In one spot, to the side of the cabin, I found a pile of rusted cans covered with vegetation. It looked like a household refuse pile; the kind of pit I'd found around old lumber camps back in the woods.

I turned over one of the rusted cans and disturbed a couple of ground wasps building a nest. It didn't take more than that to move me to another spot. I parted the weeds as I walked, examining the sand. Not far off, there was a place that looked as if it could have been a root cellar. Sand had blown in and filled the area so only the tops of the blocks could be seen. I moved around behind this "cellar," keeping my head down, eyes narrowed, looking for anything out of place. Anything man-made.

As I walked, I must have put my left foot down at the wrong angle, or stumbled on uneven ground. I fell to my knees, hands straight down to save my face. I scrambled back up to my feet, pulled the hem of my sweater from my jeans, and bent to wipe at my chin where I'd hit the ground. Sure enough—dark blood. Not a lot. The palms of my hands were both scratched and bleeding slightly along the scratches. I searched behind me for whatever I'd fallen over and saw it wasn't a thing, but a place where the ground dipped and fell inward. The depression in the sand was about six feet long and maybe three feet wide.

I called Dolly and Lucky over to take a look. Probably just another garbage pit, but it stood examining.

Dolly walked around the depression and glanced up at Lucky. "Got a shovel?" she demanded.

He nodded. "Yours," he said and left us, head down, shoulders forward. He was on his way back to the car they'd come in together. I knelt and scooped some sand from the pit with my hands. We would be waiting quite awhile for Lucky to get back. It wasn't that I was impatient, but I'd geared myself so high to get this thing moving, even an extra half hour seemed too long.

"Better leave it for Lucky," Dolly called as I poked down in the pit I'd found.

I nodded but scooped sand anyway. I figured I would find a can or old bottle. Maybe something better. I had found old bottles and old pots at the lumber campsites. Once, I even found a metal pry bar for switching train tracks.

After awhile I got up and brought a rusted can back from the other garbage dump. With the lid bent off, it made a perfect scoop.

"Me and Lucky found shredded stuff all around that house," Dolly said, motioning back toward the burned timbers. "Not old stuff. Could be tobacco, or something. Don't know. But why wouldn't tobacco have burned up with the house? Isn't that what it's for?"

I shrugged. There was no rush to do anything, and I was tired from the walking and searching. I sat beside the pit, half lying on one side, poking and scooping, then sifting the sand from the can through my fingers.

My search was languid. I had already had a terrible day. Let Dolly look over the hillocks and depressions. I figured I'd done enough, and though I could envision the Naquma family in this place, there didn't seem to be ghosts, or lingering spirits. It was too pretty, and placid, and away from people.

From where I half lay on the ground, scooping and emptying, the lake, through the brush, stretched flat and mirror-like. A couple of gulls flew high above my head. One crow—huge and dark—fluttered close above me, landing in a tree nearby and cawing his heart out.

I dipped the can into a fairly deep part of the hole and lifted it out. I was smiling up at the crow, talking to him, taunting him, when I felt the sand sift away between my fingers and something hard land in my palm.

I glanced down, thinking I'd brought up a rock—maybe even a Petoskey Stone. What lay there was not a rock. It was brown, black at one end, and long. Very narrow. I looked closer. I held a bone. Maybe the first knuckle of a finger bone.

I called to Dolly, who came bumbling up through a patch of pickers. "Yup. Bone," was all she said, bending down to take a look at what I held. "You go tell Lucky. He'll call Detective Brent and get investigators out here. God knows what you've stumbled on now. Then you go on home. When I get through I'll be over. You know, Emily, you might just've found the rest of that family."

I agreed to go, but this time I took photographs of the grave and a couple close-ups of that single bone. There had to be a lot more bones down there, but I had no right to keep digging. I took shots of the charred timbers and what was left of the house. I wasn't going to be caught short again. Not that it was easy, with Dolly shouting at me to get going every time my camera snapped.

I met Lucky coming back with the shovel. He frowned when I said there were more bones by the house. I took off with just a backward wave at him. I had a darned good story to write. The only thing missing was what else Brent's men would dig up from that grave.

# THIRTY-THREE

SORROW DIDN'T COME RUNNING when I got home. Usually, he would have worked his way back into the living room from the screened-in porch, or he would be waiting at the door as I drove down the drive, his shaggy black and white body quivering with anticipation at the sight of me.

No Sorrow. Not on the porch, not in the house, not anywhere in the immediate vicinity. This wasn't the first time he'd taken off. Being some kind of setter/Labrador mix, he'd been born with a wanderlust. But a small one. He usually stuck close to his personal supply of IAMS and dog bones.

I stood on the front deck and called his name, listening for a bark, the sound of a dog bounding through the ferns—something. I heard nothing. A loon, down at the lake, gave his wild cry a few times. Robins and chickadees sang and cackled. A black squirrel sat on a low branch above my head and chattered at me.

He'd be back, I told myself, despite a sinking feeling in my stomach. Silly dog never went too far, only down to the lake to chase a duck or two, or around through the woods, no doubt causing havoc among the skunks and raccoons and fox. I had better things to do than hunt for a dog. Calling Bill, at the paper, was first among them. I was rather proud that I'd been the one to find this grave with more bones.

"There's a new development in the bone story," I said when Bill came on the line.

Bill, a true newsman, was immediately interested. "What happened?"

"Think we found a grave with more bones out at Sandy Lake. Found the remains of a house, too. Seems a Native American hunting and fishing guide and his children—one of them Mary Naquma—lived out there about thirteen years ago. Could be whoever murdered Chet Wakowski and Mary did something to the rest of her family, too. House was burned. Nobody I've talked to has seen any of them in a long time. Except the brother. He works for the casino in Peshawbestown. I'm doing a story about the Dark Forest Cemetery for *Northern Pines*. It's all Native American, out beyond Alba. I went there today to take photos and two men chased me. One was that Lewis George and I'm sure the other was Mary Naquma's brother, Alfred. If that was really him, it could mean he had something to do with what happened to his sister and to Dolly's husband, maybe his other sister, Christine, and the father, too. I called the tribal center for information on Dark Forest Cemetery and happened to mention both Alfred Naquma and Lewis George. The woman said she never heard of them. Didn't know who I was talking about. They're covering up something."

"Christ! You think he did all of 'em in? It's happened before. Hmm. So Gaylord working on this now? And, what do you mean— chased you? Was it a problem? What did they want? Better call Detective Brent and let him know."

"Gaylord's been called. I'm writing the story about the new bones now. And I've got photographs for you." I delayed the "being chased" story due to exhaustion. I'd had enough of that whole thing.

"Good job. But what happened at the cemetery? These guys aren't after you, are they?"

"I didn't hang around to see what they wanted."

"Be smart, Emily. In something like this, you never know who the enemy is. Oh, and Emily, wait to make sure the bone you found is human. No sense running something that turns out not to be true."

"Of course," I said, indignant, "but what else can it be? I held it in my hand. I know a bone when I see one."

"Yeah, well, get it to me as soon as you have verification from Detective Brent."

I groaned. "That could be days."

"You want me to run it as speculation?" I heard, in his voice, what Bill thought of that idea.

"Guess not."

"OK. So when you know … send the photos over with tag lines. You ever consider that those two men just wanted to talk to you about the girl's bones? The Odawa are tough about the return of their ancestors or relatives. Awful things have been done to their burial sites in the past. Stuff even put up for sale on eBay. I can't say that I blame them for hanging tough on this one. Hey, there's another story you can follow—what's been done, even recently, to Indian grave sites. Maybe see what you can find on their burial rites …"

"I'm kind of doing that for *Northern Pines*." I hesitated, brain quickly searching for a different angle; a way to double dip on the same story. "Let me think about it. I just wish they weren't 'hanging tough' on me. I can't do a thing to help them."

"Maybe they don't want stuff in the paper about the dead woman."

"Yeah. But if this Alfred Naquma is guilty of something..."

We hung up. To keep busy while I waited to hear from Dolly, I cleaned the refrigerator, dumping stuff covered with purple mold into the garbage. I was into black lettuce when I heard a car in the drive and went to let Dolly in, an odd smile on her pert little face.

"Write that story yet?" she asked and gave me an even bigger, un-Dolly-like smile.

"I called Bill. We'll wait for ID. Want to make sure there's no screw up."

She shook her head and lifted her leg onto one of the stools at the kitchen island. She chuckled. "Don't have to wait. Brent said he knew 'em right away."

"Knew 'em? What do you mean?"

"Chicken bones. You hit on another garbage pit. Brent's men dug into it while I was there and came up with not just chicken bones but rib bones, some bones from a deer, and a lot of other animal bones. Maybe, when the bones disintegrated, Orly Naquma used the soil for fertilizer. Found another pit nearby. That one was filled with whiskey bottles."

I winced. *Chicken bones.*

"Brent said we should go over and talk to the tribal police. He doesn't think it would be a good idea to go back to the casino, or anywhere else, looking for those men. He said the Odawa like to handle their own affairs and, though this one isn't reservation related, they would still need to be brought into it."

"Sounds good to me. Do you think they'll help?"

Dolly shrugged. She looked around and frowned. "They're paid to keep the peace the same as I am. To tell you the truth, I'd rather have them on our side before we go looking for those others." She frowned deeper and bent down to look under the table. "Hey, where's Sorrow? I missed my usual welcome."

"Got out while I was gone," I said. "He'll be back. He never goes too far."

"Miss the big dope," she said. She stood and stretched. "You come on in tomorrow morning and we'll go see the tribal police."

I agreed. I'd had enough for one day and I was a little nervous about Sorrow. Over the next few hours I kept hearing him scratching at the door. I opened the door and looked out in all directions. I called his name again and again.

Sorrow didn't come home.

# THIRTY-FOUR

HE DIDN'T COME HOME all night. I spent a good part of the time getting up, wrapping a wool robe around myself against the cold, and standing on the side porch calling his name out toward the lake, then back toward the woods. Each time I held my breath, listening hard for his bark. Nothing.

I went back to bed, telling myself this was something dogs did. Spring, after all.

I told myself all kinds of things. I was uneasy and not happy with him. But what did I know about dogs? What did I know about people? Look how long I'd overlooked Jackson's wandering eye, ignored every phone call from an ardent "student," was blind to the late nights when he wasn't in his office at the university. It was the thong in the glove box that finally got to me. Jackson claimed someone thought they could get even for a failing grade. I mulled that one over for a day or two before visiting an attorney.

Sorrow would be back, I assured myself, trying to sleep. He was fixed. When he realized he didn't know what he was hunting for, he'd give up and come back to a full bowl of food.

At four a.m., since I was up anyway, I went to my studio and got more of Jackson's manuscript on the computer. His editor wanted it as a single file so I kept it that way, sending only the new pages I added. I got a lot of the manuscript done and then had an hour to work on my novel presentation for the Leetsville Library.

The book was moving along fast. Writing can be such a hesitant thing—work going well and then drying up. Usually when it dried up I knew there was something wrong in the work I had already completed. I didn't believe in writers' block. I believed in going back and rewriting. This morning I had no problems. My elderly attorney moved fast—in and out of his gentlemen's club where an old woman accosted him, claiming she knew who had killed Gilbert Hurley's wife. I made the woman rather grotesque: too old for the ratty, sexy clothes she wore, yet something of the "lady" about her. My attorney was repulsed by the woman, who clutched at his sleeve, trying to get money for information.

It was a good scene. Maybe this would be the one I'd read at the library, along with a synopsis of the rest of the book. I wanted people to hear only my best. With a good reading I could get over my "loser" reputation, and they'd see me as an artist, a true writer.

I leaned back in my chair, put my hands behind my head, and stared at the ceiling. I didn't owe anybody an explanation, an excuse, an apology, I told myself. And I decided to stop being hard on me. I was a damned good journalist. My novels might not be selling yet but they were good, if you discounted that one unintentional rewrite of *Fatal Attraction*.

Added to this list of fine qualities, I'd been a good wife. Still was a good friend. I was capable of living alone. And, what I liked best about me was that I learned from my mistakes. Maybe that meant I was fairly intelligent. With that bunch of metaphoric gold stars pinned to my chest, I got back to work.

———

*"Mister." The old woman in a tattered skirt and torn lace blouse pulled at the sleeve of Randall Jarvis's tweed sport coat. "Mister," she said again, frantic as he shook her off.*

*"Go away," he growled, bunching his shoulders up to his ears. The last thing he wanted was a beggar hanging on him. He had had enough trouble staying on his feet since the heart attack. If he didn't concentrate, keep one foot plodding straight in front of the other, he could fall and die there in the gutter. The worst thing he could imagine happening, here at the end of what he thought of as an illustrious life.*

*"I've got information." The old woman swiped at her nose with the back of one hand. Her eyes, lost in deep wrinkles, filled with child-like glee.*

*"You have nothing for me, ma'am." He tried to maneuver around her but she sprang back in front of him, agile for a woman of her age.*

*"Yeah? You think so? How's about something I know on that Gilbert you're working for?"*

*Randall hesitated. His client's name had been in the paper. Probably one of those mental cases allowed to roam the streets, harassing good people.*

*"I'm talking about your client, Gilbert Hurley." The woman stood directly in his path, hands planted at her waist. "I know who really done it to his wife."*

*Randall's mouth dropped open despite himself. Next would come a demand for money. He'd been through something similar before, a long time ago.*

It was so good it made me shiver. The right tone. Characterization falling into place. The chapter was easy to finish, with the old woman taking Randall to a room where she brought out bloody clothes belonging to another man. The old woman swears to Randall that the DNA they would find belonged to Gilbert's wife, Nancy.

I thought the chapter was exciting and certainly contained the heart of the novel. They would like it. A little polishing and I'd be ready for Tuesday.

I called Jackson before I left to meet Dolly in town. I told him I'd gotten a lot of his work ready and would run off a copy for him before sending anything on to the publisher.

"I can't tell you how much I appreciate what you're doing, Emily." He choked up. "It's so good to be up here with you. I guess I'd forgotten how well we fit together ..."

"I know," I stopped him.

"When you've got the pages ready I'll come out and get them—if that's all right."

I assured him that would be fine and found myself smiling. Another date with Jackson. Maybe we would move this new thing between us along. I was ready. I had to make up my mind about my future. Sure, I would miss living in the woods. I would miss the lake. I would miss Sorrow, and Harry and Dolly and Eugenia and all the others. But I could come back. I could visit.

I grabbed my bag and camera, removed the squashed sandwich I hadn't eaten the day before, and set the dog bones down on the side porch, for Sorrow, when he came home.

———

Dolly was on the phone when I got to the station. She waved me to a seat. Her end of the conversation was mostly "un-huh" and "hmm." When she hung up, her first question was about Sorrow.

"Not yet." I shook my head.

"Don't worry. That's how dogs are. Never wanted one myself."

I shrugged, a little disappointed in her. I had hoped she would take Sorrow, if I decided to leave. Finding him a home was at the top of my mental list of things to do. And other things, like not possibly missing the August daisies when the hills behind my house were speckled with them. And I couldn't miss puffball season: "slice 'em, egg 'em, coat 'em with bread crumbs, and fry 'em up in butter." And, oh my God—there was wild strawberry season at the end of June . . .

"I'll help you look for 'im after we finish in TC," Dolly said.

I thanked her and thought maybe I would enlist Harry, too. He knew the woods and places dogs went better than any other human being.

We were well on our way down 131 before Dolly said another word. She turned her head to give me a long, pregnant look, and said, "They're releasing Chet."

She checked her rearview mirror, then gave a guy in a sports car the eye as he passed us on a double yellow.

"Finally," I said. "So, did you call his sister?"

She nodded. I rolled my window down. Something in Dolly's cars always smelled just a little funky. For a while I had thought it was her, until I noticed an array of old Burger King bags on the back seat.

"She's coming up for the funeral. Bringing Chet's mom too, from Bloomington."

"They're having the funeral and burial up here?"

"That's what they say." She turned on to M72, toward Traverse City, taking the turn on two wheels just because she could. "They want me to go ahead and make the plans."

"And they're paying?"

"Well, I suppose they'll help. I'm his wife, you know. More my responsibility."

"Are you crazy?" The woman could exasperate me beyond measure. "He left you years ago. You have no responsibility at all."

We drove without speaking for a while.

"Bet they'll stick you with the entire bill," I said finally, keeping my voice low and disgusted.

Dolly shook her head. "Nope. Elaine said they'd help out, didn't want the whole thing on me, and she meant it. I thought maybe a luncheon at EATS after the cemetery. I'd like to do it right. Chet didn't go to no church so the burial will be straight from the funeral home. Sullivan said that would be no trouble."

"You've been busy." I was impressed.

"Did it all. Except the casket. Gotta pick that out. I'd like you to come with me—tomorrow morning. If that's OK? Kinda feels creepy doing it alone."

"They should be here to go with you," I muttered. "The sister and mother."

"Well, they can't be."

"So it's me?"

"Yup. Looks like that's it."

"When's the funeral?"

"Monday. Eleven o'clock."

I nodded. I'd be there, and if I got the opportunity to drop a few hints about money to that sister of his, I'd sure grab it.

The tribal police station was a low, gray stone building with spindly pines planted across the front. We went in and introduced ourselves to Detective Ray Shankwa, a tall, good-looking man in his early forties. Officer Shankwa was polite and professional, inviting us to join him at a metal desk in the corner of the large, open room. Dolly launched into the story, then told him how far we'd gotten. She brought in Lewis George and Orly Naquma and his family, including Alfred Naquma. It was Alfred's name that brought a frown to Shankwa's face. I threw in that I'd seen him at the casino and then again out at Dark Forest Cemetery. Dolly told him he was the man who'd been out at Sandy Lake when we first got there.

Ray Shankwa shook his head. "I'm very sorry if you've had a problem with someone from our tribe..."

Dolly pulled herself up as straight as she could get. "Not just a problem, Officer Shankwa. We're talking about a double murder here. If one of your people is involved, well, I'd expect you to cooperate."

Ray nodded and examined the silver pen he held between the fingers of both his dark hands. "I know the name," he said, and looked first me and then Dolly straight in the eye. "He isn't the kind of man to cause trouble. Still, since there is a complaint, I will find him. And talk to him."

He snapped his mouth shut, raised his chin, and waited for us to leave.

"He's a suspect in these two murders," Dolly said again. "And the murders didn't happen on the res. He's going to have to come with me, if you find him. You understand that? We'll need to talk to him."

Ray shook his head. "That will be determined. It might not be my call. We have our tribal council and our own courts. There will be the sovereign power of the tribe to deal with. And that's not given up lightly. You will have to understand that there are channels to go through."

"Me, too," Dolly said, a stern look on her face. "I've got channels. But we don't let people get away with murder."

Ray nodded and stood, dismissing us. "I will call you after I talk to Lewis George and Alfred Naquma."

We were out of there in thirty seconds. There was no camaraderie or standing on ceremony once our message had been delivered.

"I wish I'd gone on out to the casino one more time. Those guys could disappear," Dolly muttered.

"I think this officer's a straight arrow," I said. "He's got his protocols the same as you have. You'll hear from him."

"Yeah," she said, and got back into the patrol car. "We'll see. I'm not giving him long. I'm turning the screws on everybody."

# THIRTY-FIVE

MY HEART BROKE WHEN I saw the pile of dog bones on the porch still intact. I walked through the garden calling his name, but there was no answering bark. I walked up to the road, stood at the middle of the pavement helplessly calling out for him, but got nothing in return. For a moment I thought I heard something, but the barking came from Harry's place. His kennel dogs.

I went back to the house and sat on the low step, next to the dog bones. There was something about the quiet around me; something about the absence of an excited black-and-white dog, that tore me up. Maybe there were things more important to dogs than love and food. If he'd gone off to find those things, I wished him well, but something wouldn't let me admit I'd let him down in any way. All that happiness and enthusiasm at the sight of me couldn't have been a lie.

"Damn it," I swore under my breath as I got up.

———

"I'll come right out," Dolly said when I called. She had offered to help me search, but still I'd been ready for a refusal. She could have had a busted mailbox to investigate. Or a speed trap to plan. I was ready to remind her I was going with her to buy a casket in the morning and this wasn't too much to ask, but I didn't need any of the weapons I'd come up with. Dolly was there, tearing down the drive, in twenty minutes. In that twenty minutes I got a flyer together, complete with a picture I'd taken of him recently, and ran off twenty. While we were out looking, I'd stick them up on telephone polls and hand them out to anyone we met.

———

"Well, now." Harry scratched at his chin and stood in thought outside his little crooked house. "I'd give 'im a day or so. Spring, ya know."

"He's been gone two days. And he was fixed right after I got him."

"Just 'cause he can't do the deed don't mean he's forgot what it's all about."

He thought some more and moved his jaw back and forth. "Never saw him over here. Ya know, some dogs would be curious—I mean, all the barking. But not Sorrow. Didn't come this way once. Good thing. I'd hate to think of him crossing Willow Lake Road by hisself."

Me either. I didn't like thinking of him out on a road, or caught by a coyote or a bear. I didn't like thinking of some hunter grabbing him to use next hunting season. None of those things. I wanted Sorrow out in the woods with his nose to the ground, maybe slightly lost.

"We'd better get in the car and drive around," Dolly said, not looking at Harry. He wouldn't look at her either. They ignored each other and spoke only to me. Maybe a fresh ticket for his hybrid car was on both their minds, but I didn't care right then. They were my friends, and I needed help.

"Think it's better to comb the woods than be driving around," Harry said, grunting the words.

"Nope," Dolly said, still without looking at him. "Car's best. We'll drive wherever we can and call his name. We'll hand out flyers to anybody we see."

"Better to look in the woods first," Harry said again, digging his heels into the dirt. "That's what the dog knows."

"Why don't we start off in the car?" I said, hoping Harry wouldn't get mad. "I've been out in the woods, as far as I could walk. If I could get these flyers out..."

Harry made a face at me but shrugged his shoulders. "Whatever you say. You don't need me along in that car. Tell you what I'll do. Me and my dogs will get out in the woods and see if we come up with him. Coulda gotten hurt somehow. Dogs'll find 'im."

Since it was the smartest idea I'd heard, and it was best to keep these two separated, that's what we did. Harry was off before we walked all the way back to Willow Lake Road. Dolly and I jumped in the Jeep and started driving down Willow Lake Road, then up every two-track we came to. Everywhere we went, we called, "Sorrow! Sorrow!" and stopped to nail flyers to telephone poles. At any minute I expected to see that shaggy black-and-white body come leaping happily out of the woods.

We stopped cars and asked if the drivers had seen him and left them with flyers. Everybody we talked to assured us they'd be on the lookout and would certainly call if they found him. One man, in an old blue pickup, said his bitch just had a litter and I was welcome to however many I wanted, if I needed a dog.

For two hours we roamed the woods roads. No dog.

"Why don't we go into town and put up a flyer at the IGA, the gas station, maybe at EATS, even over to The Skunk. Wouldn't hurt to get people looking across the area," Dolly said.

Since I couldn't come up with a better idea, we headed to town in our separate vehicles.

Dolly took care of the gas station and the bar. I took the IGA and, to cover everything, Gertie's Shoppe de Beaute and the barber shop. Everyone was concerned. They said they would keep an eye out for the dog and assured me he would come back. They told me not to worry. "Hard to lose a dog from a good home," Bob, the barber, said.

We met at the restaurant. Dolly had a poster in her hands and the hammer she'd taken from the back of her patrol car. In the dim vestibule, there hung a new flyer with a gold star. I almost groaned. I was tired of that little game. From then on I was going to ignore Eugenia's family. All those outlaws might interest her, but I was bored with the whole drawn-out joke.

I pointed to a place next to the cigarette machine for Dolly to hang the poster. Lots of folks came in for cigarettes. They'd see Sorrow and maybe someone, from somewhere, would recognize him and would call me.

Dolly took a small nail from her shirt pocket and hammered the flyer up on the wall.

I was ready to go on in and grab dinner. Since it was Friday night, it could be anything. Some big sweet surprise. I'd been having dreams of pot roast with tiny carrots and gravy. There are times, though, when you get particularly hungry and almost anything sounds good. Except meatloaf.

I opened the door to enter the restaurant but Dolly didn't follow. When I turned back to see what was keeping her, she was standing in front of Eugenia's new relative, looking up, frowning and reading fast.

"See this?" She poked a finger toward the paper. "See what Eugenia's gone and done?"

I stepped back beside her and read the paper. "Dolly Wakowski's Birth Certificate" it read.

*Uh-oh*, I thought, smelling a big pile of trouble ahead.

Dolly yanked the paper down off the wall. "What in hell does she think she's doing? I'm supposed to fall for ..." She read slowly, her finger tracing the lines.

"October 3, 1974," she read aloud to me. "She's got that part right. I probably told her."

She chewed at her bottom lip and frowned as she moved on, carefully going over every filled-in place on the certificate. "Says my mother's name was Audrey Thomas. The Thomas name sounds familiar." She read on. "She was seventeen." She looked up at me.

"You think this could be real?" Her face was awash with different emotions.

I shrugged. "Why would she put it up there if it weren't? Eugenia's not a cruel woman."

"My dad's name was Harold Flynn. For goodness' sakes. I've always liked that name: Harold. He was thirty-one. Uh-oh. Maybe I'm getting an idea of why she abandoned me. Harold was a lot older than she was.

"Look here. Down here. These are my baby footprints. See?"

"Where were you born?"

"Detroit. Just the way I always thought. Woman's Hospital, it says here. One thing it doesn't say was if they was married or not. They gave me his name. Hers is different. Still ..."

"I wouldn't worry about that, Dolly. Kids come into the world all different ways. Turns out the same."

"Yeah, well, unless they aren't really wanted. Then it's always different for those kids."

All I could do was nod.

Dolly read the paper over and over, looking up to share each new detail with me. There weren't many, mostly printed words of the stock birth certificate, but this was the first time she'd seen her own. I couldn't imagine how she'd gotten into school without a birth certificate, how she'd registered to vote—so many things I imagined a birth certificate was necessary to obtain. Maybe it worked differently with an abandoned kid. Maybe abandoned kids were given a pass in our society.

"Can we go in?" I finally asked.

She nodded. "I want to know that this is bona fide and not something Eugenia came up with on her own."

Inside the restaurant, Eugenia waited behind her counter. I think the whole restaurant was waiting. A suspicious hush fell as we walked in.

"Where'd you get this?" Dolly demanded, waving the certificate over her head as she advanced on Eugenia.

Eugenia looked at the paper Dolly held, then at the hammer in her other hand. "You just be careful here now, Dolly. I did some careful work with my genealogy websites. Don't you go attacking me."

"Is this really my birth certificate?" Dolly demanded.

"Date's right, isn't it?" Eugenia demanded back.

Dolly looked it over again to make sure. She nodded.

"Place right?"

Dolly nodded.

"Then the rest is right, too."

"That's who my mother and father were?"

"Got to be. It's all there. Not hard to find."

"Got anything else?"

Eugenia shook her head. "Not yet. I'm looking."

"Do you know if they're alive?"

Eugenia shook her head. "That's all, so far."

Dolly glanced around at the eyes pinned on the three of us. "Couldn't you just give me the stuff? Why do you have to hang it up like that. Seems, if you want to do me a favor you could …"

Eugenia shrugged and pushed her big blond hair back over her shoulder. "I might want to go into the business of looking up folks. You're good advertising, Dolly. Yours is all for free."

Dolly scowled. "Next time give me a call. I'll get in here fast and get it down off that wall."

"That's not nice. I'm doing you a service. The least you can do is go along …"

Dolly waved a dismissive hand, folded the paper, and forced it into one of her pants pockets. She walked away with me behind her.

"And you put that back up there when you leave, you hear?" Eugenia called after us, not giving an inch.

Everybody in the restaurant listened to this burgeoning battle of the Titans. Flora Coy leaned over to whisper to Anna Scovil. Sullivan Murphy half rose as if he might have to pull these two apart. Gertie folded her arms across her chest, and watched with her faded blue eyes narrowed and her mouth tight and wrinkly. I could tell people were choosing up sides and there would be weeks of debate ahead.

Dolly stopped in front of our usual booth and turned to face her rapt audience. Raising her voice, she called, "Funeral for Chet is on Monday. Eleven o'clock at Sullivan's. You can ask Sullivan, there, if you want details. You're all invited. Lunch'll be back here after the burial. Pass the word along."

Eugenia, at the front, pasted on a smile, and spouted. "Going to have a full buffet with salads and roast beef, and fried chicken, mashed potatoes, gravy, broccoli, and little tarts for dessert. Don't miss it."

She turned back to Dolly and yelled across the space between them, "I would think, Miss Dolly Flynn Wakowski, you'd show a little gratitude for all my work. At least you know you got somebody. Or at least you had somebody. That's something."

"I already got somebody," Dolly called back without lifting her head from the menu. "I'm burying him on Monday."

Low conversation started up. Leetsvillians gave each other sheepish smiles and shrugs. A few rolled their eyes at me when I glanced around the room. Some smiled and nodded. The rest just went on eating... meatloaf.

# THIRTY-SIX

Tired from not sleeping the night before, I was relieved to get back home, even if the dog bones were still intact and the quiet house felt like a morgue.

In the car I had decided there wasn't going to be any giving Sorrow away to anyone. Not to Dolly and not to anyone else. He was my dog and when I got him back I would keep him forever. If Jackson and I worked out and he didn't like it ... well ... too bad. He'd just have to get used to it. If he wanted me with him, he had to take my dog. We were a team, me and Sorrow. Love me, love my dog.

First thing I did at home, after kicking off my sandals and putting the tea kettle on to boil, was check the answering machine. There might be people calling who'd seen Sorrow, or picked him up.

The first call was from Jackson Rinaldi.

"Miss you, Emily. I'm calling to see if you're ready for the next batch. Thought maybe this weekend we could catch a film. You up for it? Maybe not dinner ... I've got a lot of work to do. Well, whatever you want, give me a call." His voice dropped a few notches. "I mean it,

Emily. I miss you. Maybe this week … if you'd like, I could get over there …"

I would call him right back. But first the water was boiling. I made myself a cup of Constant Comment and, with warm mug in hand, sat at the desk to check the three other calls.

The second call was from Anna Scovil. I'd just seen her in town and she hadn't mentioned calling me. Maybe this was another part of her subversive librarying.

"Emily." Her voice was high and authoritarian. "Don't forget about Tuesday night. Everybody's going to be at the library to hear you speak at six thirty. I hate to ask, but could you bring some cookies? I'll have coffee and tea, but cookies aren't in our budget. Hope this is all right. If you can't afford it, give me a call and I'll find somebody who can." Here she hesitated. "You'll have about ten minutes to read from your work. Mr. Williams said he needs twenty minutes, at least, for the family history. Winnie Lorbach's got a lot of lady's slipper slides to show. I figured ten minutes would be about right for your fiction. Then there'd be time for questions afterward."

Another hesitation. "I'll see you Tuesday night. Try to get there a little early so we can get the cookies set out. I'll get nervous, thinking you're not coming, if I don't see you by at least six o'clock. This will be a very nice affair, Emily. I'm looking forward to hearing you read. Oh, oh, I heard the funeral for Chet Wakowski is on Monday. Guess I'll see you there first."

That was that. I was pleased I was ready for her, and for the audience coming to hear me. All I had to do was buy a couple packages of chocolate chip cookies.

The next call was a hang-up.

I thought the last was a hang-up, too, but after a few minutes of heavy breathing a deep, male, familiar voice said, "I got your dog.

243

Wouldn't a done it if you'd listened. You gotta stop this looking into things having nothing to do with you, Emily Kincaid. I'll know when you give it up."

Lewis George hung up. I played it again, then again, getting madder and madder each time.

I could hardly breathe. That SOB had taken Sorrow on purpose. My beloved Sorrow—a hostage. I knew that deep voice and all those hesitations. Sorrow had been cowed by him. Oh my God! Was he cowering now? Was that awful man feeding him or being cruel?

I pictured Sorrow's sad face. Maybe he was in a cage. Maybe he was locked in a dark room. I hoped he peed and pooped all over that man's house. If he was in a shed, I prayed he barked until he drove everybody crazy. I prayed Sorrow bit him and made a break for it, thundering through the woods, down the roads, heading home with his long ears pinned back, tongue hanging out of the side of his mouth, paws tearing up the earth.

So ... no dog was going to come bounding down the drive. No dog was about to leap at the side door, demanding to be let in. I couldn't think what there was to do. Call Dolly. No. Yes. No. Lewis George wanted Mary Naquma's bones back to bury and didn't believe I wouldn't help them. Or it was something deeper, something he was covering up for his friend, Alfred Naquma.

Where did that leave me? More and more I was sure Alfred Naquma had something to do with his sister's murder. And how many more? Where was the father, Orly? Where was the sister, Christine? Sorrow and I could be up against a multiple murderer with a friend protecting him; men with no consciences.

I didn't care about my safety anymore. They had Sorrow and that was all that mattered. I had to find a way to get him back.

# THIRTY-SEVEN

I WRAPPED MY ARMS around my body to stop the shaking. I needed to think, and think hard. Both Alfred and Lewis George had something to do with the casino. I had no addresses, but I'd seen Alfred Naquma there.

I looked at the clock over the sink in the kitchen. Eight-twenty. It would be dark in about an hour—or close to dark. Should I ask Dolly to go? Did I go myself? Where did I begin?

The casino was all I had. I was going alone, I decided. I didn't want a little woman in a cop suit, with cop rules, along. I would blend in with the Friday night crowd. There was no question that I would find one or both of the men, and when I did I wouldn't leave without Sorrow.

———

The casino parking lot was filled with cars. Couples made their way toward the big front doors with their arms around each other. Groups laughed and teased and hurried along. I was the only lone woman. I slipped into step with the group ahead of me and went through the doors, into the giant room lined with clinking, clunking, and buzzing slot machines. Lights flashed everywhere. There were shouts of joy and groans of misery. The smoke was dense enough to shut my lungs down for a month or two. I walked close behind people sitting over their machines, backs bent, eyes transfixed on grapes and apples and happy faces circling on reels in front of them.

At one end of the cavernous room was the restaurant. At the other were a gift shop and a bar. Beyond was a corridor opening into yet more rooms. In the middle were the poker tables and craps tables and pit bosses and girls carrying drink trays and small crowds milling around a winner and rows and rows of machines. It wasn't the people at the tables or machines I looked at as I did a slow stroll from one end of the room to the other. I watched the faces of men who stood at corners; men in suits, standing with their hands crossed over their genitals as if fearing a head butt. These men worked for the casino. They didn't smile, only kept their eyes on the crowd. It would be among these men in charge that I would find Lewis George or Alfred Naquma. It would be here or maybe in the restaurant.

As I walked and smiled at happy people passing, I watched every Native American face in the casino. None were the two I searched for. I went down to the restaurant and told the elderly hostess with the bent back that I was there looking for a friend. She nodded me on.

The booths were full, but neither man was there. I had to do something more aggressive or I'd be leaving without Sorrow.

I found a machine where a woman was just getting up and grabbed it before a man on a walker could beat me to it. It was a triple payoff machine with a repeat spin on the third reel. I put in the ten dollars I felt I could spare. I hit the button and watched the wheels go around while still, from the corners of my eyes, watching who walked behind me; who might be watching me. I even glanced upward, to make sure the overhead cameras got a good look. I was here and I wanted it known.

The ten dollars was gone in twenty minutes. I had to come up with another idea. I had been so sure I would be tapped on the shoulder, led to some back room, and finally brought face to face with both men. I was certain I would get a chance to demand my dog back.

Though I'd lost my money and wasn't playing any longer, I stayed in the chair in front of the machine, swinging my legs back and forth, turning down proffered drinks, and thinking. I made myself conspicuous but there were no bites.

At a tap on my shoulder, I turned slowly, expecting the confrontation I wanted, or at least an invitation to follow someone. An elderly woman with puffed white hair stood there, pouting smile on her face asking me not to get mad at her.

"If you're not using this machine, can I have it?" she asked. "It's one of my favorites, you see."

She blinked a few times as if expecting me to body slam her for the machine. I nodded. Smiled back. Muttered "Sorry," and got up.

Frustration grew. The crowd got bigger. I had to elbow my way up and down the middle of the room. Almost all of the machines were occupied. People walked slowly past, hoping to be the first to jump on a seat, should anybody get up. It looked like a big, slow game of musical chairs. There wasn't any way to find the men in this throng.

I began asking for them.

The lines at the cashiers were long. What better way to make myself noticed than to jump ahead of the others? I pushed to the front of the line, in front of a man with four quarter cups hugged to his chest.

"Hey," he yelled, "wait your turn."

I stuck a finger in the air asking for a minute, and leaned in toward the cashier. "I'm looking for Lewis George or Alfred Naquma. You know where I can find them?"

The heavyset woman scowled at me. "Get in line," she ordered.

"I don't have any winnings. I just need to speak to the men."

"Ask at Hospitality," she said, and motioned me aside.

The hospitality desk was down on the other side of the building. There was a long line there too, all waiting for their badges and whatever else they needed. I pulled the same thing, stepped to the head of the line over howls of protest, and asked for the two men.

"Ma'am," the polite little girl behind the desk said, smiling and keeping her hospitably bright voice in place.

"I'm looking for Lewis George and Alfred Naquma," I repeated.

"Ma'am, there are others ahead of you. I'm sorry..."

"They are men who work here or run this place. You have to know them. They've kidnapped my dog..."

She leaned back, narrowed her eyes, and waved her hand in the air.

Immediately, two very large guards were beside me, easing me from the line with slight shoulder pushes. I looked up into each face. No smiles on these dark faces. No anything. They were removing me from center stage, getting me to walk between them back down the crowded center aisle.

Good, I thought. Now I was getting someplace. I pushed back at the wide shoulders holding me in place.

They kept me between them without laying a hand on me. Somehow I was being hustled forward. Suddenly it dawned on me that maybe I should have told someone I was coming out here. As it was, nobody knew. If I came up missing—who would think to come to a casino?

I moved with the tall, stiff men in guard uniforms. As if joined at the hip, we made our way through the crowd. When we got close to the restaurant, they turned me toward the front door. I was being escorted out. That wasn't my plan.

I stopped dead. "I'm not going anywhere until I see Lewis George or Alfred Naquma. I know they're your bosses. If I don't see them I'm going to the police. Do you two hear me?"

They didn't look down. Their bodies came in closer. I was a sandwich filling, and a not too pleased one.

I tried to pull back, out of lockstep with the wide shoulders leaning into me. "Look you ignorant bastards, I'm not leaving until ..."

I was out the door, standing in the dusky parking lot alone. I could see the two huge mutes on the other side of the glass, watching me.

If I weren't such a delicate lady I would have flipped them the universal signal of distaste. I didn't. I only sniffed, turned on my heel, and went to my car. I was enraged and trying to think what there was left to do. Something. I had to come up with a way to find those two men everyone protected. I drove out of the parking lot, and was almost rear ended by a driver too eager to grab my parking place. My biggest regrets were that I hadn't found the men, didn't know where to look next, that I wasn't bringing Sorrow home with me after all, and that I'd lost that damn ten dollars I could have used to put gas in my tank.

# THIRTY-EIGHT

THERE WERE NO LIGHTS on in the tribal police building as I drove by, and nothing but dark around me. Lake Michigan on my right. Trees to my left. I'd planned to stop and see Ray Shankwa and raise as many kinds of hell as I could. Now I had nowhere to go with my anger and frustration. It was like looking for ghosts. I knew they existed, the two men, but they were nowhere. They found me easily enough, but I couldn't find them anywhere. As if a cloak of invisibility had been drawn around the men, no one knew them, no one recognized the names, no one offered help. I got the feeling I was being shut out of a northern club I knew nothing about. Didn't anyone care that two people had been murdered and left to molder at the bottom of a lake?

The thing about murder, to me, was the hideous arrogance of taking lives no one had the right to take. Most murderers were the worst kind of egoists: if I can't have them; if they won't listen to me; if I can gain something … why, I'll just do away with them and then I'll be happy. There always seemed to be that at the very bottom of the urge to kill: then I'll be happy.

Who was happier after killing Mary and Chet? I asked myself as I drove back down through Sutton's Bay. I curved with the road, past the Bay Theatre, Bahle's Department Store, and all the galleries, toward Traverse City.

Why would Alfred Naquma kill his sister? I wondered. Maybe because Chet was a white man. There were plenty of Indians who held grudges. Would Alfred be happier knowing he had stopped his sister from making a terrible marriage? If I understood human beings better, maybe I could fathom that one, but the human psyche, much like that of animals, was, at heart, unknowable.

Was it because Chet was a married man? I wondered. That would do it for a lot of fathers and brothers.

Could be something else. Something illegal going on out at Sandy Lake Alfred couldn't let Chet find out about. Especially with Chet's soon-to-be aggrieved wife on the local police force.

But where was Orly Naquma? And Christine, the other sister?

Why would Alfred wipe out his whole family, and why would the tribe protect him?

None of it made sense.

Thirteen years was a long time to have kept this secret. It was like peeling an old onion layer by layer; the onion was rotten but the skin didn't want to give up its core.

I couldn't go home. Not back to that silent house. Too much on my mind and I'd failed to find Sorrow. I was tired and out of ideas. In the morning I was supposed to pick out Chet's casket with Dolly. I didn't want to. Didn't want to see Leetsville for a while and didn't want some melancholy job ahead of me. I wanted to be someplace where I was an Emily Kincaid I recognized. For just a few hours.

I headed out toward Spider Lake and Jackson.

———

Stripped down to his boxer shorts, a tee shirt, and bare feet, Jackson wasn't expecting company when he came to the door.

"Anything wrong?" he asked as he unlocked the screen to let me in, maybe a little reluctantly. His good-looking face was lined with worry and irritation. I ignored the pallid greeting and walked in, slapping my purse on the kitchen counter and leaning over it, resting my hands to either side. Exhaustion hit me hard. I was tired from the night before, from not sleeping, and from the emotional stress of not finding Sorrow. Maybe even from making an ass of myself at the casino.

"What happened?" Jackson's hands were on either of my arms. He turned me to him and held me. I think I might have cried—I was that frustrated.

I stepped away from Jackson, giving him points for kindness.

"Somebody stole Sorrow," I said.

"That's terrible," Jackson frowned and drew me close again, patting me awkwardly on the back.

I let out a puff of air. Enough of that. I told him I just couldn't go home, that I was miserable, and needed a bed for the night. He looked at me oddly, then sensed I wasn't in the mood for sex. He said he would clear his papers from the spare room.

Nobody answered at the Leetsville Police Station when I called. I let it ring and ring. Finally, after about ten rings, when anyone needing help would have given up, a machine came on and I left the message for Dolly that I wouldn't be able to go with her in the morning. I said I was sure she could pick out a casket by herself and that something unsettling had come up. I said I would tell her all about it when I got back home.

I got the number for the tribal police and left a message there, too. I asked Ray Shankwa to call me and gave him Jackson's number. Maybe it wasn't smart to admit to being thrown out of the casino but that's what I said in the message, and told him why, and that I was looking for the men and that they'd kidnapped my dog and I was going to go after them, beginning in the morning when I would call the police in Sutton's Bay, in Traverse City, in Gaylord—and soon nobody would be hiding and somebody would pay for everything that was going on ... The answering machine at the other end beeped, stopping me.

I called Bill's office next and left a message on his machine about the chicken bones. I promised a new story the next day.

Jackson, lying on the couch behind me, listening, put his arms up behind his head.

"Quite a night, Emily," he said, and smiled a superior smile. "Did you really get kicked out of the casino?"

I nodded. "I want my dog back. One of those men is a murderer. If I keep quiet, who's to say they won't harm Sorrow, or even do something to me? They want the murders out at Sandy Lake hushed up and everybody in the tribe is covering for them."

"Everyone?" He lifted an eyebrow at me.

"Well, it seems to me ..."

"Maybe you've gotten a little hysterical ..."

Christ! The old "now calm down little lady" routine. I'd forgotten that part of Jackson's character. It made me wince. Too tired and angry to get mad at Jackson too, I made him move over and lay down beside him on the couch.

I never got to the spare bedroom. Never even got out of my clothes. We fell asleep like that, in each other's arms. It wasn't until near morning that I moved to a deep chair and curled up with a blanket pulled to my chin.

Jackson made pancakes with real maple syrup for breakfast. I was hungry. Anger can do that, bring on the need for quantities of food to tap down all those roiling feelings.

I don't know if he expected me to leave after breakfast, but I didn't. While he went up to his office/bedroom to work on *The Mosaic of Humanity in the Canterbury Tales*, I took a full pot of tea to his deck and wrote out a new story for Bill. Two kayakers paddled silently past, and the voices of swimming children came from down around the cove. I felt safe there, with Jackson writing upstairs, with people doing things they should be doing up north. Nobody wanted to hurt me. Maybe I was hiding, but it felt good and freeing. Soon enough I'd get it together and go home. Since I had no clothes, no toothbrush, and nothing else other than the lipstick and hair brush in my purse, I imagined I would, like Shaw's houseguests, begin to stink like dead fish—sooner rather than later.

Jackson didn't seem to mind. I stayed on through lunch and then he invited me out to Hannah's Bistro for dinner and a movie. On our way through town later, I dropped the story off at the paper without seeing anyone.

How normal. A regular life. I enjoyed the salmon at the bistro and loved the movie, though I slept through most of it. On the way home we talked about our life before divorce, back when we'd been happy.

"You were a good foil for all the academic businesses," he said, turning to smile as I reclined in his Jaguar, feeling rich and important, a woman with real things to do and intelligent topics to talk about.

"You introduced me to that world I would have been shut out of otherwise," I said. "All those professors. That was fun—the discussions, even the arguments."

"Yes," he agreed. "We made a good pair."

"Except for your need to look elsewhere," I said, unable to let him off the hook, though it was a halfhearted attempt.

He shook his head. "Mea culpa. Remnants of my teen years, I'm afraid. It is possible to be a child and an adult at the same time."

"Sounds like an excuse a lot of men use."

"An atavistic giving into impulses, I've come to think. Really, those women had nothing to do with how I felt about you."

"Oh, Jackson." I was tired. Too tired to plow old ground and sane enough to realize it had all been plowed too many times before.

We didn't talk for a while as we drove back to his house on Spider Lake.

"I've been thinking hard about selling and going back to Ann Arbor," I said, almost wistfully.

"I know," he said. "Though I have to say, I've never seen you quite as happy as you've been up here. I have thought, more than once, how lucky you are to live in the North Country. For writing, it couldn't be a better place. Tough, I suppose, to make a living. But then, that's not a worry of yours. Not with the money from our divorce, and then there is the money your father left you."

There was nothing to say. If I told him my money problems, he might think the only reason I wanted to remarry him was to get a steady meal ticket. And—being honest with myself—that could be the truth. I didn't like women like that, but now I understood, just a little, how a woman might find herself frantic, needy, and vulnerable.

"Still," Jackson drove carelessly, a wrist draped through the steering wheel, "since your books don't sell and you're only working as a journalist part-time, I can see where you might want to get back into real life."

I bit my lip—hard. When I could speak, I said, "I was thinking, perhaps we might try again."

He hesitated. "You mean marriage? Us?" The laugh he gave wasn't flattering.

"We seem to be in a different place now," I pressed on.

"Yes, that's true … but are you certain? I mean, I know I'd be a much better husband than I was." He went into deep thought as we turned on Hobbs Highway. "In truth, I've missed you. It takes a wife to plan the kinds of parties we used to give. And they were good parties. At least never dull."

I nodded.

"And, with the married professors—their wives held the divorce against me. For God knows what reason. We'd be back in the married set again. That wouldn't hurt me at the university. I mean, we all reach a point where we are one thing or another: young and on the prowl, or married and settled. I suppose we could, eventually, fall back into the exact circle of friends we used to have."

I nodded, though cringing at the clinical analysis of our chances for success. And at the heavily weighted practical pros and cons.

He turned to me as we pulled in the drive under the tall pines. "We're getting on so well now. I like our being … close, the way we are. So very … comfortable."

We slept together that night. Almost a joyous occasion, as if a decision had been reached. It looked as though my little golden house could go on the market or be rented out. That idea began to hurt a lot. I forced it behind me.

Sunday morning I lazed around for a few hours, cooked breakfast for us, and then, stretching, suggested I'd better be getting home.

Jackson nodded. "I've got a lot of work to accomplish today. Probably best for both of us if you leave."

A little too enthusiastic for my ego, but it was true. I had to get back and face the funeral in the morning, had to track down those two men, had to get that cemetery story finished and into *Northern Pines Magazine*, had to find Sorrow—a lot of things I hadn't been thinking about.

Jackson said he would call in a few days and bring over more manuscript sheets. I took his face between both my hands for just a minute. I needed to look into his eyes. There was impatience there. There was a kind of satiation. There was a cautious kindness. I didn't know about love. Maybe at our age love wasn't so apparent. Maybe we'd both learned to guard our feelings. Maybe I needed to stop looking for overt signs and settle for what was said.

We kissed good-bye and I was out of there—no bags to pack. No long leave taking.

# THIRTY-NINE

AT THE BOTTOM OF my drive, when I got home, the first thing I saw was two people meandering through my garden. Dolly and Crazy Harry. Together, but apart—one up one garden path, the other standing in the new vegetable bed with a hose in his hand, watering seedlings emerging from the hills. I would have beans and corn and pumpkins and squash by fall. Harry was bent almost double, poking with one finger into a hill while water went on the next hill. Dolly, when she heard my car, stood with her hands at her waist, glaring into the sun.

"Where the hell you been?" was her greeting.

"Out," I said. "You get the casket chosen OK?"

She nodded. "That's not what's important here. You disappeared. Never said where you were going. You with Jackson?"

I nodded as I slammed the car door and fumbled with my house key.

"Get Sorrow back?" she demanded.

I shook my head.

"Then what the hell were you doing over there?"

"I went to the casino. Caused a lot of trouble, demanding to see Lewis George and Alfred Naquma. They kicked me out."

"Dumb. Why didn't you call?"

"So we could both get kicked out?"

"So we could do things the smart way."

"You hear from Ray Shankwa?"

She nodded. "He said he got a message from you but couldn't make heads nor tails of it. Told me the men haven't been seen around in about a week. He called their homes, visited the casino, and even went to the tribal offices. Alfred works there, at the offices. He might even be in charge or pretty high up. Lewis George is a tribal chief. They call him 'gimoa.' Ray said it isn't like them to be gone, and he's spread the word for them to come in as soon as they get back."

"Back from where? They've got Sorrow. Jesus..."

"We gave it a good go, Emily, but the word is out that I've turned the whole thing over to Gaylord. When they took your dog it just got way beyond what we could do. Brent's going to work with the state police out of Traverse City."

I was happy to hear we weren't on our own anymore. "You tell them the men kidnapped Sorrow?"

"Of course."

Harry, behind us, hadn't said a word. I waved halfheartedly as he shut off the hose. The next thing he was gone. I guessed, now that I was home, his job was finished.

Dolly toed the bark path. "So, you stayed with him," she said.

I shrugged, depressed and not up to being quizzed on my love life. "I had enough of everything and everybody. A weekend away from all of this wasn't too much to ask."

"Not if that's all it was."

OK. That was the end point. The place beyond which I wouldn't let her go. Dolly wanted only the best for me, I understood that. It was her methods I couldn't tolerate.

"If Jackson and I get back together, I'm very sorry, but it has nothing to do with you, Dolly. I will run my life as I want to. Even if I end up leaving here and going back to Ann Arbor—that's my own business."

She opened her mouth again, snapped it shut, and averted her eyes.

"I don't mean to be rude or anything …," I began, feeling sorry for her.

She nodded, still looking down at the ground. "I just don't want to see you …"

"I understand that. But what I do isn't up for discussion."

She sniffed. "You're right. None of my damn business. Can I say one thing though?"

"One thing."

"I never had a friend like you before. I mean, not somebody as smart. You know, it's like you're from a different world. Guess, what I'm saying is I'm a very selfish person. Look what we're doing with these murders we come up against. Maybe not this one, so much. I know it's cost you your dog and you're probably mad as hell. Still, I …"

I put a hand on her arm and stopped her.

"OK," I said. "We needed to clear the air. Now you know where I stand and I know why you were coming on too strong. So, let's just forget it and see if there's anything more we can do to get those men and get my dog."

She nodded.

"Let's go in my house. I'll make some tea and we'll talk about tomorrow."

"Tomorrow" was the funeral. She wanted to change the topic as much as I did and funerals required a lot of discussion. Over cups of Earl Grey we talked. She seemed overwhelmed.

"Never planned anything like this by myself before," she said, sipping at her tea as she sat at the kitchen counter and I stood across from her. "The casket was bad enough. Who knows what Chet would have wanted? I mean, we never talked about stuff like that. Too young to even think about it. I got him a nice one. Sullivan said I didn't even need a whole casket 'cause it was just the bones. He thought I should go for cremation and an urn but that's not what I want."

"How much did you spend?"

"Twenty-five hundred."

I took a deep breath. "You talk to his sister?"

She nodded.

"Did you tell her how much this whole thing is going to cost? I mean, there's the luncheon at EATS afterward, the funeral home fees, grave site."

Dolly shook her head. "It's enough for them to come all the way up here. His mother's driving from Bloomington, Indiana, you know. We'll talk about it after. They'll probably stay with me a few days. Got the house pretty clean and changed the bed in my spare room."

"When are they arriving? Shouldn't you be home?"

"No. Won't see them until tomorrow morning."

"Before eleven?"

"I told them the time. Said they could make it."

"So, you'll talk to them about the cost…"

She gave me a long look. "Maybe you should stay out of this. Just like I'm staying out of whatever happens between you and the jerk. This is my place."

I sputtered. "I don't want to see you get stuck…"

"Yeah. Well, that goes two ways. So let me handle my husband's funeral, OK?"

Nothing more to say. She was right.

At the door of her patrol car, we got back to what Dolly and I shared in common.

"Are we really out of it, Dolly? I don't feel right..."

Dolly shook her head and made a face. "Naw, Brent's just our cover."

Relieved, I leaned in the window. "Then what about that sister of Alfred? Christine. Think we can find anything more on her?"

"Good idea. I'll call Lena Smith. The chief pulled her number from when she called the station. Let's see if Lena knows anything about Christine's whereabouts. Then I guess I'll start checking driver's licenses. Find if there's a Christine Naquma in Michigan or not. Go through the usual channels."

"Should we get back to the casino? Or to the tribal offices? Or even house to house out there? That's what got us a response on Lena Smith."

"Don't think you'll be welcomed at the casino for a while. The others I'd better do myself."

Dolly put the car in gear and held one finger in the air. "See you in the morning. About ten at Sullivan's?"

I nodded. I'd be there.

———

No Sorrow. No resolution. Dolly had depressed me, and there were other things. When I picked up the mail, driving in from Jackson's, there were two envelopes with my address in my own handwriting. That meant two more rejections on *Dead Dancing Women*. I couldn't believe it. I'd been so sure of that book. Dolly and I had exposed people out to kill gentle women of the woods for their own gain. It had everything: plot, characters, place. Somebody would buy it. But, I told myself, not just yet. Being a writer meant extreme patience and a firm belief in my own work. Time, I told myself. I just needed to give it more time. Which was what I was running out of.

I went to my studio and tried to write for a while. The Indian cemetery story was due and I still had research to do. Nobody would be around on Sunday, and who knew if I could get anyone with the Odawa Education Center to talk to me—now that I was persona non grata with the tribe.

What I did, when I saw the northern sky begin to darken, was to get on my bathing suit and do a cannonball from my dock into Willow Lake. A sound decision.

The water was still winter cold, with eddies of warmth. I found the eddies and floated along them, above the muck of leaves and weeds below. The water was opaque, still fogged with winter density. I lay on my back, doing only enough of a stroke to keep myself afloat so I could watch the sky, admire the speed of the dark, rolling clouds, and feel the thrill of danger. Soon lightning thrashed across the northern sky, sidewise. Then came the roll of thunder. I felt it move through the water as it shivered the air.

Time to get out, before I fried in my own lake. The storm brought in much cooler air. I shivered, wrapped a towel around myself, and hurried up my path between growing stands of thick bracken.

Once at the house, I don't know what made me look up. Maybe it was a noise. The air felt different, and not from the temperature dropping. It was more a sense of something happening by the big maple beside the door. A disturbance. I stood beneath the tree as it blew back and forth in the wind. I peered up. A dark shape huddled high on a branch. An animal, clinging near the top of the tree. I couldn't make out what it was in the growing dark. Certainly not a dog. I walked backward up the drive to where I could see better. A small brown bear clung tight to the main trunk of the maple with both front paws, his back paws on a thick branch beneath him.

I took one more look, to make sure what I saw, and ran in the house. I would call the DNR. They would come out and tranquilize him, get him out of my tree, and take him off to a place where he wouldn't bother home owners. The bear would be safer that way, I assured myself as I hurried to the phone. I couldn't simply leave him up my tree. It was too dangerous. The storm would make him nervous. Maybe he would attack me or someone coming up my drive. Thank God, I told myself without thinking, that Sorrow wasn't there to bark and make things worse. I thought again of the animal up the tree, holding on for dear life. Maybe he was like Sorrow, terribly trapped where he didn't belong.

One call flashed at me from my answering machine. I punched the button hurriedly. At first there was nothing. Then I heard barking. I held tight to the phone and listened until the line went dead. My hand shook when I reached down to call the DNR. I punched one number for Information and then hung up. I didn't need to get that bear out of my tree. He didn't need the DNR shooting tranquilizers into him. I wanted no more animals hurt or displaced because of me. The storm would let up soon. The bear would climb down. In the morning he'd be gone and I could feel all right about myself.

# FORTY

THE LOVELY MAHOGANY CASKET sat on a blue satin–draped bier at the front of the large room in Sullivan Murphy's new funeral home. This time the place didn't have the whorehouse look his mother had favored. Everything was sleek and new and understated, except for that bright blue drape which had to be Dolly's choosing.

The photo of Chet I'd seen before was nicely framed and sat atop the closed casket. There weren't many flowers. I'd forgotten all about sending them and would have to do something nice for Dolly later. Guilt settled in: for the lack of flowers, no card, and for picking on her yesterday morning when she stuck her nose in my business. At least the bear had been gone when I looked out that morning. No guilt there. Maybe, I thought, fortune was beginning to smile on me.

Everyone from Leetsville was present, the room filled to overflowing. Eugenia waved from the center of her waitresses and her two cooks. Flora Coy and Anna Scovil sat with other townswomen. In another row, Chief Barnard watched the crowd. Beside him sat Frances, and Charlie, his little boy, who, with his pink cheeks and sparkling eyes, seemed to be feeling a lot better than he had been over the last year. Gertie was there with a passel of customers, hair done up in impossible beehives. The group from The Skunk stood out for their scraggly beards and hungover red eyes. The churches were well represented, though the funeral would be from no church. I supposed people were there to support Dolly. Let her see how much she was loved in town—despite her annoying tickets.

I stood at the back of the earth-toned room with airy bisque drapes, beige carpeting, and beige wallpaper. Muted hymns came from speakers set high at corners of the room.

Detective Brent stood at the back, hands clasped over his groin—the way men stand when they are uncomfortable. He wasn't in uniform, which seemed a blessing, but wore a blue suit, white shirt, and striped tie. When he saw me, his unibrow lowered a notch as he nodded, then looked back to the front, and Dolly.

She was a surprise. The one thing we had not discussed was wardrobe. I'd imagined she would be in a pantsuit. Maybe dark blue, with a dark blue blouse underneath. Dolly in a black dress with white dickey wasn't what I expected. And she had legs. In nylons. And almost high heels. Her hair was pushed back behind her ears and held suspiciously still in a flip. I thought I recognized one of Gertie's sprayed-stiff coifs. Bangs had been cut across her forehead and she had on lipstick, blush, and just a touch of eyeliner and mascara.

The effect was startling. I'd always thought that Dolly, as dear as she was—sometimes—would look like a guy in drag if she wore "lady" clothes, and makeup. Instead she was pretty. Without the guns, she was almost soft. And gracious—nodding to everyone as she solicitously found places for people to sit.

I was proud that I'd taken care dressing. My gray and white print dress, which I'd had for years, was new to everyone up here. I'd found a gray purse in my closet and gray heels to match the purse. I thought I looked rather chic and felt that at least in this I wasn't letting Dolly down.

She smiled at me when I got through the crowd to the front and stood back, admiring her. The limit to our preening was a smile and a couple of admiring head shakes. I gave her a hug for strength.

"Chet's family get here yet?" I asked, after Dolly greeted the guys from the fire department.

She looked worriedly up at the clock on the back wall. "Quarter to eleven. They've got fifteen minutes or they're going to miss the service. Sullivan's not going to wait, and Eugenia's got the food ready to go. We're on a schedule here."

I stood beside her, greeting people as they arrived. A few leaned close and pointedly whispered they were looking forward to hearing me read from my new book. Anna Scovil cornered me on my way to a seat and murmured how the whole town was so very excited about library night and how she hoped I wouldn't forget the cookies.

At precisely eleven, Sullivan walked in and ushered Dolly to a seat. She sat, but turned nervously every few seconds to watch the door.

Sullivan raised his hands and began with a prayer—a kind of non-denominational thing that talked only about the great beyond where Chester Wakowski had gone. He talked about Dolly, said nice things about Chet, then asked anyone who would like to come forward and say a few words to do so at that time.

Dolly was the first one out of her seat. She evidently didn't get the protocols of a funeral. She went up to the front, got behind the narrow podium, and clutched the sides with her hands.

As she cleared her throat, preparing to give her little talk about the goodness of Chester Wakowski, two women walked in. The younger one was Elaine, Chet's sister, dressed neatly in a soft pink dress. The older woman was extremely thin, almost emaciated. Her back was bent and she held firmly to Elaine's arm. Her wrinkled face had light powder dabbed on in places. Her cheeks were bright circles of blush. This had to be Chet's mother from Bloomington, Indiana.

Dolly left the podium and hurried up the main aisle. She introduced herself, and led the women to seats at the front. When the women were settled, Dolly went back to the podium and gave her little speech about what a wonderful man Chet had been and how much she'd missed him all these years. After that she invited his sister and mother to come up and say a few words. Both women declined, shaking their head vehemently. Two men from The Skunk took the microphone and rambled awhile. One brought up the toilet paper incident. He was thankfully interrupted by Tom Flaherty, town raconteur, who never missed an opportunity to tell jokes in front of an audience. He pushed Jason Real aside and regaled us with an Irish joke; then a priest, rabbi, and parson joke; and finally one long story about a ticket Dolly gave him, which he didn't deserve. That seemed to unlock other tongues. A line of men formed at the microphone. The first one started by saying he wasn't one to complain, but ...

Sullivan finally took back the mike and was in the middle of inviting everyone to the luncheon at EATS when the back doors opened again.

An old woman with long braids entered and moved quietly to one side of the room, standing with her arms folded serenely at her waist. Another woman followed. After her, there came two Native American men with sun-darkened skin and deep-set eyes. They silently joined the women. Ten people in all walked in and stood as if at attention. At first there was a collective gasp from the gathered mourners. I looked toward Dolly. Her face was frozen.

These had to be Mary Naquma's people, come to pay their respects to Chet Wakowski. I looked from one to the other, and understood what they were doing. At the same time, I didn't want them to get away. If they knew what had happened out at Sandy Lake, this was our opportunity to talk to them. If they knew where Alfred Naquma was, or Lewis George, or Christine Naquma ... I looked to Detective Brent who stood back in a corner. I bit at my lip, willing him to understand how badly I wanted to ask about the men, and my dog.

Brent nodded and was on his way toward the door, probably to intercept the people as they left, when the door opened a last time and both Lewis George and Alfred Naquma stepped into the big room.

# FORTY-ONE

AN AWKWARD SILENCE FOLLOWED the entrance of the men. The other Indians stood in place, staring straight ahead, a line of determined people. Sullivan, with a brief clearing of his throat, went back into updates on going to the cemetery and then over for the luncheon. When he had finished and signaled the pallbearers to approach the casket, Alfred Naquma, with his flowing black hair thick as sea grass, in a business suit but with a bolo tie and tall boots where one pant leg had caught, strode toward the front. He stood beside Chet, rested one hand on the coffin, the other he put into the air, demanding attention.

He spoke without aid of the microphone, looking over the crowd, nodding, and saying, "I am here today, along with some of my people, to honor your friend, Chet Wakowski." He turned aside to cough in his large hand, then continued, "Chet Wakowski died with my sister, Mary. Maybe it isn't ours to ever know why..."

Here he looked out over the crowd again, but seemed to center first on Dolly, and then his eyes locked with mine, pinning me in place. I felt uncomfortable and desperately wanted to get him alone, demand my dog back, and ask why I was chosen to be the focus of their anger. Though his look was hard to take, I didn't move my eyes from his.

"My sister, Mary, cannot be buried, as she should be. We are asking the police to return her bones to us so they might be placed where she can continue her journey to heaven. This is something my people value above all else. We came here today to ask this favor, and we will now go to your law. We came, also, to show how we respect your dead, and ask that you respect ours in return. Thank you." He gave a final, stiff nod and walked back up the aisle. He didn't stop but went on out the door. I knew Brent was there, but I couldn't stand on ceremony. I pushed through the crowd and got outside in time to see Brent ushering the two men to his car. They had to be heading to the Leetsville police station. Only a few blocks. I would never be allowed to sit in on the interrogation, but I could voice my concern that they had Sorrow and were keeping him to silence me, or to stop both Dolly and me.

Dolly came out of the funeral home.

"One of us should be there." I turned to her.

She nodded. "Brent and Lucky will never let you sit in. Could screw up their case, if it comes to that."

"Then *you've* got to go."

"Me? Look at all these people. First we're going to the cemetery, then I've got to be at Eugenia's for the lunch."

"OK. OK ..." I gave myself time to think. "Look, after the cemetery I'll go to Eugenia's and you go to the station. See what's happening. Just tell them what we suspect. You know, about Orly and Christine. Tell them about Sorrow and how they've got him and keep calling, threatening me."

She looked hard at the waiting hearse, then at the people streaming down the steps of the funeral home. "One time in my life," she said. "I just can't …"

"Dolly, I'll go over to EATS. I'll do a song and dance or whatever it takes, until you get back."

"Show some respect," she spit at me.

"You know what I mean. I'll play hostess. Just a few minutes …"

"See that Chet's mom and sister get a good table." There was grudging agreement.

"I will," I promised. "Just go."

She gave me one last reluctant look as we gathered for the casket being pushed to the porch and the waiting hearse.

There were fewer people at the cemetery than at the funeral home. The Native Americans who had come with Alfred and Lewis were gone. I had the feeling that a burial and buffet lunch weren't what they'd come for.

As soon as the prayers and throwing of flowers down on the casket was finished, we all filed away from the freshly dug grave. I nodded to Dolly to get going. There was one last flash of rebellion before she hopped in her patrol car and sped off.

Many of the tables were occupied by the time I got over to EATS. Plates, in front of the seated mourners, were piled high and folks were calling across the room to each other. There was buzzing about the appearance of the Native Americans, the man who got up to speak— and "What was that all about?" There was a lot of conjecture and a lot of arguing back and forth.

I stopped at each table, telling everyone Dolly would be right along. "A little business came up …" They clucked or nodded and mumbled things about such a shame, poor Chet.

Eugenia had outdone herself. EATS actually looked pretty. The windows were open and the smoke had cleared. Each table held a small white vase filled with blue wildflowers. The buffet table, behind a line of people, stood against the side wall, covered with blue plastic paper and white ribbons. The hot pans of food were interspersed with bowls of salad, baskets of bread, and tubs of butter. Off to one side, next to the glass case at the front, was a smaller table lined with pies and tarts and fruit.

"Here she is now." Flora Coy turned from the buffet to call over to Gertie, who called out to me.

"We're all wondering what the heck was going on there, Emily? Tell you the truth, I don't blame the man. Police have no business keeping his sister from being buried." Gertie shook her head. "That girl really from the Odawa?"

"That's what it looks like. Still, there are questions…" I made my way to an empty table, hoping to hold it for Dolly and her guests.

"Nice of the Indians to come anyway," Gertie called after me, turning to talk to others around her.

"You mean 'Native Americans,'" Anna Scovil shot over her shoulder.

Elaine Wakowski and Chet's mother walked in right then, looking bewildered by the crowd. I waved them over, introduced myself, and invited them to join the buffet line.

When they came back with filled plates, Mildred and Elaine settled across from me and began to eat without another word.

"Dolly will be right back," I leaned close to them though they hadn't asked. "She had some business at her…eh…office."

"She gave Chet a nice funeral," Mildred Wakowski said, her wrinkled lips pulling into a tight line I thought must be a smile.

Elaine nodded in agreement and said, "Very nice."

That seemed to be the extent of their small talk.

"Lovely casket," I commented, smiling to show how tame I was.

"Very nice," Mildred said.

"Dolly spent twenty-five hundred dollars on it. She wanted something Chet would have been proud of."

"Really? Well, she got it all right. Chet would have been pleased—I suppose," Elaine said around a mouthful of fried chicken.

I waited just a minute. This was Dolly's business. I had no right to stick my nose in ... "And this luncheon, too," I said, unable to help myself. I looked at the filled tables and people standing near the walls with plates in their hands. "Must've cost her quite a bit."

The women glanced around the restaurant. Both nodded, though they seemed less than pleased.

Mildred leaned close to me. "We don't know a soul. I'd never have done something like this."

She looked at her daughter, who nodded emphatically.

"Will Dolly be here soon?" Elaine dabbed at her mouth. "I've got a check for her. We want to pay our fair share."

"Of course," Mildred interrupted. "We weren't expecting anything this elaborate. Chet's been gone thirteen years. It's not as if he died yesterday. I'll bet most of these people ..." She looked around the room. "I'll just bet they didn't even know my boy."

"Probably not," I said. "But they're Dolly's friends."

"Oh, oh, oh—yes," Mildred said, and blinked with each exclamation. "Still, it needn't have been so ... overdone. And to have those Indians come in. What was that about? I thought maybe we were having a powwow or something."

I bit at my lip. Judgmental voice. Smug face. Poor Chet, I told myself. No wonder he'd escaped up north.

Elaine set her fork beside her plate and fumbled in her large, black purse. "If we have to leave before she gets back, you can give her our check."

"I thought you were staying awhile?" I remembered Dolly's cleaning spree.

Mildred and Elaine shook their head as one. "We've got to get back today. In fact, we should be on the road as soon as possible."

"If you'll just hand her this, with our thanks." Elaine held the check out to me, snapped her bag shut, and pushed her plate away. "Sorry it isn't for more, but she went way overboard."

Her mother nodded firmly. "Much too elaborate."

I couldn't help looking down. Two hundred dollars. No half and half here. Dolly was going to be stuck with the greater share of everything. I palmed the check just as Dolly walked in. Later she could see what Chet's family had done to her. Right now everyone was taking her hand and expressing regret at her loss.

When she could finally sit down with us, I leaned close to see what kind of luck she'd had with Detective Brent.

"I told him everything." She shook her head at me and kept her voice low. "But it's not going to matter."

My stomach sank to somewhere down around my ankles.

"They lawyered up," she said. "Two guys came from the tribal council. I guess Brent was hoping for a confession. We've got nothing on either of them. They had to let them go."

"Crap," I said under my breath. "I figured this would happen."

"Yeah, well, two people are dead. Maybe more. I'm not letting either one of them get away with it." Dolly's little face settled into determination.

"Did Brent get anything out of them?"

"They want Mary's bones."

"Did Brent ask Alfred where his father, Orly, is?"

"The old man is dead."

"And his sister, Christine? Is she dead, too? Pretty unlucky family."

"Said he hasn't seen her in years."

"Where were they while we were all hunting for them?"

"Said out of town. Casino business."

"And nobody at the casino knew about it?"

Dolly shrugged.

"Did Brent get addresses? There is still Sorrow. I'll have to do …"

Dolly gave me a brief thumbs up then leaned in to speak to Mildred and Elaine, asking how they enjoyed the luncheon and if they thought she did Chet proud with the coffin and the service and the burial. Elaine was quick to say she'd given me a check to cover their share of the cost. Dolly smiled and said, "Thank you." I kept my face straight and took a deep breath. I was about to blurt out the figure, but stopped myself.

"Dolly," I tapped her arm. "I want those addresses."

She nodded.

"Have you got them with you?"

She nodded again. "But I can't go out there and talk to them. I'd get in trouble. Those lawyers would be all over me and Lucky."

"Nothing's stopping me from hunting for my dog."

She shook her head. "Nothing stopping you at all. I just don't want you going there alone. Your last trip didn't end so good."

"I'll get Bill to go with me."

She thought a minute, then nodded. "Then I'll go after Christine. She's got to be out there somewhere and somebody knows how to find her. I called Lena Smith on the way back here but she doesn't know a thing. She did give me the name of an old woman in Peshawbestown. Could be a relative, an aunt, to the Naqumas. Wasn't sure, but she said to go see her."

"Anything said about the gun that killed Mary and Chet?"

"Probably long gone by now. Chet and Mary were shot up close, execution style."

I took a deep breath. "Think the police will give the Indians their bones back?"

Dolly shook her head. "Brent says that's all we've got. He's calling the bones a part of an ongoing investigation."

"What about DNA? They get anything out of the bone marrow?"

"Something about mitochondrial DNA. Not as good but it'll stand up in court. Alfred Naquma offered his DNA through his attorneys. That should clear up who she is soon. But once Mary's buried, we'll lose any leverage we've got."

Dolly handed me the paper with the addresses I wanted. I folded Elaine's check in half and pushed it back at Dolly. Dolly glanced down at the check, then up at the two women, who had the good grace to redden and turn away. She looked back down at the check one last time, then slid it across the table to Elaine.

"I'll take care of it myself," Dolly said, keeping her voice low. She settled up straight in her chair. "I did what I wanted to do for him." She shook her head a couple of times. "I take care of my family."

I thought Elaine would apologize or insist Dolly take the check. She looked at Mildred, who looked back at her. Both were well pleased. Elaine picked up the check and tucked it back in her purse with no fuss.

"Guess I'll go get some of this food, since I'm paying." Dolly put her hands behind her head and stretched hard, an odd movement in her black-and-white feminine dress. She made to get out of her chair but hesitated a minute.

"I figured you two would be going right back home," she lied to the women. "No place in town for you. My house way too small ..."

They sputtered and stammered and assured Dolly they were leaving right after lunch.

Dolly said, "Good," got up, swaggered a little, and made her way toward what was left of the buffet. She stopped to talk to table after table of friends and never came back to sit with us, not even when Mildred and Elaine got up to leave, waving half-heartedly in Dolly's direction.

# FORTY-TWO

BILL'S GPS SAID WE were in front of the address we hunted for. I saw nothing. The machine urged us to turn, then sounded disappointed as she ordered us to go back. We did. The unpaved road we were on had no houses. There was thick forest on either side; no lights and no driveways leading into anything.

"Has to be the wrong address," Bill said, stopping in the middle of the road to look hard to the left and then to the right, furiously pushing his glasses up his nose.

"Would they have dared to give Detective Brent the wrong address?" I wondered.

"Be a dumb thing to do," Bill shrugged and moved the car a few yards, searching the side of the road again.

It was getting dark. The woods around us were deep and already murky as night. Somewhere, in the trees, a bird sang a nesting song, a kind of warning to the other birds. A stand of pines on one side gave that sigh they give at dusk, just before the wind dies completely. Twenty yards ahead of us a doe and her twin fawns stepped out to look around and then leap to the other side, babies tripping over their own feet.

Bill looked at me. I looked at him. "Pretty isolated place," he said.

We were out beyond Peshawbestown, down a road that connected to a smaller road and then deep into the woods.

"The GPS says the address is here. Why aren't we seeing anything?" I said.

"Want to get out and walk it? Maybe we're just not looking at things right."

I agreed. We left the car at the side of the dirt. He walked one way. I walked the other.

The empty road, the deep shadows in the trees, the quiet—it gave me the chills. I wrapped my arms around myself and walked slowly, glad for Bill close by. It was a good thing I hadn't been stupid enough to come out looking for the men alone. Getting Sorrow back was about all I had on my mind, but becoming another floating dead body wasn't high on my list of other things to do.

"Hey," Bill called, "think I found a drive." I hurried to where he pointed to a grassy opening between trees. No mailbox. No name. And so narrow we'd driven by twice without seeing it.

"I'll get the car," he said, and loped back to where the car was parked. He drove up and turned in the opening between the trees.

We left the car pulled in off the road and started up the almost invisible driveway. Bill had brought a flashlight. It wasn't very big and not very powerful, but it illuminated enough to keep us from falling over downed limbs and into deep ruts. I took Bill's arm and stayed close to his side.

Just when we were about to give up and turn back, we stepped into a wide clearing. The moon, just rising, lighted the edges of leaves, lighted the grass and the eaves of a small house.

Bill's flash picked up a huge, round fire pit in the middle of the wide clearing. At its center, a triangular stand of peeled logs held a cooking pot. The fire was long dead. The grass in the clearing was tall. In the light of Bill's flash we could see the narrow house with twin gables, but not a light, or sign of a human being, anywhere.

"Sorrow!" I called and heard my voice echo around us. "Sorrow!"

"Sorrow!" Bill called too. We stood still and listened. For a moment I thought I heard a bark, but it was more like a sound inside my head.

"Should we knock?" I whispered. Having given away that we were here, I felt exposed.

"Might as well. No car. No lights. Still, let's knock. If he's in there at least it will give him something to think about."

Nobody answered though Bill pounded hard, first at the front door and then at the back door. We waited, knocked again, and then Bill shone his light around the back clearing. Another opening in the trees, only wider than out on the road. This was the entrance. In the clearing Bill picked out where a car usually parked, where the weeds were worn down. A footpath, trampled to bare earth, led up to the house.

"You want to go?" Bill asked after we stood still awhile, listening and hoping maybe we'd hear a car pulling in or somebody talking or see a light go on in the house.

I nodded, uneasy about trespassing, as we were, here in the dark.

We picked our way carefully back around the house and out to the car.

"You got the next address?"

In the dome light, I checked the paper Dolly had given me. Two addresses. No name attached to either. I didn't know if we'd just visited

Alfred Naquma or Lewis George. And didn't know who the next one might be.

Bill programmed the GPS with the new address and we set off the way we'd come in, back up the dirt road and out to M22. At the stop sign, we made a left and kept heading north. The road where we were told to turn was about a mile or more down. We turned and soon there was a gong and the GPS said we were there.

Lights this time. A yard of lights. Lights on in a big log house. We walked quietly onto the wide, covered porch. Bill knocked as I stood back.

The door opened and Alfred Naquma filled the open space, blocking out the light behind him. He made a huge, dark silhouette.

"Yes?" he said to Bill.

Bill introduced himself, said he was from the *Northern Statesman*, then put up his hands as Alfred began to close the door.

I stepped from behind Bill. "Mr. Naquma, I need to talk to you. Not for the paper. Someone's taken my dog. I'm getting phone calls. I'm being threatened. If you know anything about this, or where my dog is, I have to know."

There was a moment of surprise, and then of hesitation. Alfred stepped back from the door. I thought he was going to slam it in our faces. Instead, he held it open, inviting us to enter.

The room we walked into was large, with a soaring, cedar-lined ceiling. Pendant lights hung on long cords, down over built-in leather sofas. The effect was of softness with a touch of gold. Native American rugs covered the floors and a tapestry depicting a buffalo hunt covered two walls. The place was beautiful.

He motioned for us to sit on one of the dark leather sofas, then took a chair, leaned forward, and set his hands between his knees. His head was down, hair hanging forward over his shoulders. He looked like a defeated man.

"What is this about your dog?" He looked up after taking a deep, sad breath.

"Someone took him. They've been calling my house saying I'll get him back when your sister's bones are returned or when I stop looking into the murders. Things like that. The last call, I heard Sorrow barking. If your people are doing this, I want you to ask them to return him. I can't do anything to help you get your sister's bones returned. I am in no position..."

"That Detective Brent said something about a dog. I thought it was a trick."

I shook my head. "No trick."

"Did you know the voice? The one on the phone?"

I nodded. "Your friend, Lewis George. He came to my house once and almost mesmerized Sorrow. I can only imagine he thought it would be easy to take my dog and get whatever you want from me."

"If it is because you don't want publicity about what happened there at Sandy Lake," Bill said gruffly, sitting at the edge of the sofa as if he planned to be out of there soon, "Emily's still going to keep writing the stories. If she doesn't write them, I will."

"I wouldn't expect her to stop. I think ... well ... let me look into what's happened." He stood up. Our signal to leave. I wasn't quite ready.

"Why would your people protect you?" I asked. "Mary and Orly and Christine were their people, too. I would imagine they'd be clamoring for you to be put in prison, if you had anything to do with the murders. Is it because you have some position at the casino? Do you always threaten people who cross you?"

I was plenty angry but Alfred Naquma looked at me in a way I hoped I'd never be looked at again. The back of my neck was yelling, "Run!"

He said nothing. He walked to the door. With his face blank and his dark eyes like stone, he said, "I hope you don't think your dog is here."

I was slow to shake my head, then looked beyond him and yelled out, "SORROW!"

No answering bark. I waited a few seconds, and then agreed that Sorrow probably wasn't there.

"I will be in touch," he said, holding the door for us, "very soon."

On our way to Traverse City, where I had left the Jeep, I assured Bill that I wouldn't hold back on any of the story.

"I didn't think you would," he said over a k.d. lang CD he'd put in for the ride to town. "And I've got something to offer you. Not much. But something. We need an obit writer—in a couple of weeks. Won't be full-time but I can throw in stories for the Sunday sections. Human interest stuff. At least you'll have a pretty steady income. With your other work ... I mean, just until one of your books sells."

I thanked him, and said I would begin reading the obits immediately, for the style.

"Nothing too creative," he warned.

I agreed to tone down the fiction. "I'm thinking real estate, too. Could I do that, do you think?"

"Don't see why not. With everything, you could make it. Might be busy in summer. But then there are the long winters to write."

As we drove into the parking lot of the newspaper, I reached over and touched Bill's hand on the wheel. It seemed only fair to warn him things might change.

"I really appreciate how you're helping," I said. "The only thing in the way is that I may be going back to Ann Arbor."

"What brought this on?" he asked, pulling his hand from under mine.

"Jackson and I..."

"Oh..." He looked confused. "So... maybe back to the *Ann Arbor Times*, eh?"

"I haven't gotten that far."

"Well, whatever you decide, I wish you luck. Keep in touch. I'll keep the obits open awhile."

I promised I'd let him know as soon as anything was decided, got in the Jeep, and drove to Kalkaska where I stopped for three bags of chocolate chip cookies for library night before going home.

# FORTY-THREE

THE LIBRARY WAS PACKED with people. Librarians from surrounding towns were there for this very special event, along with most Leetsvillians. I had arrived early, store-bought bags of chocolate chip cookies in hand. The cookies got only a minor look of consternation from Anna Scovil before being removed from the bag and piled in an orderly manner on a cut-glass plate.

Coffee and tea were ready in tall silver urns, with sugar and cream beside them. The cups weren't Styrofoam, but an assortment of china cups Anna must have scrounged from everyone in town.

The charge was three dollars each to get in for the evening—including coffee, tea, and cookies. Not a bad deal, I thought, and smiled at those assembled, tea cups in their hands.

I nodded to people who nodded formally back at me. Evidently this was a state occasion and therefore everyone was dignified, dressed in their best, and prepared to sit through family history, lady's slippers, and whatever it was I'd come up with.

Gertie had put in a busy day. Most of the women's heads were pouffed and sprayed. The gentlemen had trimmed their beards and even the long-haired men from The Skunk had their hair slicked back and stuck behind their ears.

Once every seat was taken, Anna clapped her hands and introduced Ronald Williams, who stepped forward to polite applause and slapped an enormous manuscript on the desk Anna had provided for the readers. I wondered if anyone else in the room felt like groaning, but I remembered Anna had warned him. Twenty minutes. I hoped she was going to check her watch and keep him honest.

"The Parkinsons came to this area in 1856 ...," he began, stretching his long neck out of the white shirt collar that didn't fit him. He spoke in a monotone that only got worse as he picked up page after page and read to us: dates, names of places in the East his mother's people had come from. Then we were on to the Williamses—his father's family—back to when they first came to Leetsville and how they knew the John Leets family who'd settled here first.

I sat at attention, keeping a bright look of interest pasted on my face. About the time Dolly finally got there, taking a standing position against the wall among the travel books, I began to fade. I checked my watch and saw Ronald Williams had fifteen minutes to go.

He read on. The Williamses started a farm.

Ten minutes to go. Joshua Williams opened a tackle shop in Leetsville.

Ronald's voice droned through the next two years of minutes from the church society.

Eight minutes. We learned how the one-room school got started— not early teachers or even other students, only a list of Williamses who went there.

Five minutes. I zoned out. There was a titter of laughter. Something I'd missed. A joke. He was looking over the audience, a wide grin on his face. He wiped it away and went back to reading.

Four.

Three.

Two.

One. I looked over at Anna. Surely she would pop out of her chair and move on to lady's slipper slides before everyone fell sound asleep. I'd already heard a heavy snore coming from behind me.

Ronald read on. Anna sat with her hands in her lap, in her front-row seat, a look of rapt attention on her face.

"Twenty minutes is up." Someone called out behind me. Maybe the snorer had popped awake and checked his watch.

Others added murmurs of polite agreement.

Anna Scovil rose, cheeks red, and approached Ronald, who hadn't heard a thing. She touched his forearm, then shook it. He frowned as he looked first at the hand on his page-turning arm, then up at Anna. "Your time is up, I'm afraid," she said, smiling, but not letting go of him.

"Well, I'm just getting to the part..." He pointed one long, crooked finger down at the page he'd been reading. "I know everybody'll be interested in when the Williams' barn burned down."

"Oh, I'm sure it's all interesting," Anna said, but sighed. "We have other people waiting to speak, however. Maybe another time."

Ronald wasn't about to give up that easily. One of his hands folded around the edge of the table and held on. Anna, in a smart move, let go of his arm and began to clap. Everyone joined in, clapping loudly. There were a few bravos. Ronald could do nothing but take a bow, gather his worn manuscript, and go back to his seat.

Winnie Lorbach and Anna set up the slide projector, asking people to move to one side or the other so everyone could see the screen pulled down at the front. Winnie snapped a tray filled with slides into the machine, got the control in hand, and waved an imperious hand at Dolly to hit the light switch beside her.

Winnie was a good photographer. One by one, different varieties of lady's slippers moved past on the screen. I'd never seen the beauty there, myself, but with Winnie describing them and pointing out differences and telling us where they grew and how they grew and what treasures they were, I thought I'd take another look when mine bloomed, next spring. Maybe I'd take some photographs.

Her presentation was smooth and interesting. She put up the slide that announced "The End" at fifteen minutes, not even using her allotted time. Dolly turned the lights on and people put up their hands to share stories of their own lady's slipper finds. A couple stood to show a few photos of lady's slippers they had taken and get pointers from Winnie.

Everyone was awake, but Anna Scovil stood to say there would be a break before Emily Kincaid read from a work in progress. She offered more coffee, cookies, tea.

"And don't anyone leave yet," she warned as chairs scraped back and people talked. "I'm sure you are all looking forward to hearing Emily."

Dolly came over and took the empty seat next to me. I told her about my trip out to see the two men in Peshawbestown. "Bill went along. We found Alfred Naquma, even got inside. I'm not sure he knows what Lewis George is doing. I came away confused. Maybe Lewis George is the one they're all protecting. This keeps going in circles. I feel like a dog chasing my own tail. I'm getting nowhere."

"I think I got something on Christine Naquma." She leaned close and whispered in my ear. "That old woman Lena Smith put me on to? She's a great aunt or something like that. A relative, anyway, to Christine's mother. Not one good word to say about Orly. Called him a mean drunk who destroyed his own family."

"Whew." It was so good to hear one of us had learned something. "Any idea where Christine is?"

"The old woman knows how to contact her. Belongs to a group of dancers in Colorado, she said. Guess they're well known and travel to powwows around the country. She called somebody while I was there and whoever she talked to said Christine was dancing in the West and she would find her."

"Great." I congratulated Dolly as people filed back through the rows of seats and a large woman stood waiting for Dolly to get out of her seat.

Anna introduced me once everyone settled down, calling me the town celebrity, their very own novelist, and also a journalist known to everyone in Michigan. Over the applause for that out-of-proportion introduction, I gathered my pages together and went to stand at the table, pages too far down in front of me to be seen. I gave them the synopsis of the book I'd put together, taking them through the surprise ending that I assured them would astound the reader. There was a murmur and Flora Coy, in the second row, turned around to look at people behind her. She mouthed words at somebody. I read, bending to see, as Ronald had. I squinted, filled in words I couldn't quite make out and read what I figured had to be a pretty exciting part…

*"Mister." The old woman in tattered skirt and torn lace blouse pulled at the sleeve of Randall Jarvis's tweed sport coat. "Mister," she said again, frantic as he shook her off.*

*"Go away," he growled, bunching his shoulders up to his ears. The last thing he wanted was a beggar hanging on him. He had had enough trouble staying on his feet since the heart attack. If he didn't concentrate, keep one foot plodding straight in front of the other, he might fall and die there in the gutter. The worst thing he could imagine happening at the end of what he thought of as an illustrious life.*

I read for a while, looking up to smile—as all good public speakers must learn to do.

I figured I was close to my ten minutes when someone tapped me on the shoulder. I turned to find Flora Coy standing beside me, her eyelids fluttering behind her large, pink-framed glasses. I gave her a perturbed look and kept on reading. She tapped again.

"What is it, Flora?" I hissed at her.

She leaned very close and whispered, "*Witness for the Prosecution.*"

My mouth dropped open. I gulped a couple of times. The words she'd said ran circles in my brain. *Witness for the Prosecution, Witness for the Prosecution, Witness for the Prosecution…*

I knew that title. But from where?

"The movie, dear," Flora bent to my ear. "I thought I'd better stop you. Others recognized the plot…"

I groaned. Tyrone Power. Marlene Dietrich—both the cool woman and the old tart. Charles Laughton—oh my God. My aging barrister. How far had I fallen that I didn't recognize an Agatha Christie plot? What a complete fool I had made of myself.

I looked at the faces in front of me. Most were sad. No one looked back. They stared at the floor or up at the pressed tin ceiling.

I couldn't move. I stood immobilized with my hand over my mouth until Anna hurried over to nervously thank me for my presentation. There was polite applause. Anna invited everyone to finish the cookies, have another cup of coffee, and come back often to the library where new books would be appearing soon, thanks to their generous contributions. I gathered my papers and left the building.

# FORTY-FOUR

I SAT IN A metal lawn chair, poking a stick at the fire I had built down on the beach. The water lapped rhythmically along the shoreline. Flames burned bright orange in the pit. I was invisible in the dark. Embers glowed beneath the logs as, one by one, I fed the manuscript pages to the fire, enjoying the brief white flame, the edges curling inward, the quick, bright disintegration.

There was no excuse this time. What I'd judged as superb creativity was only a flair for mimicry, or outright plagiarism. The people in my head weren't mine. They belonged to other writers; other stories. Somewhere in my brain there was a blind spot. Once I claimed people as my own, I couldn't see or recall where they'd come from. A fatal flaw in a writer. How could I trust anything I wrote?

I felt sorry for myself and mad at myself at the same time. I hadn't wanted to wait around for the embarrassed comments the audience would come up with. Sympathy wasn't good for my deflated ego. Nor were the suggestions Flora and the others might offer, like talking my next idea over with them before beginning to write. I wanted to get home, be alone, and burn something, anything, completely.

When Dolly Wakowski called my name and came out of the darkness, down the path from my house, I wasn't happy to see her. I didn't want to see anyone, maybe for days, or weeks. Dolly said nothing. She squatted in the sand and stared into the flames along with me. After a while, she grabbed a handful of the manuscript and fed the pages, one by one, into the fire, then watched as each burned.

"Everybody gets fooled, ya know," she said after a while, her voice making a small place in the quiet around us. Her profile, outlined in the red glow of my bonfire, looked old and gnarly and wise.

"Yeah," I said, not mollified, "how could I be so stupid? I think it's because of that other book, the one about you and me and those poor old ladies. Threw me off my stride."

"This wasn't the first time," she cruelly reminded me. "'Fool me once, shame on you. Fool me twice, shame on me.' Now you've been fooled twice and you won't forget again."

"Forget! I won't ever write again. That's enough." I poked at a dying log with my stick. Sparks shot into the night air. I held down burning pages as they tried to fly away. "In fact, I'm leaving here. That's enough. You people have stolen my dog, humiliated me, threatened me, put me in danger…"

She didn't say a word. When I turned to her, she nodded.

"Jackson and I might get back together," I said. "It's worth a second try. No use staying here, fooling myself that I can write a salable book. I'm tired of fighting everything and everybody."

"Yeah. I suppose you are."

She was maddening. I wanted her to argue with me, not agree.

"If lightning should strike and I sell that other book, I'll make sure you get your cut."

"Don't see me worrying." She poked at the last burning pages.

There was the smack of a bird out on the dark water. Maybe a loon. Or maybe it was my miserable beaver, watching us.

"You think I'm making a mistake," I said.

She gave something like a little laugh, but not a happy one. "You *know* you're making a mistake. Just going back to what you ran away from. Next time it won't be so easy to leave."

"Jackson's changed. He's gotten older ..."

"Yeah. Three year's worth." She stood, stretched, and started back up toward the house, calling over her shoulder, "OK. Call me when you get over the self-pity. I don't need to hear any more of this crap."

She was disappearing into the darkness when I called after her. "Thanks for coming, Dolly. I ... appreciate it."

"Knew you'd be down." She hesitated where she stood, only a shadow among the ferns. "You probably don't care but I found Christine Naquma."

I said nothing. I knew she still stood there. "You know what else?" Odd, her disembodied voice coming out of blackness. "Eugenia had my dad's discharge papers from the army up in her vestibule tonight. He was in Vietnam. Can you imagine? Kind of weird seeing papers with his name on 'em. Guess he was real after all."

Bones and Indians and murder and Dolly's mythical family had all faded to the back of my brain. Before I could come up with an answer, she was gone.

I sat on, adding logs as the fire burned to cinders. Maybe I would sleep out here, I told myself, rocking back and forth in my rickety old chair. Something so clean about water and sand and fire and night. Depression settled on me. I listened to the beaver swimming. I listened to the fire crack and spit. I left my chair and lay down flat in the sand with my hands behind my head.

I didn't see the figure silently approaching. I saw nothing until the man loomed above me, long hair across his shoulders, eyes reflecting dying flames. It wasn't Lewis George. But it wasn't anyone I wanted to be alone with, here on my deserted beach.

Alfred Naquma.

I scrambled to my knees and then held still. I found I had no fear left in me. And not even any anger. The man's face was shadowed. I didn't really feel in danger, but still I moved my hand slowly toward a log that lay half in and half out of the fire. It would make a great weapon, if he came after me.

Despite the isolation of my beach, despite what I had believed about this man, something else was going on. He bent his long body and settled silently to the sand, one hand on either knee. Still, he said nothing.

The firelight played off his face, red off glistening skin. The long black hair hung straight. With a sense of inevitability, I stayed crouched where I was.

"I came to apologize," he said, voice across the crackling fire like a voice from a cave.

I listened and said nothing.

"I have already told my people how sorry I am. For the trouble I caused them. For forcing friends to do things they would never do. I've brought shame on our tribe. I cannot let them go on protecting me."

He stopped. I held my breath and settled back on my heels.

"I am sorry about your dog. I didn't know. Nor did I know people .lied to protect me at the casino. I have put friends in danger. Not anymore. Thirteen years is too long not to speak. I have been told you are a decent woman. My poor friend Lewis, the only true father I've ever known, thought he could force you to stop the police from looking into Mary's murder. He thought he could make you keep stories out of the newspaper. Lewis thinks a father must protect his son."

"Where's my dog?" I demanded, braver and stronger.

He put up a hand.

"When my grandfather died, Lewis took me into his home. The tribe sent me to college. I have too much to be grateful to them for to hurt them now."

"My dog…"

"I heard that the police are after my sister, Christine. She had nothing to do with what I'm going to tell you," he went on. "In return for what I am about to say, I want your friends to leave Christine alone. She has a good life. She is safe and away from this place. I hope you will take me at my word and do nothing further to contact her."

I couldn't make any promises. "I'll listen, but Dolly Wakowski wants this solved. Chet was her husband. She has as much right to the truth as you have."

Alfred nodded, then threw his head back a moment and combed his fingers through his long hair. A sliver of a moon was rising. Pale white light glinted off his shining skin.

"I am the only one who knows that truth," he said.

I waited.

"Our parents died when we were young," he began. "There was only my father's father left to care for us. He had the curse of alcoholism. Long before my grandfather forced us to leave the reservation and go to Sandy Lake, he started drinking. When our people confronted him about his drinking, he got angry and took me and my two sisters away. Orly Naquma was a cruel man. We were beaten many times. He threatened to kill us if we said a word about our life there at Sandy Lake. To get to school we had to walk many, many miles. Sometimes the bus was gone before we made it to the main road. If we were late coming home, it meant another beating. We were to work the skins for him. Help him get money, but none of it was for us. I felt sorriest for my two sisters. Mary made trouble for him. Christine was too quiet." He stopped and drew a deep breath.

"The girls got to an age when they wanted a normal life. Mary stole what she could from Orly and sold hides on the side. Eventually she bought an old car and kept it way off from our house, among trees. She enrolled in beauty school. She was out of high school then and supposed to be working, bringing money home to him. When he found she was going to beauty school in Traverse City, that she had stolen his skins, he beat her. That time it was very bad. Then that last day, when she came with Chet Wakowski to say she wanted her clothes and that she was leaving, our grandfather was the only one at the cabin."

He paused a long time. I thought maybe his story was finished, stopped because he didn't know what happened next.

"I wasn't there when it happened or I would have stopped him. At least, I need to think I would have stopped him. Grandfather had been drinking all day. He was terrible when I got home. At first I didn't know what he meant when he bragged, 'I fixed her. I fixed her like I'll fix the rest of you.' I ignored him but soon I knew something terrible had happened. Something to do with Mary."

"Are you saying you didn't...?"

He looked at me, reflection of moonlight in his eyes.

"Let me finish. Then I'll answer your questions."

I waited, thinking what I should do. Dolly and Detective Brent had to know. I wasn't the authority here.

"As the day went on, Orly Naquma sat in his rocking chair, in the middle of the room. He drank, finishing one bottle of whiskey and starting another. After a while the old man began to laugh. He said he had taught Mary a lesson. Now the rest of us would know who was in charge. No child disobeyed an elder, he said. He ranted until I asked him, finally, what lesson he'd taught Mary."

Alfred took a deep breath. A shudder passed over his shoulders. "I wish I didn't ask him. To this day, I wish I didn't know what he'd done."

"What ... was it?" Like Alfred, I didn't really want to know.

"She came home to get her possessions, he said. That was when she told Orly she was running away with a white man. A married white man. She would shame us and herself, Grandfather said.

"'I fixed her.' That's what he shouted at me. 'And that man, too. He won't be sniffing around an Indian woman again.'

"It dawned on me, what he was saying. He'd really done what he'd threatened us with so many times. He'd killed Mary, a spirited, hopeful soul who asked little from life. I put my hands on him and shook him hard, demanding he tell me what he'd done. He struck me a few times; hit me with that whiskey bottle once. Then he stumbled back into his chair and began to laugh harder and harder. I prayed he would choke and die. But, God help me, he didn't."

The last words were coughed out. It took time for him to recover his voice.

"He shot my sister, and her friend, he told me. When the man was dead, he got him into our rowboat. In the rowboat he tied cement blocks to the man's feet. In the middle of the lake, he pushed him overboard, then went back for Mary.

"Mary wasn't to have even a watery burial. He put her body on the raft I'd made when we were small and towed it to the middle of the lake. He left her there, on top of the raft, for the birds to peck and the sun to rot."

He stopped, picked up a stick, and poked at the dying fire.

"I couldn't do anything," he went on. "I couldn't move. Hate rose and came out through my skin. As if my whole body was on fire, I needed to take his skinny neck in my hands and squeeze so tight his eyes would pop out of his ugly face. I wanted him dead. I told myself that I was now a man and vengeance was my right."

The voice hardened. The words came at me clipped and angry. Between us, hovering over the embers, hung the scene he was reliving. Ugliness and evil. I needed to hear what he said, but wished it weren't true, that no human being had to live the way Alfred, Mary, and Christine had lived.

"I waited until he passed out," he went on. "The way he did every night. When the chair stopped rocking and his laughter dwindled to a drool and a hiccup; when that bottle rolled from his lap to the floor..."

I sensed something coming that would challenge my sense of morality. If I could have stopped him, I would have. His voice was direct, words loosening and tumbling. He was going to tell me a terrible truth.

"When I knew he'd passed out I went outside and brought a can of gas in from the shed."

I held my breath.

"I poured the gas around his chair, where he slept. When I got to the door, I lit a match and threw it back at him. The fire caught in little rivers, circling the chair and circling my grandfather. The fire crept up his pant legs. It moved over his body. When I took my last look he was aglow with flames; struggling up from his chair. He screamed. I closed the door and slipped a tree branch through the handle so it couldn't be opened."

The voice stopped a moment. As if he was reliving that night, his face, illuminated by the last log I'd put on to burn, was horrified. He watched as his grandfather was consumed again, in my fire.

"I looked through the window to make sure he burned, and took great satisfaction in the pillar of fire writhing inside the house." He put his hands on his knees and rose to his full height. "I went back three times and poured gasoline around the cabin. Three fires. When it was over I threw tobacco on the ashes and said prayers for his damned soul.

"So you see, Emily, it wasn't my sister, Mary, or Chet Wakowski that I murdered. It was my own grandfather."

# FORTY-FIVE

"AND MARY...?" I PICTURED her poor body on that raft, in the middle of a cold, dark lake.

"You mean, did I leave her there? No. I rowed out. I tipped her body into the water. I should have brought her to shore and buried her, but I was afraid. The house was still burning. If someone saw and came back... I would be charged with murder.

"There is guilt attached to what I did to Mary, that I didn't have the courage to bury her."

"You were a boy."

He made a scoffing noise. "Old enough to kill my grandfather. Not old enough to take care of my sister's body. That's what I owe her."

"And that's why you want her buried now."

"Our people have had enough of desecration."

"We've got to go into town," I said, drawing a deep breath. "You have to tell your story to the authorities. I won't lie to you, Alfred. You'll probably go to prison for the murder of your grandfather."

"I know what I have to do. I'm ready. We had to come here first."

"We?" I looked up the path to the house. That "we" made me nervous. I didn't know what I was dealing with.

He stood and swept sand from his pant legs. "Lewis is with me. I asked him for a half an hour to tell my story." He stopped talking to listen.

I listened, too. There was a faint sound from up near the drive. Then a wild sound.

Barking.

More joyous barking came down the path at us and Sorrow was on me, paws on my chest, knocking me backward then licking my face. I grabbed his ears and pulled his matted face into mine. His breath was awful but how could I care about that? He was home. He was as happy to see me as I was to see him. Sorrow was back, soon snuffling around the campfire, then bounding back up the path as Lewis George made his way down to where we waited.

———

I followed Lewis George's pickup into town. Sorrow sat beside me in the front seat. I'd put him in the back but he demanded that his body be close to mine. I drove carefully, leaning over every few minutes to rub my head against his. I never imagined how sweet it could be to be loved this completely. And how necessary, after listening to Alfred Naquma's horrible story of life with that man. Picturing Orly burning didn't faze me now. If ever there had been justification for a death, Alfred, only a boy, had been justified. But I was uneasy. Where had Christine been through all of this? Had she been protecting her brother for the last thirteen years? How could she live with herself, knowing Mary was at the bottom of the lake?

And, if Christine hadn't lived with Lewis George too, then where had she gone? Was she sent away deliberately? There were so many questions left to answer. Alfred had been ... what? ... maybe seventeen when he killed his grandfather? Others knew, and never said a word. No one said a word.

So much Alfred hadn't touched on.

Lewis George had apologized for taking my dog. He said he expected me to press charges against him for stealing Sorrow and was ready to pay the price. I was mad enough to do it, but Sorrow seemed none the worse for his time away from me, and he responded happily to Lewis as he might a friend. I would see, I told him, when I got to town. I would see how forgiving I felt then.

I called the chief and Dolly, giving them the word that I was bringing Alfred Naquma and Lewis George to town. At first Dolly was speechless. Then she shot questions at me. I told her she would hear the whole story when we got there, and that she should call Detective Brent, tell him what was happening.

"He do it?" She couldn't help herself. "He kill his sister? What about the other guy? He do him in, too?"

"Dolly, you won't believe ... let him tell you."

Once there and both men were turned over, I left. Dolly came out to the car with me to kiss poor Sorrow on top of his head and admonish him to be more careful who he left with in the future.

"You pressing charges against Lewis George?" she demanded of me.

I shook my head. "Go on in and listen to what they have to say. I'm not adding to that. I've got him back." I patted the big head stuck out the window, long tongue drooling down the side of the Jeep.

"But there's the law, Emily," she frowned. "You can't work your head around what the law says is your responsibility to press charges."

"Yeah, sure, Dolly. You go ahead and lecture me about not breaking the law."

I left her sputtering as she headed back into the station to tape Alfred Naquma's confession.

———

After leaving Leetsville, I was much too elated to go home. I had Sorrow back. The bone mystery was solved. Alfred would be charged with his grandfather's death. It was late, but I had to share my good news.

Crazy Harry would be thrilled that Sorrow was home, but it would take a few minutes to tell him, and then he'd start talking about putting in another shot of radishes. I didn't want to be with an excitement killer.

Bill was a possibility. I'd have the story on his desk first thing in the morning—no matter what. But it was late. Bill wouldn't be at his office, and I didn't know where he lived. I drove toward Traverse City anyway. At Garfield I turned left and drove out of town toward Hobbs Highway, then around back roads to Jackson's cottage.

I parked under the pines and nuzzled Sorrow's head, assuring him I'd be right back. There were two lights on. One on the lower floor, probably in his kitchen. The other light was upstairs, in his bedroom. He could be turning in for the night. Didn't matter. I ran to the door and knocked as hard as I could. Jackson would be happy that I had my dog back, and fascinated with the story I had to tell.

When he finally answered the door, his hair was mussed. His eyes were confused. He grabbed his robe around him and held it tight at the throat, barely covering his nude body.

I rattled the locked screen. "Let me in. I've got news."

"Emily." His voice was stern and not at all welcoming. "I was in bed."

"So what? I got Sorrow back."

He had the grace to smile. "Great news. I'm happy for you."

I shook the locked door again. "You going to let me in?"

"Well . . ." He unlocked the door slowly.

"And I know who murdered who out at Sandy Lake." I stepped into the house, kicked off my sandals, and did a pirouette into the living room.

As I turned, I lay my head back and looked up. A woman, pulling a robe around her body, looked down from the upstairs balcony.

Ramona Sheffield. The woman who'd come to Jackson's dinner party with Bill.

Her mouth dropped open. My mouth dropped open. I stared at her a long time, then turned so I faced her dead on.

"Emily," she said.

"Ramona," I said.

It would have been funny if . . .

"I didn't know you were coming . . . ," Jackson started to complain.

"Obviously," I said. I think I laughed a time or two. The scene was trite, and sickening. Here I was again, the irate wife catching her husband in bed with another woman. Only I wasn't the wife. And not so much feeling irate as feeling dumb.

"Now, Emily," Jackson tried to put his arm around my shoulders. I shook him off fast. "We need to talk. I'll come out in the morning."

I made a sound somewhere between a giggle and a choke. I pursed my lips. "No you won't. The one thing we don't need to do is talk."

I picked up one sandal, then found the other under a chair. I got them on and headed for the door.

"You will finish the typing for me, won't you?" Jackson followed me out to the car.

"You know the term 'When hell freezes over,' Jackson?"

"Oh, please," he said, disgusted.

At the car, I had to battle Sorrow back. He wanted out of the car so he could give Jackson a royal greeting.

"But this thing," he motioned toward the house. "It's not what you think at all."

"Never is." I rolled down the window. "Hey, maybe this one types."

"Please, Emily. Don't let this … well … we had something. Even you agreed."

I started the car, pushing Sorrow out of the front seat and into the back. I backed out of his drive and headed toward home.

———

The trip to Willow Lake was one long stream of four letter words after another. It was interesting, after a while, to see how many I could think of and how loud I could say them. Then I went into a tear-filled rant during which I struck the steering wheel with my fists. After that I told myself how lucky I was. I had been so willing to give up everything I'd come to love. When, I wondered, had I lost my mind?

At that turn in my emotional upheaval I gave a loud "Hmmph" and laughed. Sorrow, probably thinking me certifiable, stayed away. He hugged the back of the seat, pretending to be invisible.

At home, I got a pad of paper and wrote down everything I hated about Jackson Rinaldi. It was a refresher course. Before long I was laughing at my list which included: unfaithful, arrogant, stupid, bad writer, losing his hair at the back, lousy cook, selfish lover, crappy editor, moles on his butt...

When I couldn't get beyond those moles that formed the constellation Orion, I gave up and went to bed.

Sorrow slept with me all night. Far more dependable company than what I'd sought on Spider Lake. I thought his long, warm body a great improvement over Jackson, whose hairless legs twitched and kicked. I slept like a dead lion until morning.

# FORTY-SIX

THE NEXT DAY WAS soft and sweet smelling. After I e-mailed my story to Bill, I took my tea on the front deck, going in only when the phone rang. The first call was from Jackson, who launched into a stuttering apology.

"Guess what?" I said, my cheery voice clearly a surprise to him. Even his "hello" had contained contrition. "I am glad this happened now rather than later."

"But it won't happen again," he pleaded. "Never, I promise you, Emily. This was just..."

"'An opportunity.'" I finished his line for him.

"Don't be bitter." Now came the hurt voice. I could have charted the trajectory of the call. Next would come the slightest of hints that it was all my fault.

"Bitter is not what I am. I am so grateful. You snapped me right out of a delusion I suffered from. I'm not going anywhere. I'm not marrying you again, and I'm not going back to Ann Arbor."

"Don't…" Uh-oh—I'd gotten the sequence wrong. His voice fell into something close to tears. "I counted on us being friends, not necessarily remarrying. You could get a condo. I have mine. We could work out something mutually…"

"Ah yes. 'Mutually beneficial.' Like … what do they call it … 'friends with benefits'? Tell you what, you come on up here and see me anytime. Bring all the women you want. We'll be such good friends. Don't think another thing about it. Probably more my fault than yours…"

"Yes." He was happier. "If only you'd called first this wouldn't have…"

I hung up.

The phone rang again. It was Dolly, angry that she'd been calling me and calling me and all she got for her trouble was a busy signal. I had no intention of telling her what had happened last night but she seemed to smell it anyway.

"Jackson, huh? Bastard. Told you so."

"And how are you this bright and cheerful morning," I said, hoping to piss her off and shut her up.

"Bill called me. He's coming out to see you and couldn't get ahold of you."

"What did he say?" I demanded, angry at the conspiring behind my back.

"He didn't tell me anything. I just figured it out."

"What's he want out here anyway? I got my story in."

"Don't know. He'll be there soon. Thought I'd warn you in case you're running around with no clothes on, beating your breasts and tearing at your hair."

"Yeah. That's me."

"I'm not going to say 'I told you so.' I'm not like that."

"You already did."

"Oh …," Dolly said. "I got one more thing to say. I found Christine Naquma, Alfred's sister. Told her what happened and she's flying in this afternoon from Colorado. Doesn't look like we've got the right story yet."

"That's what I thought. He wanted her kept out of it too bad. Where'd they take him?"

"He's still here. Got him in a cell."

"You heard his story," I said.

"Yeah, what he wanted to tell me."

"You think there's more?"

"Sure is. I guessed it right away. Wants his sister kept out too bad. And that Lewis George … the way he bit at his lip when Alfred talked, I could see him bursting to tell me something. Geez, I was afraid he was going to have a heart attack right there. He doesn't want Alfred going to jail. They argued more than one time in their own language. Brent's having the ashes of the cabin sifted for bones; maybe a gun. Christine's coming to the station when she gets to town. I want to see them together and hear her side of things. Could be that after all this time she wants to tell the truth about what her brother did out there. Let's hear 'em both and then decide who's lying and who's telling the truth. You're coming in, aren't you? You've been in it since the beginning …" She stopped to draw a long breath.

I sensed there was more.

"Hey, by the way," she added. "Ha ha. I told you so."

She hung up before I could think of a comeback.

The phone rang again. A very busy morning.

"Emily? This is Ramona Sheffield. Please don't hang up …"

Since I had no such intention, it was easy to get the upper hand by letting her talk.

311

"I didn't know you and Jackson were working out your difficulties. He never said…"

"He wouldn't. And they weren't 'difficulties.' We are divorced. He's free…"

"Please forgive me for any part I've had in this…problem."

"You're forgiven, Ramona. He's done this too many times for me to hold grudges against the women."

Putting her in with a long line of Jackson's "women" hurt her, I could tell, but I wasn't feeling big enough to care.

"I don't know what came over me…"

"I do. A Jaguar. A line of crap. A good-looking face. Rapt attention turned your way until he's had you in bed a few times. And on and on."

"You're probably right." Her voice was low and pained. "I'd hoped we could be friends, Emily. Bill speaks highly of you."

We agreed we probably wouldn't be friends, but still she asked me to stay in touch and assured me she wouldn't be out to see Jackson ever again. That much felt good.

I was dressed and busy doing laundry when Bill arrived in his SUV. Sorrow, thrilled at the thought of early company, was out the screen door before I could unhook it, leaving screening to flap behind him.

Bill climbed from his car and stretched his thick body one way and then the other before sticking a hand in the air to greet me.

"Ramona called," he started after I invited him in. "I heard what happened last night and I felt awful. I should have said something when you mentioned remarrying Jackson and going back downstate. Ramona told me last week that she and Jackson were 'dating.' It's just hard to be the one…I'm not in the habit of carrying tales. Then, last night. I might have spared you all that and I feel bad that I didn't."

I shrugged. We settled down on the brown couch.

"Big night," I said.

"Got the story this morning. I see you've got Sorrow back. Alfred Naquma is in jail. My guess is he'll be bound over for trial."

"Who knows?" was all I said.

His newsman's nose shot immediately into the air. "Something new come up since last night?"

I shrugged. "Could be."

"You'll get it right to me?"

I nodded.

"Tribe taking over? Is that it? They're pretty protective of their own, all that sovereign nation business."

"We'll see."

"If a jurisdictional battle is shaping up, it'll be tough. The murders didn't happen on the reservation. The old man left or was kicked off years before."

"I'll let you know."

When he left he looked worried. There was an awkward moment after I thanked him for coming to console me. He pushed his glasses up his nose and rested his hands on my shoulders.

"So you'll be staying up here after all? That's good. That's very good news. And don't forget the obits. I meant the offer."

I nodded. He leaned forward and kissed me on the cheek. Not exactly a declaration of love, but a sweet gesture. I waited a minute, stood on tiptoe, and kissed him back.

"I'll try to throw as much work as possible your way," he said, climbing back into his Explorer. "What about a column? Your garden's beautiful. Write about that. Once a month, a Sunday feature article."

"I'm no master gardener."

"Not what I'm looking for. Need somebody who just loves gardening. Get that across."

We agreed. Soon I'd be a columnist and an obit writer and who knew what else he'd assign? With a few more articles for magazines, maybe I could make it financially. There was still real estate to consider. Wouldn't hurt to get licensed. And if I listened to Dolly, I could always sell chocolate underwear.

What a full life I had ahead of me.

# FORTY-SEVEN

HARRY AND I WORKED for hours that morning. Straight on through lunch and up to the time Dolly called. Alfred's sister was on her way from the airport in Traverse City.

We edged the beds and moved the bachelor buttons busily taking over the garden. Harry rototilled more of the creeping crap I didn't have a name for. Already the stuff had rolled its way into the rose bed, up a small hill, and was nudging out the vinca. I worked on my herb garden, deciding to pull any herb I hadn't used in a year. That meant all the mint and nameless, weedy things went. The chives stayed. They not only added to salads and meats, but if I let them go without trimming back, they sprouted pretty purple pompoms.

Harry pointed to slug damage and said I'd better get myself out there next time it rained. Carry a can of salt, pick off the slugs and drop them in. "Only way," he assured me, though I was leaning toward the less violent methods of placing pans of beer or egg shells among the hostas.

At two o'clock I drove to Leetsville. Dolly's patrol car was parked behind the station. I saw Lucky's Chevy out front. Detective Brent had to be there too. A blue Michigan State Police car was pulled in crookedly next to the Chevy.

I smiled at the gaggle of cops inside the station. Brent frowned, but Dolly quickly told him she'd asked me to be there. "Been through everything else," she said. "Brought in Alfred Naquma. She's got a right."

Christine hadn't arrived yet. We sat around at the desks and at a small wooden table covered with old coffee cup rings and gouges made by pointed pencils. After a while, we speculated that maybe Christine Naquma was lost. We talked about somebody driving out to hunt for her, except nobody knew what she looked like or what she drove.

After another ten minutes, the door opened and a small woman walked in. She bowed to each of us, keeping her head turned away, hair almost hiding her face. She stood nervously with her brown purse clutched in front of her long dirndl skirt. When she looked up and pushed her dark hair away from her face, we all caught our breath. One side of Christine Naquma's face was delicate and pretty. The other side was drawn up tight into a fixed stare. The eyelid on that side was gone, or frozen in place. The skin around her mouth was puckered. Across her cheek, shiny, unmoving burned skin held her face together.

"I'm Christine Naquma. I'm here to talk to my brother," she said. Nervous fingers fluttered to the scarred side of her face, then down. Her lips were uneven, coming together between words into almost fish-like pouts. She wore a brown wool sweater which seemed much too heavy for a Michigan May, and that washed-out skirt hanging over soft brown boots.

"Thanks for coming," Brent stood up, ready to take over.

"I'm here to see Deputy Dolly Wakowski," she said to him, pulling back a little.

Dolly stepped forward and put out her hand.

Christine's handshake was tentative and quick. "I'd like to talk to you after I see Alfred."

Dolly nodded. "He's back in a cell."

Christine looked at Dolly, then at me. Dolly told her who I was. She nodded, but didn't take the hand I held out to her.

Lucky led her back to the cells. The rest of us settled down to wait.

She wasn't gone long. Lucky brought her back. Christine motioned to Dolly and then to me. She turned to include Lucky and Detective Brent.

"I'll talk to all of you with Alfred. Back in his cell, if need be. Our attorneys are coming. I spoke to them before leaving Traverse. We won't talk without attorneys again after this. Alfred made a mistake when he made a statement last night. He thought he must do that to protect me."

Brent started to sputter. He wasn't a man used to having the agenda set by a little wisp of an Indian woman. He'd already groused that this was a weak case. If the confession was rescinded, he'd have nothing to take to the district attorney.

Lucky and Dolly exchanged one quick glance. Lucky nodded.

Alfred sat on a lower bunk when we got back there. Christine sat beside him. Dolly and I went into the cell with Christine. The others stayed in the hall. Alfred was dressed in the clothes he'd had on the night before and not in jail garb. I supposed that Leetsville didn't have a big budget for wardrobe and didn't usually keep inmates for long.

Christine put a hand on Alfred's knee, forcing him to turn toward her. She gave him a crooked smile that came from deep within her eyes. The half of her face that was burned didn't move. Alfred, nervous, put a hand up to touch her face. She held that hand, and kissed it.

"I don't want you here," Alfred said to his sister. There wasn't cruel rejection in his voice, only a sad plea for her not to become a part of this terrible thing. She shook her head a final time and began to speak.

"My brother has told you lies," she said, turning to us. I heard Brent groan behind me. "Not about our grandfather. He was a terrible man and never should have taken us away from the reservation after our parents died. He killed my sister, as Alfred told you. He killed the man she'd brought home with her as protection. He would have killed any of us, anytime he felt justified. Sooner or later he would have sent me to the lake bottom, too. And then Alfred."

I heard the whir of the tape recorder Lucky had set up.

"What he is lying about is how our grandfather died. Alfred wasn't there alone that day. I came home early from school. I watched as our grandfather murdered the man who stood up to him, arguing for Mary. I watched as he shot Mary in the head after he shot the man. I watched as he took the bodies out on the lake. I hid in the woods, afraid I would be next. When I saw Alfred, I had to warn him. We went into the house together. Alfred told him we knew, and that we would go to the police. Our grandfather laughed at us. He mimicked Mary pleading for her life and said that we would be next. He thought it was funny. Grandfather thought he'd had an afternoon of great entertainment.

"Alfred and I sat across from each other in that house of hell until he passed out with his drinking. It was then that Alfred got up and went outside. I thought he was leaving me to go for the authorities and went out of my mind with fear that Grandfather would wake up and shoot me. But he came back with a gas can and poured gas over our grandfather and around his chair. I watched what he did and didn't understand until we went to the door. Alfred had a box of matches in his hands. He tried again and again to light one of the matches but couldn't. I took the gas can. I threw more gas in that cabin. Then I took the box of matches from Alfred. It was I who struck the match. I threw the match into the room. When the first one ignited, nothing happened. I struck a second match and there was an explosion." She hesitated, putting a hand to her face. "So, you see, I am the one who murdered our grandfather. Not Alfred."

Alfred protested but she stopped him with a hand up in front of her. "Please Alfred, I have enough to be ashamed of."

Nobody moved. As though the words she'd spoken came from a dark place where tremendous evil existed, I shuddered and wrapped my arms around my body. Dolly's head was down. Lucky and Brent studied their shoe tops.

"I will go to jail instead of Alfred."

"No," Alfred said. "You can't, because you're lying."

She shrugged. "My face doesn't lie. People know."

"You're lying," he said again, tears standing in his dark eyes. "Your face happened years before, when you were in the car accident with our parents."

She smiled and touched one of Alfred's hands. "My dear brother, if you keep lying, how will the police know who to believe?"

They looked at each other, sitting that way until two attorneys from the tribal council arrived, making noise out in the hall, demanding to see their clients.

A long, private discussion followed. First the Naqumas spoke to their attorneys, and then Brent, Lucky, Dolly, Christine, Alfred, and the attorneys went into a small side room and closed the door behind them. If they thought I was leaving, they were dead wrong.

I could see them gathered closely around a small table in earnest conversation. After a time the door opened and they came out together. They shook hands and nodded affably. Not what I'd expected.

"We'll wait here...," the younger of the two attorneys said to Lucky.

Lucky nodded and went around toward the back. He returned with papers. Alfred and Christine were leaving. Whatever had been decided, it seemed to please the entire group. I asked if I could take a photo for the paper and was told I could not but that they would speak to me later.

"Christine will be leaving soon, but we will gladly talk to you before she goes," Alfred said, and took my hand briefly.

After they left, it was Brent who told me they'd been turned over to the Odawa.

"This is a matter for their people to decide," he said, shrugging his wide shoulders. "Not enough evidence of anything to go to trial. And with the sister's story... well, what can we do?"

He was out of there fast. He'd gotten a call, he said. "Bar fight."

I wrote down a quote from Detective Brent, and a quote from Lucky, on his way out, about how old murders come back to haunt people. "Not that I believe in ghosts," he quickly added. "Just that secrets don't stay secrets forever."

When it was me and Dolly, settling in behind the desk with the telephone, I asked her, "You mean we'll never know for sure who killed the old man?"

"Looks that way," Dolly said.

"What about the law?" I asked her.

She reddened. "What's the law got to do with this?"

"Oh, come on. You mean nobody goes to jail?"

"You want to put the sister away?"

"Well, no, but her face proves..."

"Not according to him."

"There's that aunt of theirs in Peshawbestown. She'll know."

"Yeah. You think she'll testify?"

"Crap, Dolly. How am I going to write this? There's no resolution."

She shrugged. "Sure there is. Those two can put it behind them finally. Write that there was a tragedy out at Sandy Lake thirteen years ago and nobody knows for sure what happened."

"You're satisfied with that? What about Chet? You happy with nobody paying for his murder?"

"Who would you have pay, Emily?" She stood tall, adjusted her gun belt, sat back down, and put on her lecturing face. "This was about family. And who knows family better than me. If I could put that evil old man in prison, I'd do it in a flash. He's in a greater jail. The Odawa don't want his bones. They'll leave 'em where they are. That's as bad a punishment as any of us can come up with."

"What about Mary?" I asked.

"She's part of the deal. Brent agreed to release her body right away. Alfred and Christine invited us all to the ceremony out at Dark Forest in the morning."

"Then this is your idea of justice." I couldn't help but turn the screw a little.

"Bigger justice. Sometimes you just got to wash your hands and figure things are too far beyond you."

# EPILOGUE

UNDER THE OLD COUNCIL trees, the dark men opened the grave.

As they lowered the small, plain coffin holding Mary Naquma into its final resting place, three crows, sitting high in the oak above, cawed mournful caws. They cawed again as the drumming began, and then flew off.

To one side of the small grave, a mound of sandy dirt stood waiting. It didn't feel unnatural to me—the heap of dirt beside the hole in the ground. No artificial grass covered over what it was and no barriers hid where the mouth of Mother Earth lay open, ready to accept her dead.

Around all of us, gathered to witness that she had lived, the beat of the drummers played a quadruple cadence along my bloodstream. As though my arteries and capillaries carried sound, my heart picked up the beat. Up through my shoes, my feet, my legs; up through my body, into my neck, my head, my ears—the beat played until my body was a drum.

Alfred Naquma, in full Indian dress, began his own beat around his sister's grave, bending and dancing and bending and dancing around the grave. Soon the gimoa followed. Lewis George, with no hesitation, no doubt at his footing, in his own world, joined the man he thought of as his son in mourning for one of their family.

Behind the others—all the Indian women and men and the white women and men, behind a Catholic priest who said prayers and sprinkled incense on the wooden box holding the bones of Mary Naquma—Christine, small in her plain leather dancer's dress reaching down to her moccasins, began a sweet lament. Her voice followed the drum then rose above it and deepened into dark places the drums had opened.

I could hardly breathe. Dolly, beside me, stood with her head bowed and her hands crossed in front of her. She was here, she had told me on the way from town that morning, because the Indians had come for Chet. And more than that. When you know the sad story of a life that should have been happier, she had said, you owe that person not mourning but a celebration. She stood next to me, celebrating in her own way. We didn't dance. We didn't sing. We didn't have real prayers to recite. But we had our bodies as witness. So we were there.

After a time the drums stopped, though the beat echoed on over the ridge of white crosses. An old woman stepped from the crowd and sang a song so sad I didn't need words to know her heart was breaking.

At the end, Lewis George tore tobacco to pieces and let it sift down on Mary's final resting place. Alfred picked up a shovel and threw shovelfuls of dirt onto the box. Christine took the shovel next. Then Lewis George. Then the singing woman who, I had been told, was an old aunt of the Naqumas. Then Lena Smith. The others followed. Christine came to where Dolly and I hung back and led us forward, seeing that we each shoveled dirt into the grave. I could barely see. My eyes burned. I let the tears run down my face. I had never felt so much a part of ceremony, of a true seeing to the other side.

When the grave was covered, women came forward to pat the earth into place the way they might care for a baby, almost with soothing motions, giving no offense to the earth, to Mary, to the people who loved her.

A group of young women then picked up drums again and began an intense drumming with long spaces between the beats as Alfred lifted Mary's white cross in his large hands and pushed it straight, and firm, into the ground.

Christine stepped forward holding a small brown doll she carried, first above her head, then down to her lips. She set the worn child's doll, dressed in beaded leather, beneath the cross, straightening the doll's skirt and propping her better to sit upright.

People began to leave silently. Dolly and I exchanged a glance then tiptoed away with the others, leaving brother and sister behind us, feet planted on either side of their sister's grave, hands entwined across it, all three together for a last time.

Karen Youker

## ABOUT THE AUTHOR

Elizabeth Kane Buzzelli is a creative writing instructor at Northwestern Michigan College. She is the author of novels, short stories, articles, and essays. Her work has appeared in numerous publications and anthologies.

# WWW.MIDNIGHTINKBOOKS.COM

From the gritty streets of New York City to sacred tombs in the Middle East, it's always midnight somewhere. Join us online at any hour for fresh new voices in mystery fiction.

At midnightinkbooks.com you'll also find our author blog, new and upcoming books, events, book club questions, excerpts, mystery resources, and more.

## MIDNIGHT INK ORDERING INFORMATION

### Order Online:

- Visit our website www.midnightinkbooks.com, select your books, and order them on our secure server.

### Order by Phone:

- Call toll-free within the U.S. and Canada at
  1-888-NITE INK (1 800-648-3465)
- We accept VISA, MasterCard, and American Express

### Order by Mail:

Send the full price of your order (MN residents add 6.5% sales tax) in U.S. funds, plus postage & handling to:

> Midnight Ink
> 2143 Wooddale Drive 978-0-7387-1265-9
> Woodbury, MN  55125-2989

### Postage & Handling:

Standard (U.S., Mexico, & Canada). If your order is:
>    $24.99 and under, add $3.00
>    $25.00 and over, FREE STANDARD SHIPPING

AK, HI, PR: $15.00 for one book plus $1.00 for each additional book.

International Orders (airmail only):
>    $16.00 for one book plus $3.00 for each additional book

Orders are processed within 2 business days. Please allow for normal shipping time.
Postage and handling rates subject to change.